Wardrobe
MALFUNCTION

OTHER CONTEMPORARY NOVELS BY SAMANTHA TOWLE

Unsuitable

Sacking the Quarterback (BookShots Flames/James Patterson)

The Ending I Want

When I Was Yours

Trouble

REVVED SERIES
Revved
Revived

THE STORM SERIES
The Mighty Storm
Wethering the Storm
Taming the Storm
The Storm

PARANORMAL ROMANCES BY SAMANTHA TOWLE

The Bringer

THE ALEXANDRA JONES SERIES
First Bitten
Original Sin

Wardrobe
MALFUNCTION

SAMANTHA TOWLE

Copyright © 2017 by Samantha Towle
All rights reserved.

Visit my website at www.samanthatowle.co.uk
Cover Designer: Najla Qamber Designs
Editor and Interior Designer: Jovana Shirley,
Unforeseen Editing, www.unforeseenediting.com

No part of this book may be reproduced or transmitted in any form or by any means, electronic or mechanical, including photocopying, recording, or by any information storage and retrieval system without the written permission of the author, except for the use of brief quotations in a book review.

This book is a work of fiction. Names, characters, places, and incidents either are products of the author's imagination or are used fictitiously. Any resemblance to actual persons, living or dead, events, or locales is entirely coincidental.

ISBN-13: 978-1542959858

PROLOGUE

Vaughn

"So, Vaughn, how was it, making a movie with your girlfriend and best friend?" Bradford asks me.

I'm sitting on a studio sofa in front of a live audience with Piper Watts, my girlfriend, and Cain Acton, my best friend. *Treason* is the film we did together. It's a romantic comedy about two best friends who end up fighting over the same girl. Of course, I end up with the girl. It would have been a little weird for audiences if Cain had ended up with my real-life girlfriend. The film is due to drop in cinemas next week, so Piper, Cain, and I are doing the press rounds to promote it. Tonight, we're on *Digby's Dirt*.

No, I shit you not. That's the name of the show I'm currently on.

The most popular late-night chat show on television.

It's hosted by Bradford Digby, the television host that every celebrity loves to hate. The fucker is a rat through and through. He's like a bloodhound. He can sniff out scandal at fifty paces. God, even his name sounds pretentious.

But he's popular. His show has high ratings, hence the reason Jack, my manager—who is also Cain's manager—and the studio are having us appear on here to promote our new movie.

Pausing briefly at his question, I slide a smile in Piper's direction. "It was fun."

Hard work.

Piper bitched the whole time. I might have been with her for six months, and I'd known she could be a challenge at times, but I'd thought her diva reputation on set was sheer embellishment. It wasn't.

Honestly, it made me look at her with a whole new set of eyes. But that's a thought for later.

I'd worked with Cain before, so I knew what to expect. It was great, as always. He's my best friend. I've known him for ten years. I trust the guy with my life.

"It's always fun working with Vaughn," Cain says, smirking at me.

I know he thought Piper was a pain in the ass, too, but he'd never say it to me because she's my girl.

Piper is actually the first woman I've dated seriously since I got in this business. I just figured it was time to settle down. I'm not getting any younger, and I want to have a family someday. Piper's great—apart from being annoying to work with, which I'll make sure I never do again. I'll keep our relationship and work separate in the future.

"No disagreements? Arguments?" Bradford asks.

"Well, there are always disagreements." I give a laugh, and the audience laughs, too.

"But they were only minor disagreements, right, V?" Piper says.

God, I hate it when she calls me V. How hard is it to say my name? Vaughn. It literally rolls off the tongue.

Wardrobe Malfunction

"We had a blast filming together. And what more could a girl want than to work with the man she loves and, of course, his best friend?"

The audience sounds out with an, "Aw."

"Of course," Bradford says. "Don't forget the best friend."

Um...what? Piper loves me?

First I've heard.

I make sure to control my outward reaction to this surprising piece of news, keeping my facial expression as neutral as possible.

Inside though, I'm shocked to shit. I mean, we've been together for six months, but we haven't said *I love you* yet. Honestly, I don't think I'm even there yet. But that's beside the point. You'd think she'd have said it to me first before announcing it on live television.

God, I hope she hasn't said it to me, and I didn't hear it—or worse, that I forgot.

"So, Vaughn, how long have you and Cain been friends for now?" Bradford asks.

"Uh…" I look up.

Bradford chuckles. "Been that long that you've forgotten?"

"Probably." Cain laughs and looks at me. "Ten years, right, man?"

"Yeah. Ten years too long." I grin at Cain, and the audience laughs.

"Ten years? Wow." Bradford leans back in his chair. His hand straightens out his tie.

There's something in his tone that I don't like. Unease moves through me.

"So, I guess it must come as a hell of a blow to learn that Cain has been having an affair with Piper for the last three months."

What?

I hear a whoosh in my ears and realize it's the audience gasping.

I blink, glancing around.

Piper's and Cain's faces are frozen, like I guess mine is. And Bradford just has this smug expression on his face.

"What?" I laugh, but it sounds uneasy, even to my own ears. "You're kidding, right? This is a joke." I even look around to see if Ashton Kutcher is waiting to tell me I've been punked.

"It's no joke." Bradford's eyes flick to the big screen behind him, and there's a picture of Cain and Piper in an embrace, outside what looks like a hotel room door.

It's fake. It has to be. Because Cain would never do that to me.

I squeeze my eyes shut.

But I know it's not a fake.

Because I know this industry. I know this asshole wouldn't risk his career on a rumor or a fake picture. He must have authenticated it. He wouldn't have done this on live television without die-hard facts and the proof to back it up because he knows he'd have his ass sued if he were lying.

My heart sinks into the pit of my stomach.

"This is bullshit!" Piper snaps.

I open my eyes and look at her. She's pissed.

It's because she's been caught. And caught so publicly.

My eyes flick past her to Cain.

The contriteness in his expression is all the confirmation I need.

And I feel sick.

There's commotion all around. I can hear people yelling from off camera. Piper is screaming for them to turn the cameras off.

That's what she cares about right now.

Not me. Not the fact that my heart is being broken on live television by my cheating-ass girlfriend. But, worse, by

Wardrobe Malfunction

my friend, whom I trusted. The guy I've known for ten years.

Ten fucking years.

My head starts to cloud.

I'm no longer on live television with an audience of people sitting there.

I'm staring at my best friend, and rage is firing in my bloodstream.

I get to my feet. "Is it true?" I say to him, my voice trembling with anger.

Cain gets to his feet, facing me. "I'm sorry," he says.

Sorry?

"You're sorry?" I laugh without a trace of humor.

Then, I punch him.

Hard. In the face.

Three Months Later

Vaughn

"Up and out!"

The sound of hands clapping and Jack, my manager's, voice split through my head like an ax on wood.

Groaning, I mumble, "Fuck off, Jack. I'm sleeping." My voice is muffled by the pillow my face is buried in.

Sunlight and warmth hit my back a second later as the curtains are pulled open.

"For fuck's sake," I grumble.

"Ladies, get dressed, and be on your way. A car is waiting for you downstairs to take you home," Jack says with that no-nonsense tone of his.

I feel movement on the bed. Limbs and bodies climb over me and off the bed.

Last night...

Oh, yeah.

A party.

Alcohol. Lots of alcohol.

A redhead who could deep-throat like a champ and a brunette with legs that went on for miles.

Sex.

Lots of it.

At the party. In the limo on the way back to the hotel suite I've been living in these last few months. The sofa. The bed.

The usual.

Well, the usual for me now.

Stretching my aching body, I lift my head. The sunlight blinds me. Rubbing a hand over my face, I blink through the haze. My eyes meet with Jack's.

He's standing there, his arms folded over his chest, a disapproving frown on his face.

He wears that look a lot when looking at me nowadays.

The girls are moving around the room, picking up the debris of their clothes from last night's activities.

"What?" I bite at him.

He says nothing. Just shakes his head.

His stare is making me uncomfortable. It's the disappointment in his eyes that bothers me the most.

In a business filled with sharks, Jack isn't one. He's loyal. To me. His wife. His kids.

For all these years, I've stayed clean in a city full of dirt with his help and because of my family back home.

Well, I was clean. Now, I'm a helluva lot dirty.

My eyes flit to the girls as they quickly dress.

Shame spreads through my chest.

This isn't me…

At least, it wasn't me.

Sure, I've done one-night stands in the past. I've slept with women with no promise of more.

But this—the endless nights of drinking and fucking, and then rinse and repeat—isn't me.

Wardrobe

But, right now, it's the only thing that makes me feel better.

Well, for a time anyway.

Shame has me getting to my feet and snapping out, "Jesus, Jack, stop fucking looking at me like that." I walk my bare ass over to the closet where I pull out a pair of black lounge pants and slip them on.

"Like what? Like you're a mess?" Jack states, like he doesn't care that other people are in this room.

I can just see the headline now…

VAUGHN'S MANAGER CALLS HIM "A MESS" IN HEATED ARGUMENT

As I grit my teeth, my angry eyes quickly flit to the girls leaving my room. Neither looks like they heard or care about what Jack said, but you can never be too sure in this town.

My eyes meet with the redhead's. She gives me a smile that says she wants a repeat and drops a slip of paper on the dresser before she leaves with the brunette in tow.

Sorry, love, no repeats.

Jack walks over and shuts the door behind them.

"Since when do you mouth off in front of people?" I fire at Jack.

He's the one who always tells me to be careful what I say and to whom.

"Since you clearly don't give a shit about your career anymore."

"I care."

He laughs. "Then, sort your shit out."

"Give me a fucking break."

"That's all I've done for the last few months. That's all anyone's done. We get that you're hurting. What they did…it was shit. But shit happens, and life moves on. *You* move on, Vaughn."

"I'm moving on," I growl.

"Yeah, looks like it." He gives a pointed look at the empty box of condoms on my nightstand and the bottles of Jack littered around the room.

I feel ashamed again. I shouldn't. I'm a grown fucking man, but I know this isn't me. It isn't what I'm about.

And I care about what Jack thinks of me. I respect him.

And I know my family is worried about me. I know I'm letting them down.

I'm letting myself down.

Sighing, I drag my hands through my hair.

"You need to get it together, Vaughn." He reaches inside his sports coat and pulls out his phone. He turns it, showing me the picture and headline.

OUR STAR HAS FALLEN

Unrecognizable, Vaughn West is seen falling out of a club, held up by two women he spent the night partying with in Van Helden, along with renowned party boy and A-lister Gabriel Evans and TV star Julian Jacob.

The brokenhearted star's behavior has worsened since the outing of the affair between his former best friend, Cain Acton, and ex-girlfriend, Piper Watts, which was revealed on Digby's Dirt, *the popular late-night show hosted by Bradford Digby, where West physically assaulted Acton. No charges were filed.*

The affair between Acton and Watts allegedly began on the set of the film, Treason, *which the three actors starred in together.*

I barely recognize the bloodshot-eyed mess of a man staring back in the photos. Propped up by the two women

Wardrobe

who just left my bed, my hand clearly up the back of one of their skirts in one of the shots.

Jesus, I'm a fucking mess.

Jack swipes the screen. The next headline...

VAUGHN WEST. SEX ADDICT AND ALCOHOLIC?
OUR EXPERT SAYS YES.

And again...

A picture of me from another night, looking wasted, flipping the bird to the press, with another woman holding me up.

Then, there's a picture of Cain and Piper, the one that was used to expose them on Digby's show—the source of my pain and humiliation.

The betrayal hits me all over again.

Sighing, I turn away from Jack and look out the floor-to-ceiling window, dragging my hands through my hair again.

I hear the creak of the bed as Jack sits down on it.

"I know what they did stung like a motherfucker—Cain stung me, too—but you can't let this destroy everything you've worked for."

When Jack took me on as a client, Cain was already his client. I needed a place to stay, so Jack put me in touch with Cain, who was looking for a roommate at that time. That's how we met.

Even with the scandal, Cain was still big money for Jack, but he dropped him as a client and stayed with me.

I know I should feel thankful for that, but I don't feel thankful for an awful lot right now.

"Drinking and screwing random women isn't going to fix this, Vaughn. Getting back to work is what's going to fix it. We need to get the press and fans focused on your next movie and not your personal life."

"Personal life?" I laugh. "What a fucking joke that is! I don't have a personal life because everyone in the world is fucking privy to what goes on."

"And you're not exactly making it hard for them right now, are you?" he throws back at me.

I narrow my eyes at him. "What if I don't feel like making a movie right now?" I fold my arms over my chest, pressing against the dull ache there.

He laughs. It's not a humorous sound, and it makes me turn to him.

He gets to his feet. "They screwed you over, and it hurts like fuck. I get it. But you think this is the way to get back at them—drinking yourself into a coma and banging anything with a vagina? Get fucking real. You know this business, Vaughn. It can turn at the snap of a finger. At the moment, their popularity has crashed. They can't get work for shit. No one will touch them. They couldn't even get a call back for a toilet paper commercial at the moment...but it won't last. We've seen it before. Angie and Brad each made twice as much in the year after their affair. They skyrocketed because their publicist swung it the right way. And the way you're acting now is giving Piper's publicist her meal ticket back to success."

He swipes his finger over his screen and turns his phone to me again. There's a picture of Piper, looking tearful.

Bitch.

PIPER WATTS SPEAKS FOR THE FIRST TIME
SINCE HER AFFAIR WITH CAIN ACTON WAS REVEALED

> *"Vaughn's alcoholism and constant womanizing pushed me into Cain's arms," a tearful Piper said. "Vaughn has a vicious temper."*
>
> *"You were scared of him?"*

Wardrobe

"Yes," she answered softly, head bowed.

"Did Vaughn ever hit you?"

"Yes."

So, ladies and gentlemen, when Piper was faced with a violent alcoholic who cheated as much as Vaughn West did, then I guess it is understandable that she sought solace in another man's arms.

We'd like to hear your opinions on this. Vote on our poll: Was Piper right to cheat? Yes or no?

"That lying bitch," I seethe, my hands curling into fists. "I never touched her."

"I know that, but you hit Cain with the world watching."

"Come on, Jack, you would have hit him if you were in my situation. Anyone would have."

"You're right, but it's easy to twist and manipulate things to look differently, and Piper's proven she's good at lying. Then, there's your behavior as of late—the drinking and the women. It's giving Piper's people the tools to swing this however they want. Piper is getting sympathy by bringing you down. It's not too late to stop it, but we need to take action now, Vaughn.

"I've let you have your time to be hurt and angry, but it's enough now. I need you to clean yourself up. I need you out of the press for whom you're fucking and back in it for what you're working on next. You want revenge for what they did to you, Vaughn? Then, revenge is cleaning yourself up and getting back to work, stepping over them and climbing right back to the top."

He's right.

I know he's right.

13

This isn't me. Who I want to be.

But I've never been hurt like this before. It's almost like I don't know what to do with the hurt, so I ignore it, and when it becomes too much to ignore, I drink and fuck it away…until it comes back, and then I rinse and repeat.

Piper's betrayal hurt. But Cain's betrayal hurt way more.

He was my friend for ten years. I would've taken a bullet for the guy.

And he slept with my girlfriend.

I almost laugh out loud at the cliché of it.

Best friend fucks girlfriend for months under the nose of the boyfriend, and he has no clue.

Happens all the time.

But, when you're a celebrity, then it's the juiciest story of the decade. A story that just won't fucking go away.

To the fans and press, I'm the wounded animal.

Pathetic.

Poor Vaughn.

It's the pity and apathy that drive me fucking insane.

But no more. Jack's right.

Arms folded, I lean my back against the window. "So, what do you have in mind?"

Jack smiles. "You have an offer."

"For what?"

"More like from whom." His smile widens, making me stand up straighter. "Evans."

My heart stops. "Brandon Evans?"

"The one and only."

"Holy fuck."

Brandon Evans is the hottest director around at the moment. Everyone wants to work with him.

"What's the movie?"

"*The Lament*. It's a gangland thriller. Think *Goodfellas* 2017."

"What's the part?"

Wardrobe Malfunction

"Lead. Drew Asher, heir to the Asher family. It's a great fucking script. Brandon wrote the part with you in mind."

"You're shitting me." I'm almost breathless. My insides are lighting up like the sky on the Fourth of July. "Did you know?"

He shakes his head. "You know Brandon keeps things tight to his chest. I got the call just last night. There's no doubt that he wants you for the part, *but* he has reservations, Vaughn…your recent behavior."

"I'll sort it out. Clean up my act."

My heart is drumming, my pulse thrumming. I feel alive, like I haven't felt in a long while.

This is the part I've been dreaming of. This could take me up to the next step. From the hot movie star to serious actor, like DiCaprio did with his career.

"This could be it, Vaughn," Jack says, excitement in his voice. "This could put you at the top with no way of ever coming down. I'll do the work at my end to get rid of the shit the press has been saying about you, but you have to keep your nose clean in the meantime. No more excessive partying, drinking, or screwing around until the film is released."

"Consider it done." I pick up the paper with the phone number that the redhead left behind. I crumple it in my hand and toss it in the trash can.

Charly

I'M ADMIRING THE GORGEOUS Fendi hanging from the shoulder of the woman walking in front of me when my cell starts ringing from inside my knockoff Stella McCartney.

I retrieve it from the bottom of my bag, expecting it to be Nick—my roommate and best friend since college—but see that it's Ava Simms. She's a friend and colleague. She works wardrobe like I do.

"Yello!" I sing cheerily to her.

I hear her laugh.

"Charly, do you ever answer the phone like a normal person?"

"Why would I when I can answer so colorfully?" I say in a puzzled tone, making her laugh again. "How you doing?" I ask.

"Good," she says.

But I can tell from her tone that she's not good at all. We might not be super close, like Nick and I are, but I know her well enough to know when something is wrong. I just hope it isn't that prick of a so-called boyfriend of hers. The one she moved across the country to be with. Honestly, I can't imagine leaving New York to move to LA for any guy. Especially not an out-of-work actor who sidelines as a hand model and thinks he's God's gift to women.

I don't know what Ava sees in that guy. Granted, he's good-looking, but he's a dick, and she could do a million times better.

"What's up?" I ask.

"Are you still in Nashville?"

Okay. Not the answer I was expecting but whatever.

"Nope. I just landed in JFK." I smile to myself, looking forward to having the week off that I booked in for myself. I haven't had any time off in…forever, and even though I'm not rich, I have enough money in the bank to allow myself a week of doing nothing. "I'm actually walking through the airport as we speak, heading to grab a cab home. Why?"

"Well…I haven't had a chance to tell you, but I landed a job on this big-budget movie, and I'm the wardrobe mistress—"

"Really? Congrats! That's great, Ava!"

Wardrobe mistress is a promotion for Ava, who was a wardrobe assistant like me. She's been in the business longer than I have though, so I can't envy her promotion.

"Well…the thing is, I was wondering if you would want to come and work with me."

"When?" I have a job lined up in wardrobe on a small Broadway play after my weeklong break, but if it's after that, then I can do it.

"Well…tomorrow."

"Tomorrow?" I yell in surprise.

"Yeah, I know it's short notice—"

Wardrobe
MALFUNCTION

"No kidding. Hang on, am I an add-on? Did someone drop out, and you need me to fill in?"

Silence.

I can practically hear her wince.

"Ava?"

"It's not as bad as you're making it sound. I knew you were already working up in Nashville on *Rollers*, so I hired Millie Reed—"

"Millie Reed?"

"I know you don't like her—"

"She screwed Michael."

"After you dumped him."

"I know, but that's not the point. She was supposed to be a friend. You know, girl code and all that."

"You two were never friends; you just worked together." She laughs. "I remember what you said the first day after you worked with her. You said she was useless."

"She is useless. She's a crap seamstress. She sewed all the buttons on a shirt the wrong way—rookie mistake."

"Well, she was available—"

"She always is."

"And you weren't," Ava continues seamlessly. "I would have asked you first; you know that. But, with the timing, I knew you wouldn't be able to do it, so I asked Millie, and…"

"What happened?"

"I'm not sure. I just got a call this morning from Vaughn's manager, telling me to fire her. Apparently, she was incompetent."

"She probably tried to screw him, too," I mutter. "Hang on, Vaughn? As in—"

"Vaughn West. Oh, yes."

"Oh my God," I breathe.

Vaughn West.

Vaughn. West.

19

I can't say I'm not excited at hearing that name. I've worked with a lot of celebrities, but Vaughn West is a whole different caliber of celebrity. Aside from being off-the-charts hot—dark blond hair, hazel-brown eyes, and a body made for sex…let's just say that Vaughn has starred in a lot of my late-night fantasies. I might have a teeny-tiny crush on him.

But not only is he gorgeous, he's also a great actor. To be able to see him in action would be amazing.

"What's he like?" I have to ask.

"Gorgeous, of course. I've only met him twice, and each time was brief, but he seems like a nice guy."

I knew he'd be nice! He always comes across as nice in his interviews.

Not that I stalk him or anything.

"Where's the job?" I ask her.

"LA, for studio. Vegas, for location."

"How long?"

"Two months…three, max. The pay is really good, and it's a great opportunity, Charly. It's being directed by Brandon Evans."

"Wow," I say.

Brandon Evans is Hollywood's current golden boy. Every film he touches is gold. He and Vaughn together will be magic.

"It's a gangster film. Lots of designer dresses, shoes, bags. And I'm sure we'll be able to keep some items at the end."

My ears perk up at that. Girl knows how to get me; I'll give her that.

I love designer clothes. Only my bank account doesn't love them as much as I do.

Not that she didn't already have me at Vaughn West, but I'm not going to let her know just how easily I'm won over. Especially not when I'm coming in at second.

"Okay…I'll do it."

Wardrobe

"Yay!" I hear her hands clap in the background. "You're the best, Charly! I'll get the office to book your ticket for tomorrow, and I'll have them email it to you tonight along with the details of your hotel."

"Maybe I should just sleep at the airport tonight."

I'm half-joking. Still, she laughs.

"It's going to be so much fun, working together again. I can't wait! We're gonna have a blast. Get yourself home, and get some sleep, crazy girl. I'll see you tomorrow!" she sings.

"See you," I say with way less enthusiasm at the thought of having to fly all the way across the country tomorrow when I've only just gotten back home.

But the money...

I can treat myself to those Manolos I've been drooling over...and, of course, Vaughn West. Gorgeous, sexy Vaughn West.

Le sigh.

I drop my phone in my bag and head out to grab a cab. On the way, I call the agency that gets me jobs, and I let them know that I can't do the Broadway gig anymore.

Thirty minutes later, I'm walking up the steps of the brownstone that I call home.

Nick and I live in a small two-bedroom apartment on 95th Street on the Upper West Side. Well, calling it *small* is probably over-egging it a bit. It's tiny. I could lie down on the floor of our living room/kitchen, and my head and feet would nearly touch the opposite walls. At five-eight, I'm not exactly short, but still, it's not big for an apartment. But the rent is good for a two-bed. And it's ours, and I love it even if I don't get to see it often at the moment.

I unlock the main door, letting myself into our building, and I take the first flight up to our apartment.

"Honey, I'm home," I call out. Shutting the door behind me, I drop my bags near it.

Nick appears out of his bedroom, a smile on his face. "Hey, gorgeous."

He's a sight for sore eyes. It's been well over a month since I last saw him. He saunters over, all six foot of him, and slaps a kiss on my cheek.

"Your hair looks cool," he says.

"You think?" I finger a strand of my hair. I had lilac and pink highlights put in a week ago. It's the first time I've ever dyed my hair. I just really fancied a change, and cutting my waist-length honey-blonde hair was not an option. I have great hair. Thick with a natural wave.

"Yeah, it looks good on you. You hungry?" he asks, heading to the kitchen. "I was just about to make some soup."

"By make, do you mean—"

"Pour out of a can and heat up. Yeah." He throws me back a grin before opening up the cupboard door where we keep the canned goods.

I take a seat on one of the stools at our breakfast bar.

"Chicken noodle or lentil?" he asks, holding up the cans.

"Chicken noodle."

I watch Nick move around our kitchen—getting out bowls and spoons, opening the cans, pouring the contents into the bowls, and putting the first in the microwave.

Nick has been my best friend since we met at college. We were both studying at The Art Institute of New York City. I'd just moved to New York from Philadelphia, and Nick had moved here from Canada on a study visa. I was studying fashion design, and Nick was studying interior design. We met at the party of a girl who was on my course. That's why our tiny apartment looks so awesome—because of Nick. His eye for design is amazing. He can make the smallest of space roomy but homey, which is what he's done with our place.

Wardrobe Malfunction

He works for a small interior design company. One day, he wants to run his own interior design business.

I wanted to be a fashion designer. Wasn't so easy to land a job, as I found out when I graduated. That's how I found myself working in wardrobe. I have bills to pay, I'm a good seamstress, and I still get to work with clothes. I still design in my spare time, but I haven't done anything with my designs in a long time. They sit in my sketchpad, and no one sees them but me—and, occasionally, Nick when I let him.

"So, I have news."

"Good news?" Nick asks, leaning back against the counter, folding his arms over his chest, showing off his toned biceps.

At six foot with jet-black hair and blue eyes, Nick is gorgeous, of course, but not my type. And I'm definitely not his. I'm rocking a vagina for starters, and Nick definitely likes cock.

Makes two of us.

But Nick's not just my best friend; he's also family to me. The only family I have.

"Depends on how you look at it. I'm gonna be working on the new Vaughn West movie."

Nick meets my eyes, grinning. He knows I have a tiny crush on Vaughn West. But, I mean, who doesn't?

"That sounds like great news to me," he teases with a lift of his brows.

"Yeah, it is. The downside is, the job is in LA, and they need me ASAP, so I have to leave tomorrow."

"Bummer. And you were going to have a week off, too."

"I know." I sigh. "But Ava called—you remember Ava Simms? Well, she offered me the job. She's wardrobe mistress on set."

"Yeah, I remember her. You worked on Broadway together, right? How is she?"

"She sounded good."

"She still dating that dick? The one she moved to LA with."

"Jeremy. She didn't say otherwise, so I'd say so."

The timer goes off on the microwave. Nick gets the bowl out and puts it in front of me before handing me a spoon.

"Well, I only just got you back. The place is too quiet without you. Gonna miss you, gorgeous."

Warmth coats my skin, and my throat thickens. It's always good to know that someone's going to miss me. After never having anyone to miss me in my Philly life, it means a lot, having Nick.

"I'll miss you, too." I smile.

"So, how long's the job for?" he asks, getting a couple of beers out of the fridge. He pulls the tops off and hands me one.

"Couple of months," I answer, taking the beer and putting it down on the counter. Spooning up some soup, I blow on it before putting it in my mouth. "But the pay is good. Really good."

"I'm happy for you." He lifts his bottle to me, so I pick mine up and chink it with his.

"Thanks." I take a sip of my beer.

"So, Vaughn West, eh?" Nick gives me a suggestive look.

"Ha! As if! He's way out of my league. Like galaxies out of my league." I put my bottle down.

"You're beautiful, and you know it."

Beautiful might be pushing it. Okay, so I've never had a problem with getting guys in the past. Just not Vaughn West kind of guys.

"The guy dates actresses and supermodels. Not normal girls like me." I point a finger at myself.

"And he just had his heart broken by that bitch Piper Watts. You could fix it for him, Charly." He gives me a suggestive look. "A normal girl might be just what he needs right now."

I laugh, shaking my head. "Doubtful. The closest I'll be getting to Vaughn West is when I take his inner leg measurement."

Charly

LANDING IN AT LAX after a six-hour flight and with the three-hour time difference, I feel like I haven't slept for a week even though I slept a good eight hours last night. It's all this traveling. I'm jet-lagged as hell. My body doesn't know which time zone it's in.

I'm so ready to get a cab and check in to my hotel and sleep.

I grab my case off the carousel, hitch my fake Gucci up onto my shoulder, and head out in the direction of Arrivals, texting Nick to let him know I landed.

I walk through the open door into Arrivals.

"Charly!"

At the sound of my name, I lift my head from my phone.

"Ava." I grin.

Pressing Send on the text, I drop my cell in my bag and make my way over to her.

"Hey." She embraces me in a hug. "How was your flight?"

"Long." I chuckle. "You look great," I tell her, stepping out of her hold.

I've always been uncomfortable when people hug me. It comes from a lifetime of never being hugged, I guess.

Ava is really pretty and my total opposite. Where I'm tall and blonde, she's small and brunette. And she's a little older than me. Ava is twenty-eight, and I'm twenty-five.

"The California sun is really working for you," I tell her. "Those highlights or sun-bleached?"

"Sun-bleached." She flicks a hand through her poker-straight hair.

"I'm seriously envying your tan right now as well." I glance down at my white arms. Even though it was hot in Nashville, I didn't catch a tan. I'm one of those people who has to sunbathe for hours to catch even a little color.

"Yeah, but you look great, and I'm loving your hair," she says, moving to the side to examine my hair. "Is that pink and purple you have in there?"

"Pink and lavender," I tell her.

"I might have to get some in my hair."

"You totally should."

"Cool. Something for us to do together while we're here." She threads her arm through mine. "We should get moving. I parked in short-term."

"Thanks for coming to pick me up," I say as we walk through the airport. "I thought I'd be grabbing a cab."

"As if!" She laughs.

We push through the doors into the LA sunshine.

"Welcome to LA." She squeezes my arm with hers. "You been here before?"

"First time."

"You're gonna love it!"

She leads me over to her car, which is one of those Smart cars.

Wardrobe Malfunction

"Um, will my case fit in there?" I ask, skeptically eyeing the car.

"Course it will." She laughs a bright and breezy sound, opening the trunk.

Surprisingly, my case fits in easily, with room to spare. Guess they're bigger than they look.

I climb in the passenger seat and strap myself in. The car feels really light and not sturdy at all.

"You sure we won't blow away with a strong gust of wind?" I ask as she turns the engine on.

The sound of Machine Gun Kelly and Camila Cabello's "Bad Things" blasts out her stereo. I love this song.

She rolls her eyes at me. "Don't be hating on Sunny," she says over the music. "And do you see any wind around here?"

"First off, you named your car Sunny? And, second, you can't see wind. It's invisible."

She laughs loudly. "God, I forgot what a smart-ass you are! I've missed you, babe. So glad you're here."

There's something in her tone that doesn't sound like she's totally happy, but I don't ask. She'll tell me if and when she wants to.

"That's why you love me—my smart mouth."

"And your ability to sniff out a designer sale in a ten-mile radius."

"It's a gift." I dramatically flick my hand, making her laugh again.

"Where are you staying?" Ava asks as she pulls onto the highway.

"Um..." I dig out the paperwork I printed last night from my bag. "The Comfort Inn on Sunset Boulevard."

"God, the studio is cheap."

"I'm guessing the Chateau Marmont was all booked up." I give her a sarcastic grin.

"You could have stayed with me...but Jeremy..."

"Ava, it's fine." I wave her off. "The hotel has a pool, which is always a plus."

"And it's only a five-minute walk to the studio."

"Another bonus. See? I'll be fine. And I'll only be here for, what?"

"Three weeks max. Then, we're heading to Vegas."

"Vegas, baby! Vegas!" I cheer.

"Have you ever been to Vegas?" she asks me.

"Once. Years ago. So, tell me more about the movie," I say, quickly changing the subject. I don't want her asking why I was in Vegas all those years ago.

"Which movie?"

I give her a stupid look. "The one we're working on, you numpty. The film with Makes Me Wet West in it."

"Numpty?" She throws me a confused glance, totally ignoring my new nickname for Vaughn West.

I think it's a great nickname. I should get it printed on T-shirts. I could make a killing.

"It's British. Means dumbass."

"And you're British? Since when?"

"I'm not. I just like their curse words. They're way more fun than ours."

"You're so odd." She laughs.

"I prefer the term *unconventional*." I playfully stick my tongue out at her.

She makes a lane change, and the car in front cuts her off. She honks her horn.

"Mirrors, asshole!" she yells at the driver of the car, who obviously can't hear a word she's saying, as she angrily waves her hand around. "Fucking asshole needs to learn how to drive a car. And they say women are bad drivers. Dickhead!"

Note to self: Never piss off Ava while in a car.

"Steady there, Ronda Rousey."

Wardrobe Malfunction

She glances at me, her face moving from pissed to embarrassed. "Sorry." She grimaces. "Idiots like that just piss me off."

"No kidding. Remind me never to get on your bad side," I say, making her laugh. "So, the film?"

"Oh, yeah. I told you West is in it"—*oh, yes, you did, and he's mainly the reason I'm here*—"and that Evans is directing. It's a gangster film, so the clothes are pretty much straightforward—suits, classy dresses. Natasha Warner is in it, playing the female lead."

"Ooh, I love her." I clap my hands.

"Yeah, she's super nice as well. I met her last week. She and Vaughn are gonna steam the screens up."

"And I will be watching that scene with the utmost concentration."

I grin, and Ava giggles, her brows rising in agreement.

"Right?"

"Those two would make beautiful babies," I muse.

"Agreed. But Natasha's married, and she already has a baby, remember?"

"Oh, yeah. She's married to that hot NFL player…"

"Carter Williams."

"Lucky bitch."

We both sigh at the same time.

"So, what about you? You seeing anyone?"

"Nah." I shake my head. "I've been busy a lot as of late, and after the disaster that was Michael, I decided to give dating a break."

"Wasn't that about two years ago? And I guess you are super picky."

"I am not picky!" I squawk, affronted. "I work in the clothing industry. Most of the men I work with are gay."

"I work in this industry, too, and I managed to meet someone."

"An actor. I don't want to date an actor."

"Says Miss Not Picky. And what's wrong with actors?" She flicks me a look.

Oops.

"Nothing. I just want to date a blue-collar guy."

Honestly, I think it would be hard to date an actor, having to watch them get it on with other women on the big screen. Also, there's a high probability that said actor would screw his costar and dump me. Plus, actors are high-maintenance. I might drool over hot actors—aka Vaughn West, Chris and Liam Hemsworth…God, two brothers. Anyway, I wouldn't say no to a roll in the sack with any of them—and, yes, I know dreams don't come true. But, in reality and for the long-term, I want a nice, normal blue-collar guy who works with his hands all day long and then comes home and ravages me with those rough, callous, hard-working hands.

"Wasn't Michael a drug dealer?" Ava pipes up.

"Yes, he was a drug dealer, but I didn't know that when I met him." I frown. "He told me he worked construction. I dumped him as soon as I found out his real profession."

Of course, dumbass that I am, it took me six months to figure it out. But it's not like I could have had anything serious with Michael—or with anyone back then. And, still, not now—well, for a short time longer, that is.

"And, well, I can't be that picky, considering I went out with Michael," I add.

"Yeah, he was a dick. But a good-looking dick." She grins.

She's right. He was gorgeous.

"He had a good-looking dick, too…very *big*." I size out with my hands. "That's the only thing I miss about him."

We both giggle.

Ava pulls off the highway, heading onto Sunset Boulevard. I watch out the window, taking in the sights.

"So, who else is on the team?" I ask her.

"It's just me, you, and Logan."

Wardrobe
MALFUNCTION

"Logan?"

"Logan Cheung."

"I don't think I know him," I muse, tapping a finger to my chin.

"He's an LA native. Wants to be an actor."

"Who doesn't in this town?" I quip.

"He's lovely though. Told me he started working in wardrobe to try and get a foot in the industry. He's real good, and he has a real natural flair for style. And, God, can the man sew."

"And, without stereotyping, I'm guessing he's gay?"

"Of course." She smirks.

She pulls up in front of the hotel. I stare up at it. It looks okay. And I stayed in worse places back when I lived in Philly.

"You want me to come in with you? Then, we can go out and get some dinner," Ava offers.

"Nah, I'm knackered. I'm just gonna get room service, if they do it, and crash. All this traveling has wiped me out."

"Cool."

"Thanks for the ride." I reach over and give her a one-armed hug.

"I'll see you in the morning. Show you around the wardrobe. Oh, you'll need this to get into the studio." She reaches over into the glove box, pulls out a pass on a lanyard, and hands it to me. "Your pass to get in the studio."

"What time do you need me there?" I open the door, readying to get out.

"I'm getting in at eight thirty. Vaughn's coming in for a fitting at ten. I've assigned him to you, as he was Millie's, and I know how much you like him."

She gives me a knowing smile, and I shake my head, getting out of the car.

I hook my bag on my shoulder and drop the lanyard in it. Leaning down, I say, "I'll be there at eight thirty then. See you tomorrow."

"See you then."

I shut the door and get my case out of the trunk. I tap my hand on the roof to let her know I'm good. Then, I wave bye and head into the hotel.

Charly

MY SEWING CASE IN HAND, I'm at the studio. I arrived here ten minutes ago, and Ava has been showing me around the warehouse where all the clothes and costumes for the studio are kept.

"This is the main wardrobe and props area…and this is our section for storage."

I follow her over to the rails of clothes and storage units.

"Everything is labeled, so we know which is ours. But we have a trailer over by the studio they're filming in, so we can do fittings there. All of Vaughn's stuff is already over there. I had Logan move it over for you yesterday."

"Brilliant. Thanks."

"Here's Vaughn's sheet, listing what he'll need on which days."

"Great, thanks." I take the file from her. "What about the other actors?"

"Logan has Natasha. The rest of the cast, I've split between the two of you, and we'll work out the schedule as we go."

"And you just sit back and give us orders?" I grin.

She sticks her tongue out at me. "Because we're a small team, I'll be on set for any alterations, and I get the awesome tasks of inventory and keeping your ass in check."

"I am a handful," I tell her with a serious face.

"No kidding." She laughs, swatting me on the ass.

"Hey! Sexual harassment!" I call out with a laugh.

She shakes her head, laughing. "Come on, I'll show you the trailer and introduce you to Logan."

We walk over to the trailer. I follow her inside. It looks just like all other wardrobes I've worked in, nothing different.

Except for the hottie over by the table, who's sewing a button on a Marc Jacobs blazer.

"Logan, I'd like you to meet Charly."

He snaps off the thread and puts the blazer down. "Hey, Charly. Good to meet you."

He stands up to shake my hand. I'd say he's about five-eleven, and he has a lovely face, dark eyes, and jet-black hair. Best of all, he's dressed in a snappy suit. I love a man in a suit.

"I love your top," he says.

I glance down at it. I'm wearing my black You Can't Sit With Us cropped tank. It's my favorite. I love it. I teamed it with my ripped Gucci jeans that I got at a seventy percent off sale and my Zara wedges. My hair is down, and my makeup is light. I'm rocking the basics, if I do say so myself.

"Thanks. Love your suit. Tom Ford, this season, right?"

"Right." He smiles.

I hear a phone beep, and then Ava's saying, "Shit. I've got to go pick up Natasha's dresses. I forgot they'd be ready

Wardrobe

this morning. Charly, will you be okay if I disappear for a bit?"

"Sure"—I wave her off—"I'll be fine."

"Don't forget that Vaughn is coming in at ten thirty."

"Ten thirty. Got it."

I watch her disappear out the door we just came in through.

"I need to get this jacket to Marcus—supporting cast actor," Logan explains, "and see if it's right this time. I might be a while. He can be...tricky."

"Gotcha. No worries. I'll just familiarize myself with this place."

Then, Logan's gone, and I'm alone.

I have a look around, finding where everything is. I locate Vaughn's clothes on the rail, so I get them off and set them up on the table. I get my sewing kit all ready.

And then I'm good to go, with time to kill.

Honestly, I'm feeling a little nervous.

Of course I've worked with actors before, but this is Vaughn West.

He's a huge star.

And gorgeous.

I decide to do some work on my latest design. I pull out my sketchpad from my handbag, set my cell on the table, and start my playlist. I open my pad at the drawing I've been working on this past week.

It's a wedding dress. Strapless bodice encrusted with crystals and a lace ribbon stitched under the breast with the ends of the ribbon set with crystals as well. I just can't decide on the skirt. It's been bugging me all week.

Madonna's "Dress You Up" starts to play on my phone.

I love this song! It's my anthem.

Putting my pad down, I turn the volume up.

Then, I'm singing along and getting to my feet. Picking up a lint roller to use as my mock microphone, I'm singing my heart out, dancing around, twerking my ass off to Madge, and—

"Shit! Fuck!" I yell mid turn, the lint roller dropping out of my hand and to the floor.

Because Vaughn West is standing in the doorway—arms folded, his shoulder leaning on the doorframe—watching me.

Oh my God.

I dart over and silence the music, closing my sketchpad. "God, you scared me." I'm breathing quickly. I press my hand to my chest, my heart pounding. "I wasn't expecting you."

"Yeah, I got that."

His voice... *dear God*. Deep and raspy and sexy.

I take a good look at him, and he's even better in real life than he looks on-screen.

He's beautiful. And tall. I know he's six foot two and a half. And, no, I'm not a stalker. I read it in a magazine once.

He's dressed in blue jeans and a simple black tee that highlights the golden tone of his skin. His hair is tousled, like he's been running his hands through it. And his lips, so full and kissable... and his eyes... they're like melted chocolate with caramel in the center...

Then, I realize he's laughing at me. Well, not laughing, laughing, but there's definitely mirth in those gorgeous eyes of his.

And I'm back to planet Earth with a bang. Where I've just made a complete fool of myself in front of Vaughn West.

Someone, please kill me now.

"I am sorry about that." I jerk my thumb over my shoulder. "I wasn't expecting you for a while, and when Madonna comes on, you just have to sing along, you know?"

"Oh, yeah. Every time I hear Madonna playing, I have to drop what I'm doing and shake my ass to the beat."

Wardrobe

"Right?" I exclaim, sounding a little shrill.

I might be a tad flustered and flying high on adrenaline right now, which is why it takes me a beat longer to realize he's actually taking the piss.

"So, anyway"—I brush it off with a shake of my shoulders—"embarrassing moment aside, I'm Charlotte Michaels; everyone calls me Charly. I'm your new dresser. I'm replacing Millie. It's really great to meet you, Mr. West." I walk over to him and stick my hand out to shake his.

He seems even taller up close. I'm not exactly short at five-eight, and I've got my three-inch wedges on, giving me extra height, but I feel like a little girl standing in front of him.

Vaughn glances down at my hand like he can't quite figure me out, and then he looks back up at my face with an expression that says he thinks I'm mentally impaired—which isn't surprising, considering he just walked in on me wailing out to Madonna and twerking.

Honestly, I question my own sanity at times.

"Vaughn's fine," he says but makes no move to shake my hand.

"Okay." I awkwardly pull my hand back, trying not to feel like a complete moron. "Vaughn, it is."

Then, we're just standing there, staring at each other.

"So…" he says.

"Right. Clothes." I snap myself to attention.

I turn to the table where I left the clothes I need to alter for him, and I pick up the pants off the top of the pile. Black Armani suit pants. He'll look super hot in them.

"To start with, I need you to try these on. Ava's notes said they don't fit properly. I just need to see them on, so I can resize them for you."

He takes the pants from my hand. "In here?" He gestures to the curtained-off area.

"Yes."

Vaughn goes into the changing area, pulling the curtain across. I turn to the table and bend over, dropping my head on it with a silent groan.

Ugh. God, I can't believe I was just twerking to Madonna, and Vaughn West walked in on me and saw me. I'm such a fucking loser.

I hear the rustle of clothing from behind me. I pick my head up, righting myself.

Vaughn West is undressing and quite possibly naked, only ten feet behind me.

Holy crap.

I'm actually starting to sweat a little.

I fan my face with my hand.

Jesus, get it together, Charly.

A minute later, I hear the rail rattle, telling me the curtain is being pulled back.

I turn around, and...*holy shit.*

He's shirtless.

He's just wearing the pants.

No shoes. Just bare feet.

Sweet baby Jesus.

Bare feet and ripped chests are my kryptonite, especially if the man has nice feet—which, of course, Vaughn does—and his chest...*man alive!*

It's the kind of chest you want to spend days licking all kinds of melted sweets off. To be honest, I'd happily lick his sweat off his chest. Run my tongue over those abs and ridges, down that happy trail—

"Where do you want me?"

Is that a trick question?

I cough. "Just over here, please."

He walks toward me, and my vagina thuds in time with his footsteps.

When he reaches me, I get a whiff of male. He doesn't smell like I expected. I thought he'd be all rich cologne and expensive fabrics.

Wardrobe

But Vaughn smells outdoorsy. Like cinder and spice. Like he just got back from a stint in the woods, chopping trees.

He smells good. It's doing wonderful things to my girl parts.

I want to take a deep breath and swallow a lungful of him.

This is what two years of sex with only a vibrator and my imagination for company does.

Don't think of the imaginary sex you've had with him in your head.

Don't do it.

Of course I think about it. My brain flashes to the scene where he has me in the shower, up against the tiled wall, fucking me like a maniac. Exactly the same as what he did in the scene with Martha Vance in *Ricochet*. Lucky bitch. I just replaced her face with my own. I always come hard and fast to that one. It's my favorite.

And, now, my whole body is on fire because I'm pretty sure it's written all over my face that I'm having sex thoughts about him.

Jesus Christ.

Forcing my mind back to work, I step back and look over the pants, making sure to check the fit and not the bulge in the front.

"How do they feel?" I ask.

"Fine."

"They look a little loose around the inner thigh and crotch area," I muse, tapping my finger to my chin.

"Are you saying I have skinny thighs and a small package?"

"What? God, no!" And, of course, my eyes go straight to said package. "I just meant that the pants are slightly oversized in that area, and you need them more fitted, not that you have a small cock—package! I mean, package!"

Holy fuck, someone, please stop me.

My face is on fire, and I'm sweating like a donkey pulling a fat man on a cart.

"Chill." He laughs once. It's deep and throaty and sexy as hell. "I'm kidding with you."

"Oh. Oh, right. Cool." I take a deep breath, pressing my hand to my chest.

Needing a moment to cool my face down, I turn to the table, get my wrist pincushion, which is already loaded up with pins, and fasten it to my wrist.

I turn back to him, feeling a little more in control, and without looking him in the face, I get down to my knees in front of him, putting me at cock-level.

I'm on my knees in front of Vaughn West. Sure, I'm only pinning his pants, but still…it's one for the books.

"Okay, so if you could just spread your legs a little for me, that'd be great."

I hear those words back in my head and want to die. Thankfully, he doesn't comment and just shifts his stance, parting his legs for me.

I try to relax because I am nervous…because he's *him*.

Come on, Charly, you've done this a thousand times. He's just a man.

A hot, gorgeous, famous man. But a man all the same.

Sucking in a silent breath, I start on the right inner thigh, hemming the material in and tacking it with pins. Vaughn tenses.

Lots of people get uncomfortable when I'm doing this. I mean, it is weird, having a stranger this close who is sticking pins in the clothes you're wearing.

I shift over to his left leg, and he tenses again. Discomfort is radiating from him, which is making me feel uncomfortable.

He clears his throat.

I look up at him. His brows are pinched. He looks like he's in pain.

"Almost done," I tell him.

Wardrobe Malfunction

Now, for the crotch area.

I've been purposely keeping my eyes away from this part of his body, but now, I have no choice but to look.

And...*oh my God.*

He's got a boner. Well, not a boner, boner, but there's definitely a semi going on there.

Then, it hits me.

Vaughn West has a semi over me.

The things that is doing for my self-confidence right now.

I feel like doing an air punch. And possibly another twerk.

But, of course, I'm a professional, so I pretend not to notice. Expression schooled—and I can't even begin to tell you how hard that is, pun intended—I say to him, "Okay, a few more pins, and we're done."

I take a pin from the cushion and turn the fabric in to pin it. As I move my hand, my knuckles accidentally—and, I swear, it's an accident—brush against him. His hips jerk forward right as I'm pushing the pin in the material of his pants, and—

"Jesus! Fuck!" he yells, jumping back away from me.

I stare up at him in shock.

Oh, shit. No...

Please no.

I just stabbed Vaughn West in the cock with a pin.

I just stabbed the world's biggest movie star. With a pin. In his cock.

I snap into action, leaping to my feet. "Oh my God! I'm so sorry! I can't believe I just did that! It was an accident, I swear! I can't believe I stabbed you in your cock! I mean, penis! Oh, Jesus." I cover my face with my hands.

"Ball sack." He moans a pained sound.

I drop my hands. "What?"

"You got me in my ball sack, not my cock. Jesus, fuck, this hurts! What did you stab me with? A knife?"

"A pin. And it was only a small one."

The glare he fixes me with makes me want to piss my pants.

"I really am sorry. So, so sorry." I wince.

I'm so fired.

"Let me help you." I move toward him, but he backs away from me.

"Seriously, stay the fuck away. I can't believe you just stabbed me."

"Pinned."

He glares again.

"Sorry," I mumble, dropping my gaze.

"Vaughn?"

"What?" he snaps.

"The pin…it's still in…*there*."

His eyes follow mine down. "Jesus Christ," he groans.

"Do you want me to pull it out?"

"No, I don't want you to fucking pull it out! I'm not letting you anywhere near me ever again. You've probably just killed all my best swimmers. I swear to God, if I lose a ball because of you—"

"That's a tad dramatic. It was just a tiny pin."

I don't think I've ever seen someone as angry as he looks right now. His face his red, bordering purple.

"Okay, so let me stick a *tiny* pin in your clit and see how you get on," he grits out.

"Okay. Point taken." I clamp my thighs together.

And I watch quietly as he takes a few deep breaths before he takes ahold of the pin and yanks it out.

"Motherfucker!"

"Are you okay?"

"No, I'm not fucking okay!" he snaps.

He opens the button on the pants and carefully pulls the zipper down, and I realize he's about to check his damaged goods.

Should I look away or watch? That's the million-dollar question.

Wardrobe Malfunction

"Can you turn around?" he barks at me.

"I was just about to," I mumble, turning away.

And I swear to God I was going to.

I hear him groan.

"Christ, I'm fucking bleeding. What the hell kind of pin was that? And what the hell kind of seamstress are you?"

I have to stop myself from correcting him that I'm actually a wardrobe assistant and not a seamstress, but something tells me that wouldn't go down too well. So, all I say is, "Sorry," for the hundredth time.

A few seconds later, I hear movement and then feet shuffling.

I risk a glance over my shoulder.

I see him limping toward the changing room—in only his boxer shorts.

Holy cow! He's naked! Well, not completely naked, but…

He has great legs. Really long and toned.

And I just stabbed him in his ball sack.

That thought quickly drenches my pervy libido right back down.

"Can I do anything?" I ask quietly.

"No."

Okay then.

Out of the corner of my eye, I see him get his cell from his jeans pocket, which are hanging on the peg in there.

He dials and puts the phone to his ear, his other hand cupping his junk over his boxer shorts.

God, I can't believe I stabbed him with a pin. All these years I've been doing this job, and I've never stabbed anyone—oh, fuck. He's making a call. What if he's calling to get me fired?

"Vaughn…Mr. West." I turn to face him, not bothering to care that he's practically naked, and I press my hands together in front of me in a pleading manner. "I really am sorry. It was an accident and—"

The look he hits me with slams my lips back shut.

45

"Alex, I need a doctor," he says into his phone. "What? No, I just got stabbed in one of my balls with a pin."

He glares at me again, and I shrink in on myself.

"Yes, I'm being serious. The seamstress in wardrobe. It's not funny, you prick. Yeah, I'm still in wardrobe. Bring the doctor here. And, Alex, it goes without saying…discreet. Yeah. See you soon." He hangs up his cell.

He was calling for a doctor, not having me fired. Thank you, God.

"Thank you. I thought you were calling to have me fired."

Another glare. This one, a narrow-eyed glare. "The day is still young."

Shit.

I watch as he walks over to a chair. He lets out a pained sound as he sits down.

My natural instinct is to help him, but I know he doesn't want me anywhere near him, so I stay put.

And then I'm just standing there, like a spare part.

"Do you want me to get you an ice pack while you wait for the doctor?"

"Why? So you can freeze my balls off, seeing as though your first attempt at maiming me didn't work?"

I bite my tongue.

Asshole. I know I hurt him, but it's not like I did it on purpose.

"No." My voice is tight. "To help numb the pain."

"Fine," he grumbles, not looking at me.

I head over to the small refrigerator that I spotted earlier, hoping it has a freezer compartment in it. And, thankfully, it does.

I grab a clean dish towel, put some ice inside, and fold it up.

I take it back to Vaughn. He's quiet, his head tipped back, eyes closed.

"Here," I say softly.

Wardrobe
MALFUNCTION

He opens his eyes, his angry stare back on me.

Ignoring his anger, I hand the ice pack to him.

He rests it over his injured part, a soft moan escaping his lips.

I wonder if that's what he sounds like when he's—

Jesus, Charly.

"Better?" I ask, clearing my perverted thoughts away.

"Better would be not being stabbed in the ball sack by some crazy twerking chick who clearly can't do her job properly."

"Hey now! It wasn't entirely my fault. You did jerk your hips forward—"

"Because you groped my cock!"

"I didn't grope your cock!" I splutter indignantly. "I *accidentally* brushed it with my knuckles as I was taking in the fabric! And, anyway, if you hadn't had a boner, then I probably wouldn't have even touched it—by *accident*!"

"I didn't have a boner!" he scoffs. "You're not my type, *seamstress*."

What. A. Dick.

"I'm not a seamstress!" I yell. "I'm a *wardrobe* assistant." Who's currently yelling at the man who can have her fired with a snap of his fingers.

God, this is so not how I expected my first meeting with Vaughn West to go.

For starters, I have to stop yelling. I need to be the bigger person here. After all, I did just hurt him in the worst place possible for a man.

"Look, Mr. West"—I take a step toward him, softening my tone—"I really am sorry. For stabbing you…*there*. It honestly was an accident. I would never do that intentionally. And I'm sorry for yelling just now. I was out of line."

"Yeah, you were," he grunts.

Then, nothing. He doesn't apologize for yelling at me.

Jerkface.

47

"Are you just gonna stand there, staring at me all day?" he rasps out.

"I'm sorry." I step back, surprised.

"Look, do me a favor, *wardrobe assistant*, and leave me in fucking peace while I wait for the doctor to arrive."

Wow. Okay then.

Asshole.

Without another word, I grab my bag and walk out of there.

It's not until I'm halfway across the studio lot that I realize he never said anything about not having me fired.

Shit.

Vaughn

I'M RESTING UP ON the sofa in the hotel, watching sports on TV, when there's a knock at the door.

On a sigh, I get up, and cupping my balls with my hand, I amble over to the door.

I'm still taking it steady. This is precious cargo we're talking about here.

Not long after Ball-Sack-Stabbing Chick left, Alex turned up with the doctor.

The doctor checked me over and told me there was no serious damage, just a small puncture wound. It didn't penetrate the sack, meaning my boys are still intact. *Thank fuck.* I had feared at one point that I was going to be leaking cum out of the wrong hole.

The doctor just said to take it easy for the rest of the day, so Alex drove me back to the hotel. Then, he left to run some errands.

God, that seamstress—wardrobe assistant, whatever the hell she is, I can't believe she stabbed me in the balls.

When I first walked in on her twerking her ass off, I thought she was funny. Cute.

Okay, she's hot.

And, when she was on her knees at my feet...yeah, there was a lot going through my mind at that moment—right before she stabbed me in the balls, that is.

She might be hot, but she's a danger to cocks everywhere.

Reaching the door, I check the peephole. Never can be too careful. I might go under a pseudo name in hotels, but the fans always seem to have a way of finding me.

Nope, not a stalker fan. Her. Ball-Sack-Stabbing Chick.

I swing the door open. "What are you doing here? How did you find me?"

"Oh. Hi. I spoke to your PA, Alex. He told me where to find you."

Alex is so fired.

"What do you want?" I frown.

"To...um..." She shifts nervously, biting her lip. Her lips are glossy and painted red. She's dressed in a different outfit from earlier as well.

It's surprising that I remember what she was wearing earlier. But I do. I remember because I liked the way her tits looked in the top she was wearing.

Now, she's got on one of those jumpsuits that women seem to like wearing nowadays. It's short, showing off a gorgeous pair of long legs. She has heeled sandals on her feet. I notice her toenails are painted red, like her lips. Lifting my eyes, I see the necklace she's wearing has fallen into her cleavage.

I instantly have dirty thoughts about putting something else between her cleavage.

My dick pokes his head up.

Wardrobe Malfunction

Whoa. Down, boy. Crazy lady who tried to take one of your boys out, remember?

"Well? I haven't got all day." I'm being an ass, which isn't like me. But then again, I've never been stabbed in the junk by a chick before.

Anger flashes in her eyes, but it's quickly gone, and I'm oddly disappointed.

I kind of liked arguing with her earlier even if I was in pain. Arguing with her felt like foreplay.

"Can I come in?" she asks, her voice a little more pronounced than before.

I sigh and then stand aside, letting her in.

As she passes me, I get a whiff of raspberries and vanilla. It makes my head spin.

I shut the door and follow her into the living area.

"Nice place," she says, her eyes taking in the space.

"It's okay, I guess. So, what can I do for you?" I ask, folding my arms, leaning my ass against the back of the sofa.

She presses her hands together in front of her. "I came to apologize again, Mr. West. And, also, to thank you for not having me fired. I want you to know I appreciate it. Really, I do. And I shouldn't have yelled at you; I was totally out of line. And what happened earlier"—she nods south, at my junk—"has never happened before. I swear, I'm a total professional, and I really am good at my job."

"Opinions vary."

She sucks in a breath, anger flashing through her eyes. Then, she blows out a calming breath.

A sick part of me is enjoying this. Watching her squirm.

"How are you feeling?"

"Like someone stabbed me in one of my balls with a pin."

She grimaces. "I honestly don't know what happened."

"I do. You weren't paying attention to what you were doing."

Her mouth opens, but no words come out. Very slowly, she closes her mouth.

"I brought you something." She reaches into her oversized bag and pulls out a parcel wrapped in brown paper along with an envelope.

She hands the envelope over.

I open it and pull out what appears to be a homemade card.

It is a homemade card. A little old-style film camera, a clapper board, and the Hollywood sign—all made out of different fabrics—are glued to the front, and written in glittery gold pen at the top…

"*Get West Soon.*" I lift my eyes and brows at her.

"It was a play on *well* and your name, *West*. I thought it sounded cute at the time, but…yeah, it's pretty lame…" She trails off, looking at her feet.

It's not lame. It is actually kind of cute.

I'm being a dick.

"You made this?" I ask.

Her cheeks turn pink, and she smiles. She has a great smile. It lights up her whole face.

"Yeah. I like to make things. Clothes mainly. But I like to make cards; it's more personal than buying one, you know."

I wouldn't know. I haven't bought a card in years. It's not like I can pop out to the shops to get one. Not without a bodyguard at the very least. Alex always buys them for me.

"Is that for me as well?" I gesture to the package she's still holding in her hands.

"Oh, yeah. It's…well, it's just something I made. I thought it might help, but you don't have to use it. And I'm sorry about the paper. It was all I could get." She hands it over.

I put the card and envelope down on the sofa and unwrap the package.

Wardrobe Malfunction

Staring down at the unidentifiable black object in my hand, I toss the wrapping paper onto the sofa behind me. "Um...what is it?"

"It's a sling for groin injuries. I got the design off the Internet. See"—she steps closer and takes it from me—"this part goes around your hips." She demonstrates against herself. "And, well...this is a little bit different than the usual straps used for groin injuries, but I made a, um...well, a part for your..." She points in the direction of my dick. "And a pouch for your...balls...to support the injured one. And I also put in an inner pouch that has a cooling gel pack in it, which, of course, you can change out."

I'm staring at her, mouth open.

She made me a cock warmer.

I'm in shock. And kind of turned on right now.

I know. I'm a sick bastard.

"And I made it extra large, you know, just in case," she says, handing it back to me.

Taking it, I blink a few times and stare down at it.

The waistband part is made of soft elastic, and the cock part is made of a soft, stretchy material, kind of like Lycra.

This woman, whom I've known for less than a day, who stabbed me in the ball sack, has made me a cock warmer.

I actually don't know what to say. For once in my life, I'm speechless.

It's got to be a joke. Surely.

I blink and press my lips together. "Is this a joke?" I finally ask.

When I see the hurt flicker through her eyes, I know it's not, and I feel like a gigantic asshole.

"Um, no, it's not," she says slowly and carefully. "You know what? Forget it," she says, making a grab for it.

But I quickly move it out of her reach, suddenly wanting to play.

"No. It was really thoughtful of you." I'm fighting a smile. Then, laughter snorts out of me.

"God, you're a jerk." She frowns.

"I'm sorry, but you made me a cock warmer. What do you expect me to say?"

Her eyes narrow on me. "It's not a cock warmer. And a thank-you would've been nice. I put a lot of thought into that."

"Yeah, I can tell," I say drolly. "And, hang on, you stabbed me in the ball sack, and then you made me a cock warmer. What am I supposed to be thankful for? That I still have two balls?"

"It's not a cock warmer! It's a sling for groin injuries!" Her hands slam onto her hips.

Hips that I wouldn't mind grabbing on to while thrusting in and out of her.

I really am a sick fuck.

It terrifies me what actually turns me on.

Turns out, women who make cock warmers do it for me.

"I don't have a groin injury. I have a hole in my ball sack, thanks to you. And this"—I hold it up—"is a cock warmer. God, you are something else." I chuckle.

"And you're an asshole!"

My eyes swing to her just as she claps a hand over her mouth.

"Quite a mouth you have on you there," I say, feeling suddenly pissed off. I've never known someone who could push my buttons as quickly as this chick can. "Maybe you should put something in it to stop you from cursing out like that." I hold out the cock warmer to her. "Here, put this in there. That should help keep you quiet."

"Ugh! Stuff you, you *jerk*! I can't believe I even bothered! And have me fired because I'd rather dress a smelly tramp than you! At least he'd be more appreciative!"

Wardrobe Malfunction

She storms off, heading for the door. And I have to hold back laughter.

She's a real pistol, this one, and I just can't stop myself from stoking the fire one last time.

"Hey, Pins," I call to her back.

She swings around. Her eyes are wide and blazing.

"Pins?" she says like she can't believe I had the audacity to call her that. "God…you are…you're just *mean*! I can't believe I ever thought you were hot!"

The realization of what she just said flickers through her eyes, and her face goes bright red.

And, in this moment, with her standing here, all angry and flustered, it is the sexiest thing I have ever seen. *She* is the sexiest thing I've ever seen. And I've seen a lot of sexy.

"I am hot. And, FYI, this won't fit, sweetheart. It's too small." I toss the cock warmer in her direction. It lands at her feet with a soft thud.

Her eyes flash with something that sets my pulse racing. "You know what? You want somewhere to stuff that cock warmer? Then, you can stuff it up your ass!"

"So, you admit, it's a cock warmer?" I'm fighting back a smile, and I'm fighting hard.

I never knew arguing could be this fun. But she somehow makes it fun.

A cute growly sound escapes her. Her nostrils flare, her little hands ball into fists at her sides, and her chest heaves up and down, showing off those magnificent tits of hers. I have never wanted to fuck a woman more.

Then, without another word, she flips me off and swings open the door, and then she is gone.

And I burst into laughter. I can't help it.

She's a spitfire.

I like her.

No way am I having her fired. I have a feeling that keeping Pins around will be very interesting. Very interesting indeed.

And, no, I'm not going to fuck her. I'd have to be insane to let her near my dick. I might love sex, but I do have some sense of self-preservation.

No, I'm going to fuck with her.

Payback is a bastard…and he goes by the name of Vaughn West.

Charly

WELL, IT SEEMS, I'M not fired, as Ava hasn't said anything.

We had dinner last night with Logan, and she never said a word. Actually, she asked how it went with Vaughn.

I couldn't tell her what had happened. I was too embarrassed.

More like mortified.

I totally fibbed and said that he hadn't turned up. I know; I lied. It was crappy. But I didn't know what else to say. Telling her the truth just wasn't an option. I don't think Ava is a gossip, but I couldn't chance her telling anyone. I knew Vaughn wouldn't want news of what I had done to him traveling. With any normal person, something like that might end up on someone's Facebook status for a good chuckle. But, for Vaughn, it would end up on the nightly news. The guy can't take a crap without it being reported, and he's had enough shit lately. He deserves a break.

I might think he's a rude, obnoxious jerk, but I'm not out to hurt him.

Well, not any more than I have already done.

I still can't believe what I did. I didn't even tell Nick when he called last night, and I tell him everything. That tells you of my level of mortification.

Ava was surprised when I said Vaughn hadn't turned up, said it wasn't like him and that she'd call his assistant to rearrange the fitting.

I didn't want her to call Alex, as he knew that Vaughn had shown up and it was me who was the problem. So, I told her not to bother, that I'd call him.

That's why I now find myself having to call Alex again—not so I can go apologize to his boss again, but this time, to actually get these clothes fitted. That is, if Vaughn will actually let me anywhere near him. Good thing is, I have the fitting for the Armani pants, so I can adjust all his other pants in line with those. There's only some shirts, a few vests, and several suit jackets for him to try on for me.

Part of me doesn't ever want to see him again after yesterday. And not just because of the stabbing incident, but because of the whole cock-warmer thing.

I feel my cheeks start to heat with embarrassment at the memory.

He was totally right; it was a cock warmer.

Not that I'd ever admit that to him.

I just hadn't thought of that when I was making it for him. I'd thought I was being helpful, and I'd wanted to make amends for hurting him.

But all that happened was, I ended up yelling at him again.

I'm surprised he didn't have me fired after that. I would have had me fired. God knows what Millie did to get herself fired. I've stabbed the guy, yelled at him, and made him a warmer for his cock, and I still have a job.

God, yesterday was a total disaster.

Wardrobe Malfunction

I guess it's true what they say; you should never meet your idol because your illusion just might be shattered.

I mean, Vaughn West wasn't exactly my idol, more like a sexual fantasy, but whatever because, honestly, I wish I'd never met him.

I'll never be able to imagine him in any other way than with a pin stuck in one of his balls now.

And he's also a mean jerk.

A handsome, super-hot, mean jerk.

I stop in Starbucks on the way to the studio and grab a caramel latte, needing some caffeine before I speak to Alex. Then, I make the call.

"Alex Larson speaking."

"Hi, Alex. It's Charly. From wardrobe."

"Oh, hey. It's my new favorite girl, Pins." He chuckles.

Pins?

Ugh.

That's what Vaughn called me right before I flipped him the bird yesterday. Shit, I forgot I had done that as well.

"Yeah, it's, uh, me."

"What can I do for you?"

"Well..." I bite my lip. "I still need to fit those clothes for Vaughn—not the pants," I'm quick to say. "Just shirts, a few vests, and some suit jackets."

"Mmhmm."

"Would he be able to come in for a fitting today, as they're needed for shots tomorrow?"

"He's got meetings all morning, and then he's running lines all afternoon."

"Oh." *Shit.*

"Does he not have any space at all to fit me in? I'll only need thirty minutes, max. I can come to him, wherever, to save him the journey."

"Okay, come to the hotel at six p.m. You remember his suite number?"

"Yes." Not forgetting that anytime soon. "Thanks, Alex. You're a lifesaver."

"Anytime."

"Alex…will he be okay with me coming to fit him?"

He laughs. "Guess we'll see when you get here. See you later, Pins."

He hangs up, and I stare down at the phone, feeling a little sick.

Oh well, I don't have any other choice than to go. I have a job to do. I'll just apologize—*again*—for yelling at him, calling him an asshole and a jerk, and giving him the middle finger. I won't let him rile me up. And I definitely won't be taking him any more I'm-sorry gifts; that's for sure.

Charly

SIX P.M. SHARP, I'M standing outside Vaughn's hotel room with his clothes hanging over my arm in a garment bag, my sewing case in my hand.

I'm wearing my dark blue distressed skinny jeans, an oversized beige sweater that falls off the shoulder, and my leopard-print Christian Louboutins that I found in a secondhand charity shop in SoHo. I swear, I nearly cried with happiness that day; they were practically brand-new. I like to think they belonged to a celebrity who was clearing out her last-season items. I now make it a point to visit that charity shop every chance I get. Hanging from my shoulder is my knock off Gucci Dionysus GG Supreme mini bag. I love her. If only she were real. My hair is tied back in a sleek ponytail. My eye makeup is light. My lips are painted red.

I look good. I feel good.

I push my shoulder back, take a deep breath, fix a smile on my face, and knock on the door.

You can do this, Charly. Yesterday was yesterday. Today is a new day.

I hear footsteps approaching the door, and it swings open, revealing someone who's not Vaughn.

Oh.

Oddly, I feel a flash of disappointment. I wanted to make an impression. A good impression.

The guy looks to be around my age or a little older. With close-cropped brown hair, he has on a pair of black-framed glasses, and he's wearing jeans, a navy-blue shirt, and a pair of Vans.

"Hi." I smile wide. "I'm Charly. I'm here to fit Mr. West—I mean, do a fitting for Mr. West. I'm from the studio. I work in wardrobe. I'm a wardrobe assistant."

For fuck's sake, Charly.

I do a mental eye roll at myself.

He smiles. "Hey, Charly. I'm Alex. It's nice to finally meet you."

Oh, it's Alex. Duh.

"Good to meet you, too, after speaking to you twice on the phone." I laugh lightly.

"Here, let me help you."

He gestures to the garment bag, so I hand it to him. He seems nice. Much nicer than his boss.

"Come in," he says.

I walk past him and into Vaughn's suite. Then, I hang near the door before following him over to the dining table on the other side of the room—where I gave Vaughn his cock warmer last night.

Dear God.

"Did you get a cab over with this stuff?" Alex asks, putting the clothes down on the dining table.

"I did." I put my sewing kit and handbag next to the clothes on the table.

"How much was it?"

"Oh, like ten bucks."

Wardrobe

He gets his wallet from his pocket and pulls up a ten-dollar bill.

"No, it's fine." I wave him off. "It's my fault I had to come over here to finish the fit."

"You sure?" He checks before putting the bill away.

"I'm sure." I smile.

"Well, I'll have Vaughn's driver take you home when you're done. No need to get a cab back."

Speaking of Vaughn...

I glance around for him.

"Vaughn's just in the shower. He'll be out in a few. Can I get you a drink?"

"A water would be great. Thanks."

He goes over to a mini fridge and gets out a bottle of water.

"Thanks," I say when he hands it to me. "So, was Mr. West okay about me coming to do the fitting?"

"Depends. You're not armed, are you?"

I swivel at the sound of Vaughn's voice behind me.

He's standing in the doorway of what I'm guessing is the bedroom. His hair is wet from the shower. He's wearing black trackpants and a fitted tank. He looks amazing.

Turns out, my attraction for him is still there—pin in ball sack aside.

He walks toward me. Eyes set on mine. My heart stutters.

He stops a foot away. "We need to stop meeting like this, Pins." His voice is low, throaty. It does funny things to me. "People will start talking."

"Hello, Mr. West. And please don't call me that."

"Vaughn. And don't call you what?"

"Pins."

"Why not? I think it's cute. And apt. Don't you, Alex?" His head tips to the side as he casts a glance at Alex.

"Leave me out of this." Alex chuckles from behind me.

Vaughn's eyes come back to mine, and a smile graces his lips.

Damn, he looks good when he smiles.

"It's not apt. It's…insulting," I state calmly. "And a little annoying."

"It annoys you? Oh. Well then, of course, I'll stop calling you it."

"Thank you," I exhale, relieved.

"No problem, Pins."

Argh!

Deep breaths, Charly. He's just doing it to wind you up. Don't react.

"Right. I'm heading to my room—unless you need me to stay?"

I sense Alex move, but I can't see what he's doing because Vaughn and I are currently locked in a staring battle.

"Nah, you're good to go," Vaughn answers him, eyes still on me.

Don't blink, Charly.

"Unless Pins plans on giving me another injury. Then, I might need you to stay. I know how lethal she can be. I have the hole in my ball to prove it."

And I blink.

Mother-trucker!

He smiles a winning smile.

The hot jerk.

I grit my teeth and breathe out through my nose. Then, I fix a sickly sweet smile on my face. "I wasn't planning on puncturing any more of your tiny body parts. But the night's still young, so…maybe." I lift my shoulder, causing my sweater to slip a little further. I see his eyes go to it and then back to my eyes.

"Tiny? Ha! You crack me up. Oh, and, Pins, the cock warmer you made me—extra-large, you said? Yeah, it doesn't fit."

Wardrobe Malfunction

"Too big?"

"Funny. Too small. *Way* too small."

"I think I should stay," Alex says. "You two might need a referee."

"We'll be fine." I give Alex my most professional smile.

"Yeah, Pins and I will be just fine," Vaughn states.

God, he's an annoying, gorgeous bastard. How can I want to kiss his face off and smack him on it at the same time?

"Okay. Well, I'm just next door if you need me."

I hear the door shut, signaling that Alex has left, and then it's just Vaughn and me, alone.

Vaughn

MAYBE I SHOULD HAVE had Alex stay. Not because I fear for my safety, but because I have the strong urge to fuck her.

I spent most of last night trying not to think about her.

And having her here isn't helping anything. Arguing with her is like the best kind of foreplay ever.

Fuck, is she hot, and that mouth of hers…that fucking smart-ass, sexy mouth of hers that I would love to see wrapped around my cock.

But, nope, not gonna do it.

I'm just here for this movie. No fucking around.

I promised Jack and myself.

"So, we're doing this?" My voice comes out sounding sharper than I intended.

"Yep. Put this on for me, please," she says, holding out a crisp white shirt.

I take the shirt from her. "Should I put some music on? I know how you like to twerk before you work." I snort at my own rhyme. *I'm such a fucking loser.* "I don't have any of Madonna's early stuff, but I think I have 'Vogue' on my phone. I'm pretty sure I remember the dance routine as well, if you want me to join in?"

She stares at me for a moment, and then laughter bursts from her. The sound is like sunshine. If sunshine had a sound.

"You're such a tool." She laughs again. "Just put the damn shirt on, so we can get this over with."

A big grin on my face, I peel my tank off and put the shirt on, buttoning it up.

I notice she doesn't once look at me. She busies herself with her sewing stuff at the dining table.

"Ready?" she asks.

"Yep."

When she turns to me, she has that damn pincushion on her wrist again, and I swear to God, my balls shrink in on themselves.

"Do you have to use pins? They're making my balls twitch."

She snorts out a laugh. "Afraid so. But don't worry; I won't get you again." She steps closer, and I get a whiff of raspberries and vanilla, like I smelled yesterday. "I promise."

I stare down into her eyes. They're blue. Dark. Like the color of blueberries.

"I'll put my hand inside the fabric to protect your skin. I could have done that yesterday, but it didn't seem appropriate to put my hand down your pants the first day I met you."

I wouldn't have minded. "That sounds like a bad pick-up line I've used in the past."

Wardrobe Malfunction

She laughs again. It's throatier this time. Sexy. And I decide that, from now on, I want to make her laugh all the time.

"Looking at this, I just need to hem the sides a little. I'm just going to put my hand up your shirt—"

"I bet you say that to all the boys."

"Only to the pretty ones." She smiles, glancing up at me through her lashes.

God, I want to fuck her so bad.

She slips her hand under the shirt. Her hand is cool against my heated skin. I suck in a breath.

"Sorry. Are my hands cold? I should've warmed them up first."

Down my pants? Of course you can, sweetheart. "No, they're fine. You're fine."

I grit my teeth and stare over her head at the wall. I force myself to think about my mother and my grandma, basically anything but the feel of her touching me.

In no time, she's done and moving over to the other side of the shirt. Her hand brushes over my abdomen. She stills. "Sorry," she says, her cheeks turning pink.

"Don't be. So far, you've nailed me in the balls, seen me in only my boxer shorts, and made a cock warmer for me. What difference is a little ab-groping going to make?"

She shakes her head, laughing. "And people say I'm odd."

"I prefer the term *unconventional*."

Her eyes flash up to mine, surprise filling them.

"What?" I ask her.

"Nothing." She shakes her head, her eyes clearing. "Okay, you're done." She steps back. "I just need to measure up the vest and jacket. I can size the rest from those. You need me to help you take that off?"

I don't, but I just want her close again. "Sure."

She steps up and starts to undo the buttons.

"I meant to thank you for keeping what happened to yourself," I say.

She glances up at me, a coy look in her eyes, as she continues undoing the buttons. "How do you know I didn't tell anyone?"

"Because I haven't read about it today."

"Well, I wasn't exactly about to broadcast that I nailed Vaughn West in the balls."

"You nailed me, huh?" I grin, and she blushes.

I like making her blush.

"You know what I mean," she chastises gently.

"Yeah, well, I appreciate you not saying anything. You'd be surprised by what people are willing to tell to earn a fast buck. You could have made yourself ten grand with that story."

"Ten grand? Shit, is it too late to change my mind?" She gives me a teasing grin. Then, her expression changes. "It sucks that you can't trust people though."

"Yeah, but I think that's the same for most. I trust my family, Alex, and Jack, who's my manager. And…right now, I trust you."

Her eyes soften on me.

I want to kiss her so fucking bad in this moment. I can't remember wanting to kiss a woman more.

"Well, just not with sharp instruments," I add to pull us out of this moment.

"I didn't stab you just now, did I?"

She pushes the shirt off my shoulders. I slip my arms out of it.

No, but I wish I could stick you with something long and hard.

I watch her walk to the table and pick up a vest.

"No, but the night's still young," I tease her with her earlier words.

She walks back over to me and hands me the vest. I slip it on.

Wardrobe Malfunction

I like this. I like getting along with her about as much as I like arguing with her.

The sick part of me wants to piss her off again though. I have visions of having angry sex with her. *I bet angry sex with Pins would blow my mind.*

She fits up the vest and then the jacket, and I stand there like a good boy while she does.

"There. All done." She walks around behind me and slips the jacket off my shoulders.

I find I'm disappointed that we're finished.

I'm just about to offer her a drink when my cell starts to ring. I walk over to get it and see it's Brandon calling.

The guy is an amazing director, but fuck, he's a needy bastard. Every *I* has to be dotted and every *T* crossed. I like things to be thorough, but he's a step above me.

We spent all afternoon running lines for tomorrow. And, honestly, I'm tired. I just want to sleep, so I can be ready for filming tomorrow.

And I want to have a drink with Pins.

And not fuck her.

Or maybe fuck her.

"Hey, Brandon," I answer.

"Vaughn, have you got a few minutes? I just need to go over some stuff for tomorrow."

I hold back a sigh. "Sure, just hang on a minute." I cover the phone with my hand and turn to Pins.

She already has the stuff packed up and in her hands, ready to go.

Can't say I'm not disappointed.

"Sorry, it's Brandon. I have to take this."

"It's fine. We're done anyway."

She's heading for the door. I follow her.

She stops by the door and turns to me. "Thanks for letting me come here to finish up."

"No problem. And, hey, you got through it without maiming me." I grin.

"Shocking, I know." She flashes her gorgeous eyes at me.

"How are you getting to your hotel?"

"Alex said something about a car, but I can take a cab."

"No, take my car. I'll just call to sort it out."

"It's fine, honestly," she starts.

I wave her off.

"Brandon, give me a few, and I'll call you back." I hang up with him and call my driver, who is also my bodyguard. "Aiden," I say when he picks up, "I need you to give someone a ride back to her hotel. Her name is Pins."

I see her roll her eyes, and it sends a thrill through me.

"Pins? Are you serious?" he says in that deep voice of his.

"No, her name is Charly."

"Cool. Is she leaving now?"

"Yeah."

"Tell her I'll be in front of the hotel in five."

"Thanks, Aiden." I hang up. "My driver, Aiden, will be up front in five to take you home."

"Thanks." She smiles. "It's really nice of you."

"I'm a nice guy." I lean my shoulder against the wall.

"Yeah, sometimes."

I give her an affronted look, and she laughs.

She opens the door, and I follow her through it.

"So"—she's backing away—"I'll see you later."

"Are you on set tomorrow?"

"Probably."

"Then, I'll probably see you tomorrow."

She smiles, and my insides heat.

"See you, West." She turns and starts to walk toward the elevator.

"See you, Pins."

I see her head shake, and I laugh.

I step back inside and shut the door.

Wardrobe Malfunction

I like Pins. I really like her. She's hot and cool and witty. And nothing like the women I usually spend time with. I should ask her to dinner…and then fuck her.

My phone starts to ring in my hand.

Jack.

Jesus Christ. Can't a guy get a minute's peace while he thinks about the woman he wants to fuck but is trying not to?

I answer the call, putting the phone to my ear. "Jack, can I call you back? I've got to call Brandon."

"What were you doing with a woman in your hotel room?"

"What the hell?" I suspiciously glance around the room. "Have you got a spy cam in my room?"

"No, you idiot. I just spoke to Alex, and he said you were busy with someone called Charly. And I'm guessing he didn't mean a man."

I sigh. "She's the wardrobe assistant on the film. She came to fit some clothes for tomorrow. For fuck's sake, Jack. I'm not a kid. I can keep my pecker in check." *Mostly.*

"Yeah, well, it doesn't hurt to remind you of it. You need to keep it zipped up while you're making this film. You don't need another scandal taking the attention of your career back to who you're screwing."

"We don't need to have this conversation again, Jack. I'm going. I need to call Brandon back." I hang up the phone and sigh.

Well, if that wasn't just the motherfucking reminder that I need to stay away from Pins.

Great. Just fucking great.

Charly

I GOT IN REALLY EARLY this morning to fix Vaughn's clothes for today's shoot. I could have done them last night after leaving his hotel, but his driver dropped me back at my hotel and insisted on carrying my things to my room for me, which was really sweet of him. After that, I couldn't be bothered to go back to the studio. I don't have a sewing machine here with me, so I figured I'd go to bed early and get up early.

God, I'm such a party animal. Not.

I'm all done, his clothes fitted to size, ironed, and pressed to perfection.

Right now, I'm just heading over to his trailer to take them to him.

And I have a smile on my face.

It's a beautiful day, and I'm wearing a dress of my own design. I make my clothes when I get time. This is an oldie but a favorite. It's a hot-pink skater dress made from jacquard fabric, and I'm wearing it with a thin silver belt around my waist that I picked up at a thrift store. On my feet are my sparkly gunmetal-gray ankle peep-toe Kurt Geiger boots that Nick bought me last Christmas. He had them shipped over from the UK, as you can't get them here. They're hot as hell. The man knows me well.

My hair is up in one of those messy buns that looks like you did it in a few minutes, but you actually spent half an hour pinning and perfecting it to get it like this.

I look good.

I also feel good because fitting Vaughn last night went better than I could've hoped. At first, I'd thought it was going to be pistols at dawn, but then, shocker, we'd started to get along. It was nice. I liked talking with him. I was kind of a little sad to leave. He's actually quite funny. Quick-witted. I like humorous men. Especially the hot ones.

And, when he said he trusted me…it felt big. It made me feel valued…worth something.

That doesn't happen to me often.

Today is going to be a great day; I just know it.

Reaching what I hope is Vaughn's trailer—Ava gave me directions to it—I knock on the door and wait.

Alex opens the door.

"Hey." I smile.

"Charly, good to see you again."

"I have Vaughn's clothes." I lift them up as proof.

"Come in." Alex steps aside. "He's just in makeup."

I step inside his trailer, and…*wow*. It's really nice. Nicer than my apartment.

It's done in dark wood. A real masculine feel to it, which is perfect for Vaughn. A circular seating area with a table has an open laptop on it. Next to it is a comfy-looking sofa with a large TV fitted to the opposite wall. There's a kitchen area, and a little further down, there's a dressing table with a large mirror lit up with bulbs. And that's where

Wardrobe

Vaughn is, sitting down on a chair while a woman is doing his makeup.

I walk over to Vaughn. "Hey." I smile in the mirror at him. "I have your clothes. Where should I put them?"

He flicks his eyes at me and then immediately looks away. "Anywhere."

"Okay." I step back and look around for somewhere to hang them, but I don't see a hook. "Is there a closet anywhere, so I can hang them?" I ask him.

"Just put them on the fucking table." He throws a hand in the direction of the table where Alex is sitting with the laptop.

His hard tone takes me back a step.

I swallow back my discomfort and surprise. "I just don't want them to get creased. I spent a long time pressing them."

"I'll put them in the closet in the bedroom for you." Alex takes them from my arms, a look of pity on his face.

"Thanks," I say quietly to Alex.

"Knock, knock," a cheery voice calls. Natasha Warner, Vaughn's costar in the movie, walks in.

It's the first time I've seen her—in real life, that is.

She's taller than I expected. I'd say she's about my height. But she's just as beautiful in real life as she is on-screen. Thin but athletic, she looks like a swimwear model. Shiny black hair sits perfectly on her shoulders. With huge bright blue eyes, her oval face is heavy with makeup, but I know that's for the film. Even still, it doesn't diminish her beauty.

She's stunning.

I feel like a little kid next to her.

And she's wearing a Stella McCartney dress that I know for a fact costs a thousand bucks.

How the other half lives. Sigh.

"God, you're still in makeup?" She laughs, walking over to Vaughn. She stops at the back of his chair, putting her hands on the top of it, while the makeup artist continues to do his makeup. "You men take longer to get ready than us women do."

"What can I do for you, Natasha?" His tone isn't much friendlier than it was with me, which makes me feel a little better at the reception I got from him.

"Isn't he a darling in the morning?" she says to me, playfully rolling her eyes. Then, she sticks her hand out to me. "We haven't met. I'm Natasha."

"Charly Michaels." I take her hand and shake it. "I work in wardrobe. I was just dropping off Mr. West's clothes. It's really great to meet you, Ms. Warner."

"Natasha, please. God, Vaughn, you don't make this lovely girl call you Mr. West, do you?"

His eyes momentarily flick to me, and the look in them is filled with annoyance.

Jeez, who pissed in his cornflakes this morning?

"No." He looks back at Natasha. "I've told her countless times to call me Vaughn. What do you need, Natasha? Or did you just come for a girlie chat?"

She laughs; it's light and airy. "I need you to run lines from act four with me again, Mr. Happy. I can't get them to stick."

"Sure. Whatever. Give me five minutes."

Then, he looks at me again. It's a look that tells me he wants me to leave.

"Okay, so I'll be going." I start backing away. "If you need me for anything else, Vaughn, have Alex call my cell."

He doesn't even bother to respond.

Alex does from his seat at the table where he's working on the laptop, "No worries, Charly. I'll call if we need anything."

"It was nice to meet you." Natasha smiles at me, taking a seat at the table. "Oh, and I love your dress."

"Oh. Thank you." I run a hand down it. "I made it."

Wardrobe

"You made it? Wow. It's really good. Are you a designer?"

"No." I shake my head. *I just want to be one.*

"Well, you should be. It's amazing. Do you have any other designs? I'd love to see them."

"Jesus Christ," Vaughn growls, getting up from his seat, pulling the tissues that protect his clothes out of the collar. "I feel like I'm in a fucking episode of *Project Runway*."

"You watch *Project Runway*?" I stifle a laugh.

"No, of course I don't fucking watch *Project Runway*," he barks at me. "Now, are we running these lines or not?" he says to Natasha.

And that's me being dismissed.

The makeup girl catches my eye, giving me a smile—the one people like us who work in the movie industry share, which says that all actors are stuck-up assholes and not to take it personally.

But I am taking it personally.

Because, after last night, for a crazy moment, I actually thought he was a nice guy.

The Vaughn who got his driver to take me home so that I wouldn't have to get a cab—what happened to him?

Apparently, he was an anomaly.

I won't make the mistake of thinking he's a good guy again.

"Bye," I say in general.

I get responses from everyone, except for Vaughn.

I step outside, back into the bright sunshine. Pushing my hands into the pockets of my dress, I walk back to wardrobe, my steps a lot heavier than they were on my way here.

Vaughn

SEX SCENES.

Fucking hate them. First day of filming, and Brandon wants to jump straight into them.

Those clothes that Charly spent time getting ready for me are to be taken off by Natasha.

I'm trying not to think about how weird I feel about that.

Dressed by the woman I currently want and can't have—as Jack so kindly reminded me of last night—and undressed by my costar and friend.

In the movie, she's a stripper, and I'm a hard-ass Mafia guy. In this scene, I'm going to be fucking her on the bar top in the nightclub where she dances while people watch us. Alongside those other actors, fifty crew members will also be watching us simulate having sex. I'll be butt-ass naked, apart from the cock sock I get to wear. All the while,

Brandon will be firing out orders at us on how to fake fuck correctly.

Not fun at all.

I've worked with Natasha before, but this is the first time we'll be doing a sex scene together. And a sex scene like this is always tough, especially on the first day of filming.

Brandon says he likes to get the important and difficult scenes done first, so there's time to come and revisit if needed.

Honestly, I just feel weird. Doing sex scenes in general feels strange. But that's not what's bugging me most.

Charly is.

Or how I feel about her…

Basically, how much I want her.

I can't remember wanting a woman this much before. Especially not one I've known for such a short amount of time.

Seeing her this morning didn't help anything. She was in that sexy little dress, which, as I heard, she'd made herself. I don't know why I find that hot, but I do. And those boots…*Jesus Christ.* I have visions of her wearing nothing but them—her long legs wrapped around my waist, the heels digging into my back, while I fucked her hard.

I can't seem to stop obsessing over what it would be like to fuck her.

But I can't. I need to keep my mind on this film and nothing else.

So, I was distant with her this morning. I figure, if she thinks I'm a moody asshole, then she won't try to be my friend. The last thing I need is for Charly to try to be my friend.

But that still hasn't stopped me from thinking about her since she left my trailer this morning.

Wardrobe Malfunction

I'm on set, and we've already shot the first scene, which was Natasha dancing for me. Now, we're getting ready for the sex scene.

I have to change from the suit I'm wearing into another one of the exact same, but that one will have some marks on it.

I go into the changing trailer on set, where Alex put the spare clothes for me. Ava's in there. But no sign of Charly.

"Hey," I say to Ava.

"Change time?" she asks with a smile.

"Yeah. Where are the clothes? Never mind," I say as I see them hanging off the rail.

I grab the suit and then look inside the garment bag for the cock sock.

"Ava, there's no cock sock in here."

"There isn't?" She comes over to look. "Was it in there earlier?"

"I don't know. Alex got the first set of clothes out for me."

"Oh, no worries. I'll see if I have one here."

She goes off rummaging through drawers. I slip off the jacket, tossing it onto a chair, kick off the shoes, and start unbuttoning the shirt.

"I don't seem to have one. But don't worry. I'll call Charly and have her run one over for you."

While I'm happy that I'll get to see Charly, I'm not exactly thrilled at the fact that she's coming to bring me a cock sock.

I step into the changing room and pull the curtain across.

I hear Ava on the phone while I change.

"Charly, the cock sock is missing from Vaughn's items needed for today's take. No, it's okay. Don't worry; no problem at all. Yeah, that's fine."

Dressed, I pull the curtain back and step out with the rest of the clothes, tossing them onto the same chair as the jacket.

"Charly's just on her way back to wardrobe now. She'll be about ten minutes, so she's going to bring it to set for you, if that's okay?"

"That's fine." I push my feet into the shoes and head for the door.

"See you later," I say to Ava.

I walk across the lot and back onto set where Natasha is having her makeup retouched.

I sit down on the seat beside her. She's wearing a dressing gown. She has it worse than me. She's been dressed in a bra and panties all morning. At least I've gotten to wear a suit for most of it.

A makeup artist comes over and starts retouching my makeup.

"How are you doing?" Natasha asks.

"Good."

"Feeling okay about this next scene?"

"Fake fucking in front of fifty-plus people? Walk in the park." I slide a look at her, and she laughs.

"Never gets any less weird, does it?"

"Nope," I reply. "How's the family doing?" I ask, changing the subject to something lighter.

"Good. Brody just cut his first tooth." She gets her cell from the pocket of her gown and pulls up a picture to show me.

I lean over to take a look. "Good-looking kid. See he takes after you and not Carter."

"I'll tell Carter you said so."

I laugh. "How is Carter?"

"He's good. It's just hard for me, being away from him and Brody so soon after having him, but I couldn't pass up this opportunity to do this film."

"Yeah, I get that." And I do.

Wardrobe Malfunction

"How's your family?"

"Good," I tell her. "My sister is finally getting married next month. They've only been together for fifteen years and have three kids."

"Better late than never." She laughs. "That's your oldest sister, right? The one who got engaged a while back?"

"Yeah, Sasha."

I have two sisters, both older than me—Sasha and Meg. Both the bane of my existence growing up, but now, I couldn't imagine life without them.

Sasha and Greg, her fiancé, are going to get married at my parents' place, where I grew up, in Keno, Oregon. My mom and dad have a farm there; it's been in my family for generations. It's also where I have my ranch—the only home I own. Not many people know about it. I had it built out on the furthest reach of my parents' land. It's private, just like I wanted.

I'm really close to my family—my mom and dad, Sasha and Greg, Meg and her husband, Vic, along with my nieces and nephews, and my grandma. She's the best. Absolutely batshit crazy, but I love her for it.

My family is the only sane thing I have in this fucked up existence I call my life.

"Vaughn."

Her voice touches me like her hands have brushed my skin.

I glance up to see Charly standing beside me.

God, she's stunning.

"I have the sock for you." She holds the cock sock out for me.

And the moment is killed.

I take the sock from her. "Thanks."

I want to talk more to her, but I need to keep my distance, and I really need to get my head in the scene.

"I'm gonna go put this on," I tell Natasha.

I get up and walk away, heading for the restroom, without acknowledging Charly even though it pains me to do so.

Vaughn

THE CAMERAS ARE ROLLING. Music is pumping out in the makeshift club on set, The Weeknd's "Starboy" thrumming in my ears. Natasha—or as I should say, Lexi—is currently gyrating on my lap, dancing for me—well, for my character, Drew Asher.

Only thing is...I can't seem to get my head in the scene and off Charly.

I don't get why she's infecting my thoughts so much. It has to be because I can't have her. Forbidden fruit and all that.

I force myself back into character. On cue, Drew gets to his feet, picking up Lexi, and carries her over to the bar where he deposits her on the top, none too gently.

Personally, I would take a little more care of my woman, but this isn't me. This is Drew, and Drew's an asshole; therefore, I'm currently an asshole.

Well, I am an asshole, too. Just not in bed. I like to make sure my woman is happy and taken care of, putting her needs before my own.

Lexi pulls Drew into her body, using her legs wrapped around his waist.

Drew kisses her hard. His fingers buried deep in her hair, controlling the action.

A flash of kissing Charly like this appears in my mind.

Holding her like this, pushing my tongue into her mouth.

I can feel myself start to lose hold of Drew, imagining this is me kissing Charly.

Jesus Christ. Drew is kissing Lexi. Get with the fucking program, Vaughn.

It's not like me to lose character like this.

Dragging myself back, Drew grabs ahold of Lexi's legs and pulls them from around him. Stepping back, sliding his hands down her legs, he parts them wide, hooking each of her heeled feet onto the barstools on either side of them.

My eyes come up.

Charly.

She's standing there, right in my eye line, watching.

What the fuck is she doing here?

I know she has to be on set, but couldn't she stand somewhere else?

This scene is hard enough to do as it is without the current source of my dick's desire right where I can see her.

I feel a rush of anger at her.

Unable to do anything, I throw the feeling into my character.

Fixing his eyes on Lexi, Drew yanks his jacket off, throwing it aside. He rips off the shirt he's wearing, sending the buttons scattering. His shoes are kicked off. Belt buckle is the next to go. The zipper is pulled down, and the pants are off.

And then Drew is standing there, stark fucking naked.

Wardrobe Malfunction

There's always that moment when my brain catches up to the joke—that it is actually me who's naked, but for a cock sock, in front of all these people.

Quick as a switch, I flick my brain back to Drew.

Drew doesn't give a fuck that people can see him. Or that he's about to fuck a stripper on the bar in front of them all.

Stepping back up to Lexi, Drew rips her panties off, making her gasp.

Leaving her in just the bra she's wearing.

And Natasha with only a nude patch covering the part that no other man but her husband should be seeing.

I really fucking hate this part. More than I hate having to get naked myself. I hate having my friend out here, naked with pretty much everything on show.

But then she's not alone.

We're in this together.

But Natasha, being the professional she is, stays in character.

Lexi reaches up, hand going to the back of Drew's head, and drags him to her mouth, kissing him.

And then they're fucking. Well, Natasha and I are fake fucking. But for Drew's and Lexi's characters, they're going at it, right here on the bar in this Vegas nightclub, with everyone watching.

And no one stops them.

Because he's Drew Asher, and he does what the fuck he wants.

Unlike me. Who can't fuck anyone until this film is done.

Lexi is moaning like it's the best sex she's ever had. Drew is pounding into her. His head comes up from her shoulder, and his eyes meet with Charly's.

For a brief moment, I forgot she was there.

Fuck.

I need to look away. Back to Natasha—Lexi, whoever the fuck.

But I can't take my eyes off Charly.

The look in her eyes…she looks turned on.

And it's turning me on.

Then, she bites her lip.

Jesus.

I groan, closing my eyes.

I need to get out of my head—or get Charly out of my head.

Drew.

He opens his eyes, but when he looks down, he's not staring at Lexi.

I'm staring at Charly.

What the actual fuck?

I shut my eyes tight.

Opening them back up, I see Natasha.

But I need to see Lexi.

Fuck, my head is so messed up right now.

Drew kisses Lexi, his hips pumping hard against hers. Her legs move, coming around his waist, the stilettos of her heels digging in his back.

Charly's boots.

My mind flashes back to that scenario of fucking her with only those boots on.

Oh, Jesus, no.

I've got a hard-on.

I've got a fucking hard-on.

Think of something to get rid of it.

Mom. Grandma. Grandma naked.

Fuck! It won't go down.

It's because I haven't had sex for so long.

Now, he's up, and he's not going anywhere.

Natasha slides her hand into my hair, bringing her lips to my ear, which is now concealed by her arm. She whispers, "You okay?"

Wardrobe

She can feel my erection.

How could she not when it's poking her in the thigh?

God, I'm mortified.

I'm fucking this up—literally.

This has never happened to me before.

It's all Charly's fault for being so hot and being right here.

I need to get a handle on this.

"Cut!" Brandon calls.

Thank fuck.

"What happened?" Natasha asks, tipping her head back, staring me in the eyes.

She looks uneasy, and I feel like a fucking pervert.

I close my eyes on an embarrassed groan. "I'm so sorry."

She laughs. "Don't worry. It's fine. It happens."

"Not with me, it doesn't." I've never gotten a hard-on while doing a sex scene. "It's not you," I reassuringly tell her.

"I don't know whether to be insulted or relieved by that statement." She laughs again.

"I've got your robe, Natasha," Logan says from beside us.

"You okay to move?" Natasha asks me.

"Um…" I glance around for the current source of my problem because she'll be the one with my robe.

God, this situation is so fucked up.

I see her approaching with my robe in hand.

"Sure." I shift back a little, allowing Natasha room to move. I help her down from the bar, making sure to keep my pecker pointed in the direction of the bar and nowhere else.

"Here's your gown," Charly says from beside me. "You want me to help you put it on?"

"No, I got it." My voice comes out sharper than intended.

I take the robe from her without looking at her.

I can't look at her right now.

I just need to get the fuck out of here and clear my head for a few minutes.

That, or go and tug one out.

I pull the robe on my arms, but it feels tight.

"Why doesn't this fit?" I bark, finally looking at her.

"Oh, I'm sorry. I must have mixed up gowns with Logan."

She laughs, and something inside me pops.

All I want is to get my cock covered and get the fuck out of here and away from her because I want her, and I can't have her, so somehow, now, this is all her fault.

"You think this is funny?" I snap. "I'm stark fucking naked. All I ask for is a fucking robe that fits, and you can't even get that fucking right!"

Hurt flashes through her surprise-filled eyes. Those gorgeous blueberry eyes.

Guilt lances across my chest, leaving behind a painful ache.

The whole set is silent.

I can feel my face prickling with shame and residual anger.

Anger that I directed in the wrong place.

I'm such a prick.

I see movement in my peripheral. Logan is handing her a robe. She takes it from him and holds it out to me. Her arm stiff. Her expression fixed. But her eyes can't hide the hurt.

"Charly…" I softly say her name, taking the robe from her.

Suddenly, I don't care so much about putting it on. I just want her to forgive me.

And, anyway, my erection is gone. Apparently, my cock doesn't like me hurting her either.

Wardrobe

"Do you need anything else, Mr. West?" Her voice sounds strong, but I hear the slight waver in it.

It makes me feel like shit.

I swallow down. "Pins…"

"No? Well, okay then," she says in an overly loud voice, "I'll take these to get laundered." She quickly picks up my discarded clothes that I removed in the scene, clutches them to her chest, and strides away, leaving the set through an exit door.

"What the hell was that?" Natasha says in a low voice, coming up beside me.

I pull on the robe, tying the belt. "I don't know." I sigh.

"That wasn't like you, Vaughn."

I look her in the eye. "I know," I say.

Something flickers in her eyes.

"Ah, you like her," she says. "That's what caused the chubby."

"Chubby? Jesus, Natasha."

"What?" She laughs. "I'm a mom now."

I shake my head.

"So, you like the girl. Go for it. She seems sweet."

"I can't." I sigh, leaning back against the bar that Drew just screwed Lexi on. "I promised Jack and myself that I'd keep my pecker clean while I made this movie."

Understanding passes over her face.

"Well, no matter what, you owe her an apology."

"Yeah"—I sigh, looking over at the door Charly just exited out of—"I know."

Charly

I DON'T CRY.

It's not something I ever do.

The one and only time I remember crying was when my grandmother died.

That was twelve years ago. I haven't shed a tear since.

I think my tear ducts are defunct.

When I do get hurt or upset though, I get angry.

And, right now, I'm seething fucking mad.

What a wanker Vaughn West is!

Yelling at me like that in front of everyone. All I did was accidentally pick up the wrong robe. It was an easy mistake to make. And, honestly, I was just feeling all flustered after watching that scene he did with Natasha, and I wasn't paying full attention to what I was doing.

And don't think I didn't spot the erection he was sporting after the scene. Sure, it must be hard, being a guy and grinding up all over a beautiful woman, but she's married with a kid, and he got a hard-on over her, which is gross.

But then he did get an erection before I stabbed him in the balls. Maybe he just gets hard when he's close to a woman. He does like to put out, as the press has recently reported.

Ugh. He's a pig!

He's off my Christmas card list—not that he was ever on it.

This morning, after I thought on it, I figured he had probably been off with me in his trailer because he was tense over doing that scene. So, I was going to let it go. But, oh no, super asshole comes out to play after the scene is over.

It's official. I really, *really* dislike the hot jerk.

I'm in the main warehouse where we store all the clothes. Ava asked me to put away the shoes from today's shoot. After I wheeled them over here in a cart, I reach inside and grab a pair of men's brogues.

Even though I know these shoes are not Vaughn's, I still slam them onto the rack like they are his. If I can't take my anger out on him, then the shoes are getting it.

Sorry, shoes.

"I've been looking for you."

I whirl around at the voice, my heart making a break out of my chest.

Vaughn.

"Jesus, you scared me." I frown at him, pressing my hand to my heart, trying to settle it.

"Sorry, I didn't mean to frighten you."

"Yeah, well, you did." I turn away from him and grab another pair of shoes—Jimmy Choos this time. I'm a little more careful with putting these ones back. No way can I abuse a pair of Choos.

"Did you need me to do something?" I add with attitude.

Wardrobe

"I want to apologize. For earlier. I was an ass."

My heart skips. But I don't let it show. "Yeah, you were. A monumental one."

"I know."

"Okay."

"Okay, as in you forgive me?"

I shrug.

"Jesus. Can you turn and look at me while I talk to you? It's no fun having a conversation with your back."

I look at him over my shoulder. "Yeah, well, it's no fun being yelled at in front of the whole crew."

"I said I was sorry."

"Oh, well, that's okay then," I retort.

"Jesus, woman, what do you want? Blood? I said I was sorry. I can't do any more."

Anger lancing through me, I spin around to face him. "I don't want anything from you. You said you were sorry. We're good."

"From where I'm standing, it doesn't look like we're good."

"What do *you* want? You want me to do a little happy dance or something?" I do a little dance on the spot, waving my hands around.

He laughs. "You're fucking crazy."

I stop dancing and frown. "Maybe because you make me crazy."

"Right back at you, Pins."

"Will you stop calling me that?" My hands go to my hips. So do his eyes.

"No," he says slowly, dragging his gaze back up to mine.

"Fine. Then, I'll just call you…Boner!"

I see a flicker of annoyance in his eyes. He knows I saw the hard-on he had earlier while filming.

His expression narrows. "You know, you should speak to me with more respect than that."

"Why? Because you're a big movie star, and I'm just a wardrobe assistant? Yeah, well, you know what you can do with that notion? I only give respect to people who earn it."

"Oh, I've earned it all right." His face is tightening with anger.

"You haven't earned a dime of respect. You're just an arrogant, jumped-up—"

I don't get to finish my sentence because he cuts me off.

Well, his arm cuts me off when it reaches out, grabs ahold of me, and yanks me into his body.

Then, his lips are on mine.

Soft and sweet. Nothing like I was expecting but so much better. Pressed there, but he doesn't make a move to kiss me further.

I pop open an eye. "Um, what are you doing?" I ask, breathless. Because I am breathless.

Vaughn West's lips are currently on mine. Vaughn West, the movie star. Vaughn West, whom I've more than once used as a mental prop when spending alone time with my vibrator.

The fangirl in me is jumping up and down—even if he is an arrogant jerk.

His eyes open and stare into mine. "I'm kissing you. Is that okay?"

"Mmhmm." I nod lightly, my lips still attached to his. "Totally. I was just checking because—"

"Pins."

"Yeah?"

"Shut up, and let me kiss you."

And I do. I let him push me back up against the shoe rack and kiss the hell out of me.

And, God, can the man kiss.

His tongue lightly sweeps over my bottom lip, and then he nips it with his teeth, making me moan.

Wardrobe Malfunction

One hand is cupping the nape of my neck; the other finds its way to the hem of my dress. His fingers brush over my bare skin, making me gasp.

He stills.

There's a fraction of a beat where he just breathes against me. Then, he dives in again, and all bets are off.

His hand grabs my thigh and lifts. Hooking my leg around his hip, he presses into me.

And he's hard.

I already saw his size earlier. It's impressive.

And it's even better pressed up against me.

I wrap my arms around his neck, crushing my breasts to his chest. My hips start to move against him without my control. It's instinctual.

I suck on his tongue, and he groans.

"You feel so fucking good, Charly," he says into my mouth. "Taste so good. Better than I imagined."

He's imagined this?

My confidence skyrockets. Well, it's not every day that a man like him tells you he's imagined kissing you.

We're going hard at it, kissing like we've been starved of each other, his body molded to mine. I feel his hand wander to my ass, my dress lifting, and I wonder just how far this is going to go.

How far will I let it go?
Do I want him?
God, yes.
But in a warehouse?
No, I don't think so.

Then, a door bangs, jolting us apart.

We're staring at each other, chests heaving. His lips are swollen from my kiss, his cheeks flushed, his hair tousled. He looks like pure sex.

Good sex.

Hot, dirty, all-night-long sex.

I want him. Badly. Like I've never wanted a man before.

Footsteps start to come our way. I see panic fill his eyes, so I grab his hand and lead him away from the approaching footsteps, to the far end of the aisle and up toward the exit.

We fall out through the door, and I close it behind us.

It's dark out, the area lit by one of the many streetlamps that dot the studio.

"So…" I lean back against the door.

"We shouldn't have done that. I mean, I shouldn't have done that."

Oh. I deflate. All the good, amazing feelings I was having are gone, like the pop of a balloon.

"Okay," I say. And I don't really know what else to say or do, so I just start to walk away.

"Pins"—he catches hold of my hand from behind me, turning me back to him—"that came out sounding wrong. I wanted to kiss you. God, I want to kiss you."

His eyes move to my lips. I wet them with my tongue. It's automatic, but I won't deny that the flare of lust in his eyes sends a thrill zinging to my clit.

"It's just that I need to keep my name out of the press. I promised Jack, my manager, and I promised myself, no fucking around while I do this film. Brandon wanted me for the movie, but before he offered it to me, he had reservations because of the way I'd been living my life. I need this movie. I need the focus to be on this movie and not who I'm sleeping with."

"We're not sleeping together." My voice comes out a little sharper than intended.

Okay, I intended it to be sharp.

"I know. I mean, I want to sleep with you…"

He moves closer, and my breath catches.

"Well, what I want to do with you wouldn't require any sleep. I want to fuck you until neither of us can walk. But I can't. Not right now." He steps back, dropping my hand. "I can't get involved with you even though I really want to."

"It's fine, Vaughn. I get it." And I do. Only my libido isn't feeling too happy about it. "Friends." I hold my hand out to him, forcing a smile onto my face.

He stares at it for a beat, and I remember how he rejected my hand the first time I met him.

I'm just about to pull away when he slips his hand into mine. Electricity fires up my arm, the feel of his rough hand reminding me of how it felt on me just those few minutes ago.

He looks at me. "Friends," he says.

And he smiles, but it doesn't quite reach his eyes.

Charly

IT'S AROUND TEN, AND I'm lying in bed, wearing my pajamas—a tank and boy shorts. I'm watching a *Sex and the City* rerun, eating chocolate.

Hey, don't judge. I'm feeling a little sorry for myself over Vaughn.

When there's a knock at my door, I stop chewing.

Who could that be?

My eyes go to the door like it holds the answer.

Putting my bar of chocolate down on the nightstand, I slide my legs off the bed and quietly pad over to the door.

I put my ear to the door but can't hear anything.

I swallow the chocolate in my mouth. "Who is it?" I ask.

"Vaughn."

Holy Jesus.

What is he doing here?

My heart bangs hard against my chest as I take ahold of the handle and open the door.

And there he is, looking beautiful, wearing a Lakers ball cap pulled low over his eyes, light-blue jeans with his hands pushed into the pockets, and a midnight blue V-neck sweater that looks soft to the touch. I'm almost certain that it's Armani. That sweater more than likely costs more than my whole month's rent.

"Hi," I say softly, curling my fingers into the hem of my shorts.

His hands pull from his pockets, going to either side of the doorframe where he grips it. "So, it turns out, the friends thing isn't going to work for me."

"Oh." I sag a little. "Why not?"

"Because it's not enough. I need more. I want more…I want all of you."

My heart soars, and my panties mentally drop.

A second later, my face is in his hands, and he's kissing me like he might die if he doesn't. I know I'll die if he stops. Then, he's walking me back into my room, kicking the door shut with his foot.

His tongue is in my mouth, fighting mine over whose belongs where. I push his ball cap off, letting it fall to the floor, and my fingers tangle in his hair, clutching and pulling at it.

His hands find my ass and lift me. I wrap my legs around his waist.

The next thing I feel is my back against the wall. And Vaughn is pressed up against me, taking my mouth like it belongs to him.

Because, right now, it does. For this moment in time, I'm his to do whatever he wants with.

"You taste like chocolate," he murmurs against my lips.

"Was just eating some before you got here." I can barely get the words out.

Wardrobe

You've got to cut me some slack here. I currently have Vaughn West's body molded to mine. My libido is throwing a fucking fanfare.

He runs his tongue over my lower lip, making me shiver.

"Delicious. But I bet your pussy tastes even better."

Holy God. He's a dirty-talker, and it's so hot.

"I want you so fucking bad," he rumbles.

I want you so bad, too.

I make a garbled sound of agreement. It's all I can manage at the moment.

"Charly, are you with me?" He rests his forehead to mine, eyes watching me.

"I'm with you," I pant, breathless.

"Good." A sexy-as-hell smile slides onto his face. "Because I'm about to fuck you into oblivion."

Oh, sweet Jesus, yes.

He carries me over to the bed and deposits me onto it. He kicks off his shoes and lies over me. He kisses me again, and I spread my legs, making room for him. He pushes up against me, making me moan.

He pulls back and thrusts against me. My head tips back, pressing into the bed. His lips find my neck, kissing me, his tongue trailing over my skin.

"You smell good. What is that? Raspberries and..."

"Vanilla," I pant. "Raspberry shampoo. Vanilla body wash."

"Mmm. I like it." He moves down my body, giving a kiss to the valley of my breasts and then one on the skin of my stomach where my tank has ridden up.

On his knees, he puts his hands on my thighs. Then, he puts his face between my legs and inhales, making me squirm. "But you smell even better here."

Holy God.

He runs his nose up and down the seam of my boy shorts before pressing it against my clit, making me gasp with need.

"You like that?"

"God, yes." I slide my fingers into his hair, gripping the strands. My legs are shifting restlessly on the bed. I need him to touch me.

He climbs up my body and kisses me, deep and hard. He pulls back and looks into my eyes.

I know I must look wild-eyed and wanton. I'm so turned on, it's not even funny.

"You're so fucking hot, Pins."

He touches his thumb to my mouth, rubbing it over my lips. I catch hold of it with my teeth. Then, I suck it into my mouth, not breaking eye contact with him. His eyes flare with lust, and I see the exact moment when his patience snaps.

"I need to taste you. Now."

He's moving back down my body, and I'm shivering with need.

He gets to his knees, fingers hooking into my shorts and panties. I lift my ass, and he pulls them off together. Then, I move my legs, so he can get them off. He tosses them aside and stares down at me.

He looks like a god up there. An impossibly beautiful god that no woman could ever deserve.

And he's about to go down on me.

Whatever I did in a former life or this one to deserve this, thank you, Jesus. Thank you!

I'm also thanking the heavens that I shaved yesterday, leaving a little landing strip, and showered before getting ready for bed.

But what if Vaughn likes his women completely bare down there?

"I haven't seen this in a long time."

My vagina? When has he seen it previously?

He runs his finger over the little bit of hair on my folds.

Wardrobe
MALFUNCTION

Oh.

"You don't like?" I ask, feeling a little self-conscious.

That vanishes when his eyes meet mine. The desire in them is evident, and it makes my belly clench tight.

"Oh, I like it all right. I like it a lot. It's good to see a real woman for once."

I have no idea what that means, but he likes it. I lose all train of thought when he goes down, parting me with his fingers and running his tongue up my pussy to my clit.

"Ohmigod!" My legs try to come up, but he holds my thighs down with his hands, and then his tongue goes to town on me.

He's licking my clit, fucking me with his tongue, and it's amazing. Otherworldly. Like nothing I've ever felt before.

My hands are curled into the bedsheet, my toes digging into the mattress.

It's been so long since I came at the hands—well, in this case, at the mouth of a man. And this is Vaughn West in between my legs. The chances of me not coming in less than thirty seconds will be a fucking miracle.

"Oh, Jesus…Vaughn…that's so good. God, don't stop. I'm so close…so close…*fuuck*!"

And I come like a rocket shooting off into space. And then I come some more, his tongue relentlessly licking me, wringing me dry, until I sag into the bed, spent.

He promised oblivion. Oblivion, he gave.

I'm dying. And I'm dying a happy girl.

Vaughn kisses his way up my body, his hand pushing up my tank. I feel his mouth come down and suck around my nipple.

"Mmm," I moan, sliding my fingers into his hair, opening my eyes.

Okay, so apparently, I'm easily brought back to life.

He gets to his knees, straddling my stomach, and pulls my tank up. I lift myself to allow it over my head.

I lie back down and get a good view of his erection straining against his jeans. I reach out and press my hand to it. Curling my fingers around, I squeeze gently.

Vaughn moans, his eyes closing.

"You're still fully dressed," I say, moving my hand up and down.

His eyes flash open. His sweater is off a second later.

My hands go to his button and zipper, pulling it down. I tug on the waistband.

Vaughn gets to his feet, which are nicely bare.

Is it odd that I like the fact that he doesn't wear socks with his sneakers?

Standing between my legs, he puts his hands in his jeans pockets, takes his phone and wallet out, and tosses them on the nightstand.

He takes his jeans off.

And then he's naked.

Of course I've seen Vaughn naked before. Earlier today, on set.

But this is different. One thing, I'm getting an unprecedented view of his cock. And what a cock it is. Thick and long, straining upward. And so ready for me.

I get a thrill, knowing that I've made him this hard. That he wants me this badly.

He's so ripped. A six-pack and that deep-cut V that makes girls like me lose their panties.

I sit up and run my fingers over his abs. Then, lower, I run them over his stomach, not far from his cock.

I hear him suck in a breath, and it makes me smile.

Moving my fingers down his stomach, I trail them over his cock, tracing the veins running through it with my fingertips.

His hand goes to the back of my head. Fingers gripping my hair, he tips my head back, so I'm staring up into his blazing eyes.

Wardrobe Malfunction

"Which one did I get?" I ask, running a finger over his balls.

His lips lift at the corner. "The right one."

"Guess I should kiss it better then." I kiss my way across his hip bone until I'm face-to-face with Vaughn West's cock.

Holy hell.

Lowering my head, I press a soft kiss to the ball that I injured.

"Better?" I tip my head back and look up at him again.

His jaw is tight, eyes heavy-lidded.

He shakes his head.

Smiling, I lean back in and kiss it again. "Now?" I ask.

"No," is his rough response, his grip on my hair tightening.

I lick a path over his balls. "Now?" I whisper.

"Suck it," he commands.

A shiver runs through me, and the place between my thighs gets slicker with excitement.

I do as he said, gently sucking on it. My fingers move up his shaft, and I start jacking him off.

"Yes," he hisses.

Needing to taste him, I lift my head and lick the head of his cock, tasting pre-cum. I hum over the head of his dick.

"Open up," he says.

He's so bossy. And I love it.

I lift my eyes to his and open up my mouth.

He slides his cock inside, seeming to know when to stop, how much of him I can take.

He's so thick and big, my mouth barely covers half of him. So, I wrap my hand around the rest, and then I basically bring out my A game, trying to give him the best head of his life.

This man has slept with supermodels and actresses. I want him to remember this...remember me...because, at the end of the day, I'm no one special. I'll just be another notch on Vaughn's bedpost. But, to me, no other man will ever compare.

He's basically screwing me for life.

And I honestly don't care.

"Fuck, Charly. Yeah, that's it...suck me harder...good girl."

His hot, dirty commands are making me wetter and needier. I slip my free hand between my legs and start playing with myself.

"My job," he says.

The next thing I know, he's pulling out of my mouth. I'm flat on my back. Vaughn is grabbing a condom from his wallet, ripping it open, and putting it on in a nanosecond.

Then, he's back on top of me. His hands hold my face, and he kisses me deeply. My eyes slide closed.

"Eyes open," he murmurs over my lips.

I open them, staring into his, and he slowly pushes inside me until he's buried to the hilt.

Holy shit.

I've never felt anything like him. I feel so full of him. He's everywhere. In me. On me. My lungs and head are filled with him.

"You're so tight and hot," he groans.

"And you're so big and hard."

His eyes meet mine, and we both laugh.

It feels nice. Not awkward, like the first time having sex with someone can be. It feels like we've always been doing this.

"You're okay?" he asks.

He sounds calm, but I can see the restraint that he's barely holding on to by the tightening in his jaw, the tension in his brow.

"More than okay. Fuck me, Vaughn. Please."

He brushes his lips over mine and whispers, "Yes, ma'am."

Wardrobe Malfunction

I smile. But it's quickly gone as Vaughn starts to move, fucking me slowly, then quicker and quicker, and harder and faster. The headboard is banging against the wall, surely denting it. I'm panting and groaning. Our flesh is slapping loudly together. The room next door must be able to hear us, and I can't find it in me to give a shit.

Because, Jesus, the man can fuck.

He's like a machine. A fucking machine.

I never want this to end.

His hand goes behind my back, and he moves, sitting up on his haunches, bringing me with him, so I'm straddling him, putting us face-to-face.

"Ride me," he orders.

I wrap my arms around his neck and curl my fingers into the hair at the back of his head. I kiss him and then rise up onto my knees before slamming back down.

"Fuck yeah, that's it," he groans into my mouth.

His hands grip my hips as I start riding him.

"You're so fucking sexy." His hands slide down and grip my ass, urging me onto his cock harder.

My clit is rubbing against his pelvic bone, driving me wild.

"Oh God, Vaughn."

"That's it, baby. Come on my cock. I don't come until you do."

Then, I might hold it off forever.

But, unfortunately, my body disagrees with that, and I'm coming seconds later. And I'm coming hard.

I'm officially ruined for all other men.

My head drops to Vaughn's, my body sated.

Hand at my back, he throws me back onto the bed, fucking me like a madman, jackhammering into me. "I'm coming, Charly…Jesus…fuck…"

He growls a sound so erotic in my ear, I feel like I could come again.

He sags onto me, his big body heavy but not crushing, his skin warm against mine.

And I'm in a holy-fuck moment. I just had sex with Vaughn West. Way better than it was in my imagination.

Way, way, way better.

He lifts his head, staring into my eyes. The look in them makes my heart skip a beat. He looks happy. Exactly how I feel.

"That was..."

"I know." I touch my fingers to his cheek. *Amazing. Out of this world.* I'll never experience anything like it again.

"I can't move," he says.

"So, don't."

He watches me for a long beat, and I worry that I said the wrong thing. I know some guys just like to fuck and leave. Vaughn is probably one of those guys.

"Good, because I'm not ready to leave yet. But how long will you let me stay for?"

A year. Two maybe.

I put my finger to my lips, looking up, like I'm thinking. "Hmm...ten minutes, if you're lucky." I smile, so he knows I'm teasing. I really like that he's not ready to leave yet.

"I can do a lot in ten minutes."

"I bet you can."

Vaughn

TEN MINUTES...

Honestly, right now, it feels like ten days won't be enough to do everything I want to do with her.

That's crazy because, normally, once I've had sex with a woman, I'm done. And I don't mean that in a bastard way. I mean, I'm sated. I don't need more. Well, not for a few hours at least.

But, with Charly, I feel like I could go again now.

And, from the way she's looking at me right now, I don't think she'd be opposed to it.

First things first though, I need to get rid of this condom.

"I just need to go clean up," I tell her.

I ease out of her. Catching hold of the condom, I pull it off my cock. I roll off of her and out of bed.

I see her getting up. "Where are you going?" I ask, stopping by the bathroom door.

Her eyebrow quirks up. It's cute.

"Um, to the same place as you. I need to clean up, too."

"Get your ass back in bed, and stay there." I point at her.

She gives me a pissed off look, but there's a smile on her lips, and she complies.

And, from what I already know of Pins, if she didn't want to do something, she wouldn't.

I slip into the bathroom, toss the condom, and quickly wash up.

I look around for a cloth and find one on the bath. I rinse it under warm water, wring it out, and take it through to the bedroom.

She's lying there, on the bed, looking like a fucking goddess.

All that long, colorful hair of hers is spread out on the pillow.

"Spread your legs, gorgeous."

Her lips curve up in question, but she pushes her legs up a little, so her feet are flat on the bed, her knees slightly bent, legs parted and open for me.

My mouth waters.

Resting a knee on the bed, I reach over and press the warm cloth to her pussy, cleaning her.

Her eyes close. "That's nice," she murmurs.

"Yeah?"

"Mmhmm. No one's ever looked after me like this before."

Her eyes open, locking on to mine. I feel something flicker in my chest.

"Then, you've been spending time with the wrong kind of men," I tell her, surprised at the irritation I feel at the thought of her being with other men.

Wardrobe Malfunction

I've never been the jealous type. But then finding out that your best friend has been fucking your girlfriend will change that in a man.

I press a kiss to her lips and then pull back. Taking the cloth to the bathroom, I toss it in the sink.

I go back to the bedroom and climb on the bed, lying on my side next to her.

She turns to face me. I hook my hand under her leg, lifting it over my hip, and I pull her closer.

Then, I reach over and grab the blanket, covering us both.

"You staying?" she asks.

"Do you want me to?"

"I asked first."

"I'll stay if you want me to stay."

"I only want you to stay if you want to stay."

I smile, unable not to.

Battle of the wills. Neither of us wants to be the one to admit the truth. That she wants me to stay. And that I want to stay with her.

I know this is how it's always going to be with Charly and me. And I like it. I like the challenge she gives me.

But, right now, I want to make her happy more than I want to spar with her.

I brush the tip of my nose over hers. "I want to stay here with you."

She smiles, and I feel it right in the center of my chest.

"Good, because I want you to stay." She presses her hand to my stomach, her fingers crawling up to my chest. "I can't believe we're here, in bed, together," she says softly.

"Because I'm so good-looking and rich and famous? And have a big cock? Don't forget my big cock." I'm teasing, but I keep my expression straight.

She stares at me. "You're being an ass, West."

"According to *Cosmo*, I have a hot one. The Hottest Ass of 2016."

"Ugh! Just when I think you're actually a nice guy, you—"

She tries to get up, but I roll over onto her, pinning her down with my body.

"I'm playing with you. Jeez, I'm not that fucking arrogant."

She stares up at me, her gorgeous blueberry eyes blinking up at me. "You were kidding?"

I cock my brow. "Mmhmm. I do that sometimes."

"Sorry." Her cheeks turn pink. "I'm probably just still feeling a little sensitive after this afternoon."

"Did I say I was sorry enough for that? Because I am." Knowing I must be crushing her, I support my weight on my arms, and my hands frame her face. "So, this should show you how sorry I am. I'm about to tell you something completely fucking embarrassing."

"Okay…"

"Well, the reason I snapped at you earlier—and, again, it wasn't your fault, just my fucked up brain taking it out on the one person I shouldn't have—well, it was because I'd gotten a stiffy while filming."

Her eyes dim. "Yeah, I spotted that."

"I gathered…Boner," I remind her of what she called me back in the warehouse.

She blushes.

"Thing is…my erection…it was because of you."

"Me?" She looks surprised.

"Of course it was because of you. You've been driving me crazy these last few days. I haven't been able to stop thinking about all the ways I wanted to fuck you. When I was doing the scene with Natasha, I looked up, and there you were, watching. I was trying to focus on what I was doing in the scene, but I couldn't get you out of my head. I just kept thinking about fucking you, and…I got a hard-on."

Wardrobe

She giggles, her hands sliding down my back. "So, you got an erection over me while simulating sex with another woman?"

"Yep. Messed up, right?" I screw my face up.

"Kinda. But, oddly, it's sweet. In a messed up way."

She grins up at me, and warmth spreads across my chest.

Also, my dick perks back up, ready for round two of fun, which reminds me...

"Pins..."

"Do you have to call me that?"

I frown. "Do you really hate it that much?"

I knew it bugged her, but I thought she actually liked it.

I fucking love the nickname. It's cute. It's her.

It's ours. It's my name for her.

I know it's stupid, but it's the caveman in me that wants to keep on calling her it.

Her eyes soften on me. "No, I don't hate it." She presses her hand to my face, her thumb brushing over my lips. "You can keep calling me it."

"Thanks." I smile.

"I'll just call you West." She shrugs.

"Or you could call me Big Dick. Rock-Hard Cock."

"Makes Me Wet West," she chimes in, laughing.

The sound rolls through me, making me laugh, too.

"Did you used to call me that?" I tease.

"Of course not!" she says.

But she won't meet my eyes, and I instantly know she's lying.

"Tell the truth." I tickle her side.

She cries out, squirming beneath me, rubbing against my cock, and it feels amazing.

"I didn't!" she squeals.

"Liar!" I tease, tickling her harder.

"Okay, okay!" she pants, breathless, and I stop tickling. "Once. I called you it once."

"I knew it! You're a fangirl."

"I am not a fangirl. You were just...nope, I can't say it." She covers her face with her hands.

I grab them and pull them away. Her face is bright red. Her reaction is hilarious, and I'm dying to know what's making her so embarrassed.

Then, it clicks in my head.

"Pins...was I a sex toy in your mental spank bank?"

She groans, covering her face with her hands again, turning her face into the pillow.

"I was, wasn't I?"

She groans again louder. "Ugh! This is fucking mortifying!"

"Don't be embarrassed." I laugh. "I'm not. I'm used to being a sexual plaything for women."

She pulls her hands from her face and frowns at me. Then, she grabs the pillow beside her and hits me with it. "Ugh, you're a jerk!"

I laugh again, and it feels good. She feels good. Better than good. She feels incredible.

I grab the pillow from her and toss it aside. "Aw, Pins..." I turn her back to me, holding her hands down. "If it makes you feel any better, I spent the better part of last night jerking off to thoughts of you."

Her hips shift under mine. "You did?"

"Mmhmm." I bring my mouth down to hers, softly kissing her. "And I came so fucking hard. But, baby, nothing could've prepared me for the real thing. Being inside you...I've never come so hard in my life."

"Me neither," she whispers.

And I feel like a fucking king.

I shift, pressing my cock against her wet pussy, and it feels like heaven.

I rock my hips upward, my cock sliding between her lips, and I wonder how it would feel to be bare inside her. I've never gone bare inside a woman—ever.

Wardrobe Malfunction

Charly groans the sexiest sound I've heard leave her mouth so far, her eyes closing, head pressing back into the pillow.

I want her again. I want to be deep inside her. Buried in her all night.

But there's something I need to say, something I tried to say before, and I don't want to forget. But I also don't want to piss her off. But it's a risk I have to take.

But, being the selfish prick I am, I allow my cock another couple of slow slides over her soaked pussy.

"Pins..."

"Mmhmm?"

"I need to say something, and I don't want you to take it the wrong way."

The gentle movement of her body against mine stops, and her eyes open, wariness in them.

"We need to keep this between us," I say the words in the least dickish way possible.

"No worries. I wasn't exactly going to broadcast that we had sex, West."

I should be relieved she agreed so easily, but it still prickles at me.

"Oh, thanks!" I laugh. "You know, there are women who would be more than happy to tell the world they fucked me."

"But isn't that why you chose me? Because you know you can trust me?"

Her expression is so earnest, and I realize that I do trust her.

But I didn't pick her.

I didn't stand a fucking chance against her. From the moment I met her, this was always inevitable. We were always going to have sex, no matter how hard I fought it. Not that I fought it very hard.

"I trust you," I tell her, my fingers brushing her hair from her forehead.

She takes hold of my hand and places a kiss to the palm. "Thank you. But it's fine, Vaughn. You told me earlier about what you had agreed with Jack, and I get it. I do."

"It's not just for me though. I don't want you thinking I'm a selfish prick who wants to keep you hidden for my own agenda. If people knew that you and I had sex, the press would be in your business before you knew it. Asking questions, offering you money for details of our night together, digging into your life. We'd be married, and you'd be pregnant with my baby by the end of the week, if they had anything to do with it."

Something flickers through her eyes. Worry, dismay. I'm not sure, and it's gone before I can catch hold of it. But I worry that she thinks I just want her for this one night. That's not the case. One night is nowhere near enough to cover what I'm feeling for her right now. How insanely bad I want her.

"Okay. So, we'll keep this night just between you and me," she says easily.

"Just this night?"

"There'll be more?"

I move my mouth down to hers, cupping her face in my hand. "I want more nights with you, Pins." I let my lips brush over hers as I say, "The question is, do you want more nights with me?" I tip my head back, staring into her eyes.

"I want more," she says without hesitation. Then, she smiles.

And I just have to kiss her again. And again.

Then, before I know it, I'm putting on my second condom of the night, and we're having sex again. Even when I'm deep inside her, it doesn't feel like it'll ever be enough.

Wardrobe Malfunction

I don't know when will be enough with Charly. All I do know is, I have to have her as much as I can, for as long as I can.

Charly

I WAKE UP, SURROUNDED by heat.
Vaughn.
I turn my face to him. He's sound asleep.
He looks beautiful. His lashes are enviably long against his cheekbones.
And then I have a what-the-fuck moment. I was wondering when this was going to happen.
I'm in bed with Vaughn West!
Holy fuck!
Vaughn West!
He was inside me last night. A lot.
We had sex three times, and I had countless orgasms until we passed out.
I had sex with Vaughn West.
I have to stifle a giggle.
I stretch out my deliciously sore limbs. The kind of soreness that only comes from great sex. Amazing sex.

I turn over and reach my hand out to my cell on the nightstand to check the time.

Twenty-five past seven. I have to be on set at nine. My alarm is set to go off soon. I turn it off, so it won't wake Vaughn.

Then, my bladder screams at me.

Easing out of bed so as not to wake him, I grab the nearest item of clothing near me, which happens to be Vaughn's sweater, and I pull it on.

It smells of him. I lift the collar to my nose and inhale. His scent elicits memories of last night, and my stomach clenches.

And then I realize what a creeper I must look like right now, smelling Vaughn's clothes.

I chance a look at him to make sure he's still sleeping. Then, cell phone in hand, I go to the bathroom.

I glance back at Vaughn before I go inside.

Vaughn West is in my bed.

Holy sweet mother of Jesus.

I quietly close the door behind me, locking it.

I pee and then wash my hands. Then, I decide to brush my teeth. Teeth squeaky clean, I rinse with mouthwash.

I decide to call Nick.

"Hey, gorgeous," he answers cheerily.

"Hey," I whisper.

"Why are you whispering?" he mock whispers back.

"Because I'm in the bathroom."

"And the acoustics are bad in there?"

"No, smart-ass. I'm whispering because Vaughn West is sleeping twenty feet away in my hotel bed."

There's a marked silence.

And then, "Holy fuck."

"Right?" I giggle quietly.

"You had sex with him?"

"Three times." I smile wide.

Wardrobe Malfunction

"Charlotte Michaels...this is the one and only time that I will ever say this to you, but...I hate you."

"Hey!" I call out and then quickly cover my mouth.

"Just kidding. You know I love you. And I totally knew he'd go for you."

"You did not." I laugh.

"Yep. I called it. Remember at our apartment, I said you should get it on with him?"

"That's not calling it."

"Um, I think you'll find it is. And I expect your first kid to be named after me."

"Jesus, Nick, we just had sex. We're not getting married."

Nick laughs. "Well, not yet, you aren't. But give it time."

"What's that supposed to mean?"

"It means, I know how easy it is to fall in love with you. He'll be a goner in no time." His voice has softened, and a lump triggers in my throat.

When Nick says lovely stuff like that to me...I can't express what it means to me. I've never been good at expressing my emotions. But just to know I'm loved by someone...it means everything.

"Are you crying?"

"Of course I'm not. I don't cry, remember?"

"Yeah, I know. Chandler Bing." He chuckles. There's a beat of silence, and then he says, "So, Vaughn West..."

"Yeah." I let out a dreamy sigh.

"I have to ask—"

"Big. Thick. Huge," I cut him off, knowing exactly what he was going to ask.

"Lucky bitch."

"I know."

I hear movement in my room. "I'd better go," I whisper. "And I know you won't say anything, but I have to ask—"

"I'll keep it to myself. You know I will. Anyway, you and Vaughn…it'd be in the papers. They could find out…"

"I know." I pause. Then, I say, "I love ya."

"Love ya, too. Family forever, right?"

"Family forever." I hang up and leave my cell on the bathroom counter.

Then, I open the bathroom door and head back into my room.

Vaughn's awake.

He's sitting on the edge of the bed, the sheet covering his lap.

"Hi," I say, feeling suddenly shy.

"You're wearing my sweater."

I curl my fingers into the hem of it. "It was the closest thing on the floor that I could grab to put on."

"I like you in it. Although I'd prefer it much more if you were wearing nothing. Come here." He beckons to me.

I pad toward him, stopping between his open legs. His hands go to the backs of my thighs, sliding upward, and stop just under my ass.

I thread my fingers into his hair. He looks up at me. Those stunning eyes of his are sparkling with lust. My tummy flutters.

He grabs my ass in his hands and lifts me, bringing me on top of him so that I'm straddling his lap. He's already hard beneath me.

We're nose-to-nose. I stare into his eyes.

"Hi." He smiles.

"Hi yourself."

He slides his nose along the side of mine and brings his lips to rest on mine.

Then, he kisses me, tongue slipping into my mouth, as his hands grip ahold of my waist.

"You taste good in the morning," he murmurs.

"The power of toothpaste." I smile against his lips.

"Yeah, it's like magic, that stuff."

Wardrobe

I chuckle at his humor and kiss him back. I graze my teeth over his lower lip and then swipe my tongue over it. He catches hold of my tongue and sucks on it, making me moan and squirm on his lap.

I feel everything when I'm with him like this.

Every touch from him, I feel in every part of my body. I don't know how he does it, but it's amazing, and I love it.

His hands start creeping up my back, taking his sweater with it.

"I need to get in the shower and get ready for work," I tell him.

I can't believe I'm pulling the brakes on having sex with him. But I really do need to get ready for work.

"Yeah, I should get ready, too. I need to be in the studio in an hour."

"You can shower first if you want," I offer.

He gives me a bemused look. "We'll shower together, Pins."

"We don't have time to shower together."

"And why will showering together take longer?"

"Because we'll more than likely end up having sex."

"Hey, nympho. You might have a one-track mind, but I was thinking of time efficiency and also of the environment when I suggested showering together."

"Is that so?" I raise a brow at him, my lips fighting a smile.

"Yeah. Save water. I do care about the environment, you know. I'm not just a hot face and body."

I can't help it; laughter sputters out of me.

"You are priceless!" I climb off his lap. I hold a hand out to him. "Come on then, Mr. Environmentally Friendly. Let's go save the planet and shower together."

"I still prefer Makes Me Wet West, just so you know."

"Jerk." I laugh as he gets to his feet, taking hold of my hand.

The sheet slips away, and I'm treated to a view of naked Vaughn again.

Nice.

We walk to the bathroom, hand in hand. I let go to turn on the shower to warm it up, as this shower takes ages to get hot.

Realizing that Vaughn doesn't have a toothbrush, I offer him mine. "You wanna use my toothbrush? I don't have cooties."

He smiles and takes it from me. "Thanks." He rinses it under the faucet and puts some toothpaste on before he starts brushing his teeth.

Vaughn West is using my toothbrush. He has my toothbrush in his mouth. And he's had that mouth elsewhere, too. On some pretty awesome places, doing epic things with his tongue.

I know I sound like a teenage fangirl, but it's hard not to have those what-the-fuck moments every now and then.

"Pins, you're staring, and you have a weird look on your face."

"What?" I come to, realizing that I've actually been staring at him in the mirror while he's been brushing his teeth.

"Sorry," I mutter.

He chuckles softly.

I grab one of my hair ties off the bathroom counter and tie my hair up into a messy bun. I peel off Vaughn's sweater and hang it on the hook on the back of the door. Then, I grab my shower cap and put it on because it's not hair-wash day today.

I test the shower with my hand to see if it's ready.

Perfect temperature.

I climb in, getting under the spray.

"Um...what the fuck is that?"

"What?" I turn to him getting in behind me.

I move to the side to give him space under the water.

"This." He tugs on my shower cap.

Wardrobe Malfunction

"It's a shower cap," I say slowly. "My hair doesn't need washing, so I use this to keep it dry."

And then I realize that I'm in the shower with Vaughn West, and I have a fucking shower cap on my head.

God, I'm so lame.

"Yeah, Pins, I got that it was a shower cap, but is it supposed to be"—he peers closer—"a crown?"

I die a little inside.

"Uh…yeah. It's my Queen of the Shower cap," I mutter quietly.

Why did I tell him that? God, I'm a fucking moron.

I blame Nick. He bought it for me.

"It's, uh…pretty."

He's fighting laughter. I can see it in the tightness of his eyes and the pinch of his mouth.

Bastard.

He picks up my shower gel and flips up the cap. "So, can you get King of the Shower caps, too?"

"Ugh." I roll my eyes and take the shower gel from him.

"What? I'm being serious. I was thinking we could get matching ones."

"You're such an asshole." I shove him.

"Aw, Pins! I'm just playing." He catches my chin with his hand. "You're pretty…and sexy and hot. *So* hot."

His eyes darken, and his breathing changes. So has my own.

"Even with the shower cap crown?"

He grazes his teeth over his lower lip. "Even with the shower cap crown. No one but you could pull it off."

"Now, I know you're taking the piss." I pull my face from his hand.

"I'm serious. You look hot as fuck." His hands grab my waist, and he yanks me closer, my stomach pressing to his hips.

Oh. He's hard.

"Yeah"—his eyes glitter down at me—"this is all you. You could wear a trash bag, and I'd be hard for you. I've been hard since the day I met you."

Oh, wow.

I turn him on even when I'm wearing a ridiculous shower cap. Go me!

"So, now that you've made me hard with your sexy shower cap crown, I think it's only fair you service your King, Princess."

"Queen. Get it right. And I don't see you wearing a crown. Real royalty outranks Hollywood royalty. So, get down on your knees, King of Hollywood." I smirk, totally teasing him.

His tongue sweeps over his bottom lip, his eyes flaring with something hot and dirty, making my thighs clench.

"As you wish, my Queen." Then, he drops to his knees, lifts my leg, hooks it over his shoulder, and puts his mouth on me.

"God," I moan, dropping the shower gel, my hands going straight to his head.

"King, baby, and don't you forget it. And, if you're a really good girl, after I make you come with my mouth, I'll let you sit on my throne." He flashes me a grin and then puts his mouth back on me.

Cocky bastard.

But he can be because he's that good.

And the King of Hollywood spends the next thirty minutes making me come with his mouth and then fucking me from behind like I'm a whore, but the whole time, he still manages to make me feel like a queen.

Vaughn

I WATCH CHARLY AS she brushes her hair in front of the mirror above the dresser. I love the colors in her hair. So different. So her.

She's wearing this white sweater that stops halfway down her thighs. I think it's supposed to be a dress. But the killer is the boots...black and over the knees...destined to be wrapped around my waist.

God, she's so fucking sexy. I want her again already, and I only just had her.

She finishes up with brushing her hair and puts the brush in her bag. "Right. I'm ready." She turns to me, swinging her bag over her shoulder, the ton of bangles on her wrist clanging together. "Do you want me to leave first? Or you?"

My brows draw together. "Um, neither. We're going together. I texted Aiden. He's on his way to pick us up and take us to the studio. Alex is bringing me some fresh clothes from the hotel, so I'll get changed when we get there."

"Um"—her eyes practically bug out of her head—"Aiden knows where you've been? And Alex, too?"

"Yeah." I give an easy laugh. "How do you think I got here last night? And how do you think I knew which room you were in? Aiden brought me, told me your room number. And of course Alex knows where I am. He's my PA."

"I thought you didn't want people knowing about this." She gestures a hand between us.

"I don't," I say softly, still feeling like a monumental dick that I'm hiding her like I'm ashamed of her when it couldn't be further from the truth. "But they're my inner circle, Pins. They work for me. I can't *not* tell them where I am. And I trust them. They've both been with me for years."

"Okay," she says easily. "But I can't drive in with you."

"Why not?" I frown.

She rubs her forehead with her fingers and pins me with a look. "Because nothing says we're fucking like your driver bringing me to the set."

Okay, she makes a good point.

"How do you normally get to the set?" I ask.

"I walk."

"You walk?" I say, aghast, not feeling particularly great about that.

"Yeah, I was born with those amazing things called legs. I use them every day to get there."

"Funny. You could get mugged, Pins."

"It's broad daylight, West. And it's only two blocks away."

"It's Hollywood."

"Yeah, the land of dreams." She gives me jazz hands.

I laugh. It's impossible not to laugh at her.

Wardrobe Malfunction

"You're crazy. And I think you mean, the land of opportunists. Just because it's Hollywood doesn't mean it's glamorous, Pins. West Hollywood has the highest crime rate in the nation. Rape, murder, robbery." I tick off on my fingers.

"Okay, Mr. Statistics, take it easy." She holds her hands up. "I live in New York. I do know how to take care of myself."

"I don't care. You're not walking around here alone again. And, hang on, you live in New York?" I didn't know that, which is weird, considering I spent most of last night and this morning inside her.

"I do."

"City girl, huh?" I grin, liking the idea for some reason.

"What's with the grin?" she asks, suspiciously eyeing me.

"Nothing." I shrug, still smiling as I walk toward her. "You living in the city is just kinda hot, is all."

"Seriously? I'm starting to think that you find most things hot."

Reaching her, I slide my hands around her tiny waist. "When it comes to you, that's true."

I kiss her glossy pink lips. They taste like strawberries.

When I pull back, her eyes are all soft—just like I like her.

"So, where's home for you?" she asks me, fingers curling into the collar of my sweater, which now smells like her. I also like that a lot.

"Oregon."

"Oregon?"

"Yeah. Why do you look so surprised?"

"I just figured all you celebs lived in the Hills. So, why Oregon?"

"Because that's where my house is."

"Funny." She lightly jabs me in the arm.

"Hey! Careful with the merchandise. This makes me my living." I gesture to my body, playing with her.

She rolls her eyes, and I just have to kiss her again.

"Oregon is home. I grew up there," I tell her.

"Sounds nice." She smiles.

"It is. So, what was it like, growing up in New York?"

Her eyes change, hardening, and her body tenses in my arms. "I didn't grow up in New York. I moved there when I was eighteen."

"Okay. So, where is home?"

"New York is home." She looks past me. "But I grew up in Philadelphia."

Okay...

So, I'm taking it, home wasn't the best place for her.

And that pisses me off, making my gut tighten.

"Is your family still back in Philly?" I ask carefully.

She shakes her head. "I was raised by my grandma, and she died when I was thirteen. I went into foster care. My foster parents weren't bad people, but they didn't give a shit either. They were just in it for the money. They had a bunch of us kids living with them. So, when I turned eighteen, I was out of there. I applied to an art college in New York; it was where I had always wanted to go. I got accepted and moved there. Then, I met Nick."

She smiles fondly, and jealousy lances through me.

"Nick?"

"He's my best friend," she says. "He's my family. We have an apartment together."

"Okay, so not to sound like a jerk...but Nick...have you and he ever..."

She laughs. "No. For one, I'm not his type. You are."

Ah.

"And, even if he were straight...I don't see him like that. He's like my brother."

Wardrobe Malfunction

"Good." I move my hands to her ass and squeeze, pressing a kiss to the tip of her nose. "So, what about your parents?" I ask.

Then, I wish I hadn't because she freezes in my arms.

I lean back, looking her in the face.

"My mother died when I was two. She was murdered…by my father."

"Jesus, Charly."

She shrugs her shoulders like it doesn't hurt her, but I can tell it does. Of course it would.

"Shit happens, right? And it's not like I remember her. Or my father. He's still in prison. He will be for the rest of his life. After my mother died, I went to live with my grandma. She was the only living relative I had. She did her best, but she was old. I think it was hard for her, seeing me every day. I look a lot like my mother. She never hurt me. I was always well cared for, but she wasn't exactly the loving type."

I wrap my arms around her, hugging her, and she stiffens, but then she slowly relaxes in my arms, her arms sliding around my back, holding on to me.

I can't even imagine what her life has been like. My family is amazing. I grew up knowing I was loved. There wasn't a day my mom and dad didn't tell me that I was loved with either words or actions.

My cell starts to ring in my back pocket.

I sigh. Loosening an arm from around her, I slip it out and glance at the screen. It's Aiden.

Charly steps away from me. I frown. I don't want her going anywhere.

"Yeah?" I answer.

"I'm outside," Aiden says.

"Okay. I'll be down in a few." I hang up and slide the phone back in my pocket.

She's standing over on the other side of the room, her butt resting against the dresser, fingers curled around the edge of it.

"Aiden's here," I tell her.

"Okay. We should probably leave separately."

I don't see the point, but I don't argue.

"So, I'll see you later?"

"Yeah." She smiles, but it doesn't quite reach her eyes.

I don't like this. I don't like her like this. Distant.

She's only a few feet away, but right now, she looks like she's thousands of miles from me.

I feel like a dick. And I really don't want to leave with her feeling like this.

I shouldn't have probed about her family. It's not like me to be so fucking nosy, but I guess I just wanted to know her.

And, now that I do know a little, it's made me want to know more.

Knowing how hard her life has been makes me want to take care of her.

It's not a feeling I've ever known with a woman, especially not one I've known for such a short space of time, but it's there.

I walk over to her. I take her face in my hands and kiss her.

Her body goes lax against me, and she opens up her mouth for me, moaning softly.

Forcing myself to break away, I press a kiss to the tip of her nose.

Crossing the room, I pick up my ball cap and pull it onto my head.

Hand on the door handle, I look back at her. "Don't make any plans for tonight that don't include me, Pins, because you'll definitely be seeing me later." I wink, and then I disappear out the door.

Charly

"DRINKS TONIGHT?"

"What?" I look up from the shirt I'm sewing, my thoughts not actually on what I'm doing but on something else.

Someone else.

Vaughn.

I can't seem to get the man off my mind...and what he did to me last night and this morning...

"I said, drinks tonight?" Ava repeats, cutting into my sex thoughts. "You, me, and Logan. I thought we could go to that new bar on Sunset Boulevard."

"Oh, I can't. I already have plans."

"Don't make any plans for tonight that don't include me, Pins, because you'll definitely be seeing me later."

I get shivers, just thinking about his departing words. And I do really want to see him. And it's not like I can exactly bring Vaughn along for drinks. Surefire way to blow our cover.

Blow.

I want to giggle.

I'm such a pervert.

I'll just have to make it another night for drinks with them. Tomorrow night.

"Ooh, what are you up to?" she asks before I can suggest tomorrow night.

Looking at her, I see a gleam in her eyes, and I instantly know what she's thinking.

She thinks I have a date. And she's not far off. I do have a date, a sex date with Vaughn. And I can't freaking wait.

"Oh, I, er…" *Think, Charly.* "I said I'd call Nick. Then, I was going to wash my hair."

That's the best you could come up with?

I give myself a mental slap.

She laughs. "So, call Nick early. Then, wash your hair, get dressed up, and come out with us." She rests her elbows on the table, her chin in her hands. "I'm not taking no for an answer, Charly. You need to go out and have some fun."

From the look in her eyes, I know she means *she* needs to have some fun, and then it makes me wonder what that jackass Jeremy has done to upset her this time.

And I know I can't say no. I'll have to put Vaughn off.

My vagina cries out in protest.

Sorry, girl. Hos before bros.

"Count me in," I say.

She smiles big.

And I feel good that I've made her happy…even if my vagina is in pain right now.

"You want a coffee?" she asks.

"Homemade or Starbucks?" There's one just across the street from the studio. And Ava's coffee is like mud.

"Starbucks."

Wardrobe
MALFUNCTION

"Then, yes."

She sticks her tongue out at me, and I laugh.

"Can you grab me a sandwich as well?"

It's way past lunchtime, and I haven't eaten anything. I reach for my bag, but she waves me off.

"It's on me. What do you want?"

"Anything with turkey in it and a caramel latte."

"Turkey. Caramel. Got it. I'll be ten." She waves and disappears out the door.

My phone chimes, so I grab it out of my bag, expecting it to be Nick. We've been texting all morning about you-know-who.

When I check the screen, Vaughn's name is lighting it up.

Butterflies swoop in my stomach, and I feel like a giddy schoolgirl with a crush.

I guess I am, except I'm no schoolgirl.

I swipe the screen, opening the message.

> *Vaughn: I was serious about tonight. I need to see you.*

Need. And the butterflies go mental. Then, they drop at the remembrance that I can't see him tonight.

> *Me: I can't do tonight. Ava has corralled me into going for drinks with her and Logan. I think she's feeling a little down. I couldn't say no. Sorry. I'll make it up to you.*

I press Send and set my cell on the table, waiting for his reply.

It comes immediately. I pick my phone back up.

> *Vaughn: Unacceptable, Pins. My cock desperately needs your attention.*

I laugh out loud.

> *Me: I'm sure your cock can manage one night without me, West.*

Vaughn: Nope. I don't think you realize the seriousness of this situation. I've had a boner all morning. I can't stop thinking about those fucking boots you're wearing and how good they'll feel wrapped around my waist.

I look down at my boots. I didn't even know they had an effect on him. Then, I smile, thinking that I'll have to wear these boots more often.

> *Me: Tomorrow night? I'll wear the boots and nothing else.*

Vaughn: You're killing me here. I'm gonna have to go jerk off in the bathroom.

> *Me: Aren't you on set right now?*

It's a closed set today for some reason. I was told to take the clothes over and then leave. I don't know what they're filming, but they didn't want many people there to watch.

My mind instantly goes to another sex scene, but they didn't close the set for the one yesterday, and that was as explicit as I've ever seen, so it can't be that. I'll have to ask Vaughn when I see him. Tomorrow.

Sigh.

Vaughn: Yep. Just taking a break. In the bathroom. With my hand. Picturing you.

> *Me: Perv!*

Wardrobe
MALFUNCTION

Vaughn: I don't deny it. Then again, you could come here and give me a hand…

> *Me: Sounds like you're doing just fine yourself.*

Vaughn: I'm so hard, it hurts, baby.

Baby. What is it about a man calling you that, that makes you turn to jelly?

> *Me: I can get rid of your hard-on right now with a few words, if you want me to?*

Vaughn: Not possible. But you can give it a try.

> *Me: I'm hemming a shirt. Using pins.*

Vaughn: And it's gone.

I laugh again and then send him a laughing emoji. He pings back a text seconds later.

Vaughn: You're fucking awesome. ☺

> *Me: I know.* ☺

Vaughn: Babe…I have to go. I'm needed back on set.

A second later, I get another text from him.

Vaughn: Where are you going tonight anyway?

> *Me: Some new bar on Sunset Boulevard.*

I don't hear back from him again, and I'm guessing he turned off his phone to go back on set.

Ava turns back up a few minutes later with my sandwich and coffee. We sit and eat and talk about the night ahead of us. All the time, Vaughn is ever present in my thoughts.

Charly

THE MUSIC IS PUMPING OUT, and I'm having a great night. Originally, I was disappointed about not getting to spend it with Vaughn—I might be a little bit addicted already—but it's so good to come and let loose. Ava is, as always, so much fun, and Logan is really great.

We've snagged a table near the dance floor, and we're drinking, talking, and people-watching. I'm having a great time. I'm also on my third drink of the night, and we've only been here for an hour, which is some quick drinking for me. I'm drinking a cocktail that looks as pretty as it tastes.

Calvin Harris and Rihanna's "This Is What You Came For" starts to play. I love this song.

"Dance?" I say to them.

"Hell yeah!" Ava says.

"I'm not a dancer. I'll watch the drinks," Logan replies.

"You're sure?" I check.

"Go dance, and have fun."

I jump down from my stool and grab Ava's hand. I lead her onto the dance floor and into the crowd. We start dancing.

It's hot and crowded but amazing. I'm having so much fun.

The song eventually ends, and another comes on that's not so good, so we head back to our table. Logan's on his phone.

"Sexting?" Ava nudges him with her elbow.

"I wish. No, I'm checking Twitter to see what's happening here."

"Um, can't you just look around," I quip, "and see what's happening?"

"There was a commotion upstairs, smart-ass, and I couldn't see what was happening, hence checking Twitter for the deets."

He points, and my eyes follow to look up at the upstairs balcony that circles the whole of the bar. But I can't see much of anything.

"What kind of commotion?" Ava asks him.

"Just some screaming. And I saw some big, burly guys walking around."

"Oh, maybe there was a fight." Ava grins.

"Yeah, probably." Logan puts his phone down on the table. "I can't see anything on Twitter. I thought maybe a celeb had arrived."

"Like Ryan Gosling?" Ava asks.

"Now, that would be heaven. I swear, whose dick do I have to suck to get a job on one of his movie sets?" Logan chuckles, making us laugh.

"Probably his wife's," I joke.

Out of nowhere, I feel a tingle on the back of my neck. Then, voices around us seem to get louder. And I see a few people looking at the upper balcony. Others are pointing. A few are getting their cameras out.

Wardrobe Malfunction

"What is going on?" I ask.

"Celeb for sure," Ava and Logan say at the same time. They laugh and fist-bump each other.

"Please be Gosling." Logan presses his hands together, praying.

I swivel on my stool, looking around upstairs, and then I see *him*.

Vaughn.

He's upstairs, leaning on the railing, bottle of beer in his hand, and he's looking down…right at me.

His lips curve into a sexy smile.

It hits me right in the chest—and panties.

Then, he pushes off the railing and walks away.

He's here. What's he doing here? And why did he just smile at me and walk away?

"Was that Vaughn?" Ava asks in my ear.

Dragging my eyes from where he was, I turn back to her. "Yeah, I think so."

"Makes sense with all the squealing that went on. Is it sad that I'm not excited he's here?" She giggles. I think the drinks are going to her head. "I mean, I see him at work every day, so it's not as exciting anymore."

"No," I say. "I get what you mean."

But it's a lie because I am excited that he's here. I could never tire of seeing Vaughn.

"I wonder who he's with," Logan says.

"We should find out," Ava says. "He could be with Julian Jacob and Gabriel Evans." Her voice goes all dreamy while saying Gabriel's name, making my ears perk up. "They're who he parties with now since Cain shit all over him with Piper. We should go up there, see if we can get in. You should go first, Charly."

"Me? Why?" I feel a whip of paranoia that she knows I slept with Vaughn last night, but I quickly scrub that off, knowing I'm being stupid.

"Because you're his dresser. You know him better than we do."

"Um, I know him exactly the same as you do. Less because I've been working on set less time than you guys."

Liar, liar pants on fire.

"Ah, come on, Charly. You're braver than we are. There's no way I can go up there and ask to go in, but stuff like that doesn't bother you."

Doesn't it?

No, she's right. I'm not afraid to do stuff like that usually. I'm just feeling weird that he's here, and I'm here.

Maybe he thinks I followed him here. I mean, surely, he doesn't because I didn't even know he would be out tonight. But he knew I would be, and…

Hang on, when he asked, I didn't exactly tell him the name of which bar I was going to, but I did tell him I was going to the new bar on Sunset. This is the *only* new bar on Sunset.

Did he come here because he knew I'd be here?

Now, I want to go up there because I want to know the answer to that question.

"Fine. I'll see if I can get us in." I slip off my stool, grabbing my purse and drink. I tuck my purse under my arm.

I head for the stairway, which is unsurprisingly crowded, with Ava and Logan at my heels. I have to push my way through to get up to the top, which is now roped off. It wasn't earlier.

The power of celebrity.

There are two security men at the top, and nearby, I spot Aiden, but he's just a little too far away for me to call to.

Reaching the top of the stairs, I smile at the security man. The huge guy makes me feel like I'm the size of a toddler.

Wardrobe Malfunction

I decide to just go with the direct approach. "Hey, I work for Vaughn West. Can you let us through?"

He stares down at me, his eyes hard. "Yeah, and I'm Barack Obama. Michelle will be along any minute now."

I do laugh at that. "You're a funny guy. But, seriously, I do work for Vaughn. Indirectly. On the set of his new movie. I'm his dresser."

"She really is," Ava pipes up behind me.

"I dress Natasha Warner," Logan chimes in.

"Well, that's real nice for you all. I dressed myself tonight." He sweeps a hand down himself. "And this area is still closed off to the general public. I can't let you through."

He turns his back on me, which pisses me off. I'm actually considering pulling my cell out and just calling Vaughn, but then I realize, to Ava and Logan, that might look like I'm a little too familiar with him.

And, anyway, Vaughn knows I'm here. If he wanted to see me, he would have come and gotten me.

It's not like we're dating. He just wants to fuck me.

God, he probably doesn't even want me up here.

Not wanting to look like a stage five clinger, I turn, ready to tell Ava and Logan that we should go back downstairs, when I hear a voice that sends tingles running through me.

"Let them through."

I spin back around, and I'm greeted by the sight of Vaughn. Then, immediately after, there's the deafening sound of screaming behind me.

I smile at him. He doesn't smile back. Just looks at me like he wants to devour me whole.

I have to stop myself from visibly shivering.

The security guy unclips the rope and lets the three of us through.

"Hi," I say to Vaughn. "Thanks for letting us in."

He finally smiles, but it's a secret smile. One that says he's seen me naked and he's thinking about getting me naked again real soon.

My stomach starts flipping around like a fish out of water.

"Yeah, thanks, Vaughn," Ava says, glancing around like she's looking for someone.

"Thanks, man," Logan says to him.

"No problem," Vaughn says, eyes on me.

"Is that Gabriel Evans?" Ava asks in that weird voice again, making me stare at her.

"Yeah, it is. You want to meet him?"

"Really? He won't mind?" she squeaks, her face brightening.

I laugh to myself. I've never seen her get all fangirl over a celebrity like this before. I think someone has herself a crush.

Vaughn starts walking toward Gabriel, and we follow behind.

It's like stepping into a whole other world.

There are quite a few people up here, some cast members and some people I don't recognize.

I find myself watching Vaughn's ass as he walks. It looks good in the jeans he's wearing.

I had my hands on that very ass last night while he pounded in and out of me.

Holy shivers.

His shirt is molded to his body, and I just want to rip it off. With my teeth.

Vaughn stops at a group of guys. One of them is Gabriel Evans, and I recognize the other as Julian Jacob. Both of them are actors. Gabriel does movies. Julian is in TV. He does this big show about this cop who dies and comes back to life to avenge his murder. Unsurprisingly, it's called *Dead Cop*. I haven't seen it yet, but I've heard it's awesome.

Wardrobe Malfunction

The three of them are the golden boys of Hollywood. And it's easy to see why. I know Gabriel is part Italian, and it shows in his dark looks and lean, muscular body. Julian is the all-American boy with blond hair and blue eyes. Both are tall.

And Vaughn is Vaughn.

He just shines the brightest. Something about him pulls your attention straight to him.

"Guys, this is Ava, Logan, and Pins."

"Pins?" Gabriel chuckles.

I frown at Vaughn. "Charly. Nice to meet you, Gabriel."

"Call me Gabe."

I watch his eyes brush over Logan and Ava. Then, they stop on Ava, who's looking like a deer in headlights right now.

"Seeing as though this jackass isn't going to introduce me, I'm Julian." He shoulders Vaughn.

"I know who you are." I smile at him.

"Yeah, it's good, really good, to meet you," Logan says. "I love *Dead Cop*! Big fan! I have to ask, are you and Meredith ever going to get it on in the show?"

Julian winks and taps his nose.

"I knew it!" Logan cheers.

I think I need to watch this show if it has Logan that excited.

Vaughn introduces us to the rest of the group. A few are Gabriel's friends, and others are what I like to call celeb hangers-on.

I somehow find myself standing next to Vaughn while Ava chats with Gabriel and Logan chews Julian's ear off about his show.

"Thanks for coming over and letting us in. That security guy wasn't budging."

"I told him not to let any stalkers in, and you do look like a stalker."

"Ha! Says the man who came to the bar he knew I was going to. The *only* new bar on Sunset."

"Are you saying, I followed you here?" He gives me an affronted look.

Keeping my eyes on him, I tip my head to the side, a smile teasing my lips. "Well, didn't you?"

His arms fold over his chest. "Technically, I didn't follow you. But…yes, I did know that you might possibly be here."

"Aha! I knew it! You little stalker!" I laugh, secretly feeling thrilled that he wanted to see me tonight.

"It was my cock," Vaughn says. "He smelled your scent and followed you here. He's a needy bastard like that."

Laughter bursts from me.

He smiles, his eyes shining.

"You're weird." I laugh.

"It turns you on though. Admit it."

I measure out an inch with my thumb and forefinger.

"I hope you're not sizing up my cock there, Pins, 'cause I'm gonna be seriously offended if you are."

"Stop it." I laugh, playfully pushing my hand to his chest, feeling giddy from the drinks.

He moves a little closer to me. "Are you drunk?"

"No. I'm only on cocktail number three."

"Good." He leans in close. "Because I like my women to be alert when I'm fucking them."

"Them?"

"You."

My stomach clenches, and I feel my panties getting wet, making me press my thighs together.

His eyes skim down my body. "I like the dress and the heels, but I miss the boots."

I press a hand to my dress. It's one I made myself. A red lace body-con dress. Him saying he likes it makes me feel good even if he does know zero about women's fashion.

Wardrobe

"The boots needed a rest. I wore them all day." I flash him a smile.

He leans in again, speaking into my ear, "I want you wearing the boots later. Them and *nothing* else."

He tips his head back and stares into my eyes, taking a swig of his beer, and I nod my head in agreement, like an eager puppy.

Vaughn

I SWEAR TO GOD, THIS night is never going to be over.

I've wanted to leave the bar since I saw Charly.

I knew she was down there. Of course I knew. But I wanted her to see me and come to me.

And she did.

We've all been drinking and talking and dancing for hours. Well, I've only had a few beers. I don't like to get too tanked, and I need to be in good working order, as I plan on spending the rest of the night inside Charly.

I've noticed that Charly has slowed her drinking down, too.

I haven't been able to keep my eyes off her all night. I just want to be alone with her. I haven't been alone with her since she first arrived and we spoke for a few minutes. After that, she was off dancing with Ava and chatting to people she knew from the cast.

I just want to pick her up and carry her off, so I can have her to myself.

And thank fuck we're finally leaving.

I'm going to grab Charly, put her in my limo, strip her clothes off, and fuck her all the way to her hotel. Then, I'll get her inside her hotel room and fuck her all over again.

My dick has never been so eager.

"So, we're leaving then?" Gabe slaps me on the back. He's drunk, of course.

"Yep."

"Cool. Well, I told my driver to take the night off, so we'll grab a lift back with you. Is that cool?"

No, it's not fucking cool. It's not fucking cool at all.

I know my expression has gone tight, so I school it. "Sure," I say with a casual tone.

He stares at me for a beat and then laughs, his eyes sparkling. "Cool." He pats me on the shoulder. "I'll let Julian know we're leaving. The others are heading off to a club."

I watch him walk off, cursing the motherfucker to hell.

A hand touches my arm. "So, we're gonna head off." Charly's voice comes close to my ear.

I turn to her. *God, she's fucking gorgeous.*

"Ava's drunk. I need to get her home."

"Sure thing. I was planning on getting you in my limo and doing all kinds of dirty things to you in there, but fucking Gabe has just invited himself and Julian for a ride home."

"It's fine." She smiles. "I'll grab us a cab."

"No. I'm in the limo. I'll have Aiden drive you guys home."

"You sure?"

"Course." I move in closer, leaving a sliver of air between us. I love the sound of the breath she sucks in at my nearness. "But I'm dropping you off last. Then, you and I are going back to your hotel. Okay?"

Wardrobe Malfunction

"No." She shakes her head.

"No?" I frown.

"Drop me off first. Well, I mean, drop Ava off first, then Logan, and then me, and—"

"Um, am I fucking missing something here? You ditching me?"

She laughs, the sound light and airy, but I'm feeling kind of pissed off right now, so it doesn't have the effect it normally does.

"Don't be stupid, West. Of course I'm not ditching you, you needy bastard." She grins, and I can't help but smile back at her using my term. "It'll just look suspect if I'm the last one left in the car with you. It'll look better if you drop us off first and then your boys. Then, you can come back to my hotel once you're alone."

"Good call."

She's smart, my girl.

My girl?

Hang the fuck on. When exactly did I start thinking of her as mine?

No need to go getting carried away, West. You're just fucking her, remember?

"I'm a genius. What can I say?" She puts her hands on her hips and does a little wiggle.

"And a little devious, Pins. But I like it. It's fucking hot."

We round everyone up and head out the back exit of the bar to my waiting limo.

Of course the paparazzi are out there.

"Vaughn, look this way! It's been a while since you were out partying. Have you missed it? Who are the girls?"

"Julian, where's your costar tonight?"

"Gabe, is it true you and Marti Shaw are together?"

"Vaughn, are you still bitter about what Piper and Cain did to you? I hear they're getting married. Will you be at the ceremony?"

The questions are like bullets firing at us.

The sad thing is, it's fucking normal for me, Gabe, and Julian.

We all bundle into the car, shutting the door on the vipers. But they still have the cameras to the windows, trying to get pictures.

"Aiden, get us the fuck out of here," I tell him.

He nods from the front, and then the car is moving slowly, his horn honking to move the fuckers out of the way.

I slump back in the seat, feeling pissed off. Not about the Piper and Cain comments. I couldn't give a shit if they were getting married or not.

It's just the fact that I can't go out to a bar with my friends without getting hounded by the press.

It was probably a good thing that I didn't get in the car with just Charly. That would have been spread all across the Internet within minutes, and any chance of keeping me and her on the down-low would have been blown out of the water.

I look at her sitting on the seat across from me, a drunk Ava half-asleep on her shoulder and Logan sitting on the other side.

She gives me a soft smile, and the annoyance instantly just ebbs away.

I can't wait to be alone with her.

"The pictures are already online," Julian says from beside me, showing me his phone.

"Fuck, they're quick," Gabe says from my other side, leaning over to help himself to a whiskey from the minibar in the limo.

"The power of technology." I sigh.

"Love 'em or hate 'em, they keep our name in the press and keep us relevant," Gabe says.

He's right. But it doesn't make it any easier.

Wardrobe Malfunction

Sometimes, I just crave privacy. To not have to hide whom I'm sleeping with.

I couldn't even take Charly out on a date if I wanted to because we might be seen.

It's fucking ridiculous. And it's my life.

"Where am I heading?" Aiden calls back to us.

"Is it still okay to drop off Ava first?" Charly checks with me.

"Of course. Just let Aiden know her address."

Charly turns to Aiden and tells him where Ava lives.

Ten minutes later, we're pulling up at Ava's. Logan and Charly get her out of the limo. I'm pretty sure she's asleep.

"We'll just get her inside, and we'll be right back," Charly tells me.

"No worries. Take your time."

She shuts the door. I grab a bottle of water from the minibar.

"So, she works on set?" Gabe asks.

I unscrew the cap and take a drink. "Who?"

"Charly."

"Yeah, in wardrobe. She's assigned to me."

"You fucking her?"

I feel my chest tighten. "No."

"Mind if I do?"

I stare at him hard, my insides turning over. I grit my jaw. "No, go ahead."

I've just got to pray that Charly tells him to fuck off, or I'll be in jail for killing Gabe.

"But you're probably not her type," I add.

He laughs, eyes grinning at me. "I'm everyone's type."

"You're not mine," Julian says.

Julian's gay. But in the closet. Like a lot of actors in Hollywood. The studio doesn't want him out because they think it'll damage the show.

Stupid if you ask me, but what do I know?

I'm currently hiding the girl I'm sleeping with and telling my friend he's okay to hit on her when he's most definitely not.

"I'm fucking wounded." Gabe laughs, slapping a hand to his chest. "And don't worry, West. I'll leave your girl alone." He pats my leg.

"She's not my girl."

"Sure she's not." He laughs, and so does Julian.

I want to tell them I'm sleeping with her…that she is mine. But, after what Cain did to me, it's just hard for me to trust anyone.

I've known them both for years. But then I knew Cain for ten years, and he shit all over me.

The door opens, and Charly and Logan climb back in.

"She okay?" I ask.

"Yeah. Her boyfriend was home; he put her to bed," Charly says.

"Not that he didn't fucking complain about it," Logan says. "I don't know what she sees in that jackass."

Charly pats Logan's leg with her hand.

I know Logan is gay, but I still feel a spike of jealousy at her touching him, which is so strange to me. I've never been a jealous kind of guy.

Maybe it's because of what happened with Piper and Cain.

Or maybe it's because I never cared enough about a woman before to be jealous over her.

I'm going with option number one.

We drop off Logan. Then, it's Charly's turn.

"Thanks for the ride," she says to Aiden. Then, she climbs out of the limo. "Thanks for a great night, guys." She smiles at everyone before her eyes finally connect with mine. "I'll see you later."

Yes, you fucking will. Sooner than later, baby.

She shuts the door and is gone.

Wardrobe Malfunction

Right, let me get these bastards home, and then I can get back here.

"Aiden, Julian's next," I tell him.

He pulls off, knowing the way to Julian's, as he's dropped him off plenty of times.

"Anyone wanna come in for a drink at mine?" Julian asks.

"Nope," I say.

"Gee, thanks, West. You sure know how to make a guy feel wanted."

Gabe laughs. "I'll come for a drink, but don't be getting me drunk and feeling me up while I'm passed out. I know how bad you want me."

I laugh, shaking my head at Gabe.

"Fuck you." Julian laughs.

"I know you want to, but I'm a giver, not a taker." Gabe grins.

"Why do we hang out with him?" Julian asks me.

"Beats me." I shrug.

"Because I'm fucking awesome, and you know it." Gabe spreads his arms out, spilling some of the whiskey in his glass.

We pull up at Julian's house.

"You coming in then, fuckface?" Julian asks Gabe.

"Nah, I'll head home."

For fuck's sake, I've got to drop Gabe off now. It'll be the fucking morning before I get back to Charly.

"Cool. See you later then. Thanks for the ride, man."

We do the guy handshake as he passes by before climbing out the limo.

"Later, Julian."

He shuts the door.

"Aiden, to Gabe's place now."

The car pulls off again. It feels like he's driving at a snail's pace.

I'm tapping my foot, drumming my fingers on my thigh.

"You look tense, West," Gabe says, pouring himself another whiskey.

"Not tense, just tired."

"Sure." He smirks. "You want one?" He lifts the whiskey bottle.

"Nah. I'm good with water." I take another drink.

Then, I stare out the window, watching the houses pass by.

How long does it take to get to Gabe's place from Julian's? Five minutes normally.

Why does it feel like we've been driving for ten fucking minutes then?

Why aren't we there already?

Then, we finally turn onto his street, and I nearly exhale with relief.

Aiden stops the limo outside Gabe's apartment building.

I open the door. "Hit the pavement, pretty boy."

"Hey, I haven't finished my drink."

"Take it with you."

He smirks. "Anyone would think you were eager to get off."

"I am. I've got an early shoot."

He laughs. "Is that what we're calling it nowadays?"

"I have no idea what you're talking about."

"Sure you don't." He chuckles. "Great night, West. Thanks for the ride." He slings an arm around me, giving me a guy hug. "Love you, man," he slurs, patting my back before letting go.

Gabe always gets affectionate when he's drunk. It's usually funny. Right now, I just want him out of my fucking car, so I can get back to Charly and screw her brains out.

"Sleep it off, man." I laugh, shoving him in the direction of the open car door.

Wardrobe Malfunction

He stumbles out, glass still in hand. He rights himself on the pavement. "Don't do anything I wouldn't, which isn't much!" He laughs at his own joke, stumbling slightly.

I shake my head at him, laughing. Honestly, at this moment in time, I don't give a shit if he does know I'm going back to Charly. I just want to go.

"Get to bed, and sleep it off," I say to him. "Make sure he gets inside all right," I tell his doorman, who is standing outside, holding the door open for Gabe.

"Will do, Mr. West. Come on, Mr. Evans, let's get you to your apartment."

I shut the limo door to the sound of Gabe singing Lukas Graham's "7 Years" loudly. His neighbors must fucking love him.

"Back to Charly's hotel," I tell Aiden. "And drive fast."

"Will do." He chuckles.

He pulls off, the tires squealing as he slams on the gas.

It takes for-fucking-ever to get there.

I swear to God, we hit every red light. It's like someone is out to torture me.

I'm climbing the limo walls by the time we finally pull up at her hotel.

"Pick me up at eight a.m.," I tell Aiden.

He hands me my ball cap. Pulling it on, I'm out of the limo the second it stops.

Then, I'm jogging—I'm fucking jogging—through the hotel and up the steps and along the corridor to her hotel room.

I've never needed to be inside someone as much as I do her.

I don't know what the fuck she's done to me, but I like it. A lot.

Then, I'm knocking on her door. Fucking finally!

I wait a few seconds, and then the door pulls open.

And there she is.

Standing there, looking like a fucking goddess.

A leather-boot-wearing goddess.

My mouth waters as I take her in.

"I thought you were never going to get here," she says.

I grip ahold of the doorframe, restraining myself from pouncing on her. "Me neither. I was ready to commit murder if it meant getting back here sooner."

She laughs, and my cock stands up to attention. Not that he wasn't already paying attention at the sight of her in those goddamn boots and sexy red lacy underwear.

She's like every man's fantasy.

She's my fantasy.

And she's about to become my reality.

"Babe, not that you don't look sexy as fuck, but I believe I expressly said, boots only."

Fighting a smile, she lifts her chin, and with those vixen eyes fixed on mine, she unclips the bra, slides it down her arms, and throws it to the floor. Then, she hooks her fingers into the elastic of the panties and pulls them down her hips and over her boots before kicking them aside.

Her hands go to her hips. "Better?"

She's standing there in nothing but those boots. The hotel door is still open. Anyone could see her, and she doesn't give a fuck.

Her liberty is intoxicating.

I want to inhale it. Snort it...*her* into my lungs and breathe her for the rest of my life.

"Almost," I growl. I stride through the door, slamming it shut behind me. I pick her up, loving the feel of those boot-covered legs going around my waist. "Now, it's better."

Then, I kiss her like I've wanted to kiss her all night. Hard and deep.

Charly

THESE LAST FEW WEEKS have gone by in a blur of laughter, fun, and sex with Vaughn. It's been amazing.

We spend evenings watching movies and eating room service. And I've just started watching Julian's show with Vaughn. But we don't spend every evening together. Sometimes, we're on the film set until late. Other times, Vaughn has dinner with Brandon and Natasha, or he goes for drinks with Gabriel and Julian. Some evenings, I go out with Ava and Logan or just Ava. We go out for dinner or to the movies or just out for drinks.

But, at the end of every night, Vaughn and I end up in bed together.

We haven't spent a night apart since the first night we slept together.

We generally always spend the night at my hotel. It's less likely that we'll get spotted. It's more likely that people—hotel staff—would notice if I kept frequenting Vaughn's room. He can slip from here, going unnoticed.

I don't really know what it means. Or what's happening between us.

I mean, I don't think we're dating because we can't exactly go out on a date together, which does make me a little frustrated at times. But it also works for me, too, because I can't have the press delving into my personal life right now.

And, because I don't really know what Vaughn and I are doing, where we're heading—if anywhere at all—I can't have my life upended.

We might not be dating, but I figure we're fuck buddies, and I think we're exclusive. Well, I hope we're exclusive. I don't think he's seeing anyone else, and the fact that he ends every night in my bed tells me the same.

And I'm glad. More than glad.

I'm happy. Happier than I can ever remember being.

But one thing I do know is, when this thing with Vaughn does come to an end—because all good things end—it's going to hurt like a bitch.

Because I like him. A lot.

We're at my hotel tonight. Vaughn is working on his laptop, and I'm watching *Romeo + Juliet*, the Leonardo DiCaprio version, while working on that wedding dress I've been designing for a while now. The skirt has been evading me, but I think I finally have it. I'm going for a pleated chiffon skirt. Simple but elegant.

"I like it," Vaughn says from over my shoulder.

I cover my drawing with my hand. I didn't realize he was watching. This is the first time I've drawn in front of him.

"Don't hide it." He comes to sit beside me, pulling my hand from it. "It's really good."

"Thanks," I say.

"I didn't know you designed. Why didn't you tell me?"

Wardrobe

I shrug. "It's not important. It's just something I like to do."

"May I?" He gestures to my sketchpad.

I tentatively hand it over to him. He starts looking through my designs.

"These are amazing, Pins. Why don't you do it professionally?"

"I tried. After I graduated from college. But it's not an easy industry to get into. So, I took a job temping with an agency, and the first job I got offered was in wardrobe. I'm good with clothes, and I was always a good seamstress—"

"Except for when you're stabbing innocent guys in the balls."

I stick my tongue out at him. "Are you ever going to let that go?"

"Probably not." He chuckles, continuing to look through my designs. "Well, I think you should try again. I'm no fashion expert—"

"No kidding." I laugh.

He pretends to ignore me and seamlessly carries on, "But I think you should try again. You've got real talent. It'd be a tragedy to let it go to waste. I know some people I can put you in touch with."

"I don't need any favors." I sound touchy. I don't know why.

"Friends help each other." He frowns.

I want to ask if that is what we are—friends. Is that all we are? Friends who fuck and fall asleep in each other's arms?

But, of course, I don't.

"I know. I'm just used to doing things on my own. I want my success to be on my own merit."

"And it will. But it doesn't hurt to have someone put you in touch with the people who can help you get there."

I stare at his face, his expression so earnest, and something inside me ruptures. I feel like I'm bleeding out. I can feel my face heating up.

I swallow, take my sketchpad from him, and close it up. "Sure, that'd be good. Thanks."

I put my pad down and rest back, watching the TV.

I can feel Vaughn's eyes on me, but I don't say anything.

It's at the part when Romeo and Juliet are getting married, and that cute kid starts to sing "When Doves Cry."

"I love this song," I murmur.

"The Prince version or this one?"

I turn my face to him. "I like this one, but nothing beats Prince's version. I can't believe he's gone."

"I know." Vaughn sighs. "I was lucky enough to meet him once."

"Really?" I turn my body to his. "What was he like?"

"Cool. Awesome as fuck. Everything you'd expect him to be. I was at this party of some big music producer, and Prince was there. He and a few other musicians started doing an impromptu jamming session. I got to see him sing live. It was amazing."

"I can only imagine."

"It's one perk of my lifestyle." He doesn't sound happy when he says that.

"I'm sure there's more than one."

He glances at me, and his eyes stay on mine. "There are a few things. Meeting you was, of course, one."

"Of course." I grin.

He picks up his phone and starts playing with it. A few seconds later, Prince's "When Doves Cry" starts to play.

He mutes the TV and stands up on the bed, holding out a hand to me. "Dance with me?"

"Dance with you?" I stare up at him.

"Yeah. I know how much you love a good twerk."

"This isn't really twerking music, West." I smile.

Wardrobe Malfunction

"Well, maybe I just want to dance with you, so I can use it as an excuse to grope your ass."

I laugh. "Like you need an excuse."

"Come on, dance with me, Pins." He moves his open hand closer to me.

So, I slip mine in and let him pull me to my feet. He brings me close to him and starts to move us on the bed.

I link my arms around his neck. His hands go to my back and then slide lower where he squeezes my ass, grinning at me.

I laugh, shaking my head. "I don't think you know how to be serious."

"Hey, I can be serious when I want to be."

"Like when?"

"Like when I'm licking your pussy and making you come. I'm seriously concentrating then."

"Okay, I'll give you that."

"And when I'm fucking you. I'm serious then."

"Any examples that don't involve sex?"

He presses his lips together, giving it some thought. Then, he looks down at me and says, "Nope."

And I laugh again.

"Whose idea was it to dance on the bed? Because this isn't fucking easy," he says.

"I could've told you that."

"Dance on beds often, do you?"

"No, I just have this thing called common sense, and common sense says it wouldn't be easy to slow dance on a squishy mattress."

"Harsh, Pins. You've hurt my feelings."

"You have feelings?" I tease.

"You're an evil woman," he grumbles. "Good thing you're hot."

"Right back at ya, West. You don't think I'm sleeping with you for your brains, do you? I just want you for your hot body and big cock."

"I fucking knew it!" He lifts me up before taking me down to the bed, making me squeal.

I wrap my legs around his waist. He lifts his head, staring into my eyes. Then, he kisses me.

He kisses me like he always does. Intensely. Like he'll die if he doesn't.

I've never been kissed in this way before. And I don't think I ever will again if it's not him I'm kissing.

The song moves onto Cigarettes After Sex's "Nothing's Gonna Hurt You Baby."

Vaughn removes my T-shirt and bra, and then he pulls his own shirt off, tossing it to the floor.

He's straight back to my mouth, kissing me again. His hand goes to the zipper on my jean shorts. He opens them and then shifts, pulling them down my legs and off. My panties go next.

He reaches into his pocket and gets out a condom. Then, he removes his own jeans.

I don't take my eyes off him once.

Then, he's suited up and back between my legs.

Eyes on mine, he pushes inside me. No words spoken.

I push my head back into the mattress, my eyes closing.

"Eyes open."

I blink them open.

"Eyes always on me," he says, thrusting into me, taking me to that place no one else can but him.

And I keep them locked on him the whole time until we're both exploding together.

Then, later, when we're lying in bed in the darkness, and I'm in his arms, sleepy and sated from the orgasm he gave me, he says, "Pins, I've just thought of something I'm serious about."

"Oh, yeah? And what's that?" I ask, yawning.

"You," he says.

And, suddenly, I'm not so sleepy anymore.

Wardrobe Malfunction

Does he even mean that the way it sounded? Or is he just fucking with me like usual?

He kisses my forehead. "Night, Pins."

"Uh…night, West," I say, my heart pounding.

He pulls me closer and sighs a sleepy sound.

He was joking, right?

Yeah, he was definitely joking.

I mean, he wouldn't just say it like that if he actually meant it, right?

Right.

But, even still, I can't sleep, and I lie there for ages, feeling confused as hell.

And, when his breathing has evened out and he's sleeping, I trace my fingers over his cheek. "I'm serious about you, too, West," I whisper, knowing he can't hear me.

Because, even if he didn't mean it, I do.

And it scares the hell out of me.

Vaughn

I STEP OUT OF THE shower in my trailer. In that last shoot we did, I was covered in fake blood. It's a motherfucker to get out of your hair, so I was in there for ages, scrubbing it out.

I dry off and pull on a pair of jeans. I forgot to bring a shirt in with me.

Toweling off my hair, I wander out of the bathroom to grab a shirt.

"Hey, V."

I freeze. Slowly, I turn around.

Piper.

"What the fuck are you doing here?" I toss the towel aside, not caring where it lands.

"It's good to see you, too, V."

"How did you get in?"

She laughs and rolls her eyes. "It's not exactly hard. I am Piper Watts. Not some scum off the street."

"Opinions vary."

Her eyes sharpen.

"Well, it wasn't nice seeing you, so…" I gesture to the door.

Ignoring me, she steps forward. The look in her eyes is telling. "I want you back," she says.

I laugh. "You're insane. And I definitely don't want you back. In fact, I don't want you anywhere near me."

"I made a mistake."

"You screwed my best friend for months. Hardly a mistake. How is Cain by the way?"

"I wouldn't know. I haven't seen him since the show. I've regretted so badly what happened. I've wanted to come see you so many times, but I knew you were angry, and you needed to get that out of your system."

"You mean, my drink and sex addiction. Oh, and my tendencies toward violence. You told them I hit you, for fuck's sake, Piper."

"I never said any of that, V. You know the press; they make shit up." She steps forward and wraps her hands around my wrists. "I miss you."

I yank them away and step back. "Yeah, well, I don't miss you. I don't even like you. I'm not sure I ever did."

"Do you remember how good we used to be together?"

"No. I remember I used to like fucking you, but that got old fast."

Her brows draw together. I'm surprised they can move with the amount of Botox she has done.

"You don't mean that."

"I really do. What are you here for, Piper? Really?"

"You, I told you."

"No, you're after something. But, honestly, I don't care. There's nothing you can do to hurt me. Now, if you don't mind, I have things to do." I nod in the direction of the door.

Wardrobe Malfunction

"V, listen to me; the only thing I want is you. I want you back." She's in my space in seconds and presses her hands to my chest.

"Yoo-hoo! It's me! You'd better be decent…or not…"

Charly's soft laughter tickles my ears just as I've caught hold of Piper's wrist to try to get the crazy bitch off me.

But, instantly, I know how this will look to Charly.

And it's not good. Not good at all.

She looks frozen to the spot. The hurt in her expression is so clear and evident and like a punch to the chest.

"Charly." I shove Piper aside.

She seems to snap back to attention, her face and eyes clearing of all emotion. "I just came to drop off your clothes for tomorrow." She drops the garment bag in her hand over the chair by the door. "Sorry to interrupt."

And, before I can say another word, she's gone, back out the door.

I'm going to fucking strangle Piper.

"You." I turn on her. "Out. Now."

She laughs, her eyes going to the door that Charly just exited, and in this moment, I can't see one thing that I ever saw in this woman. She's a total bitch.

She looks back at me, a twisted smile on her face. "Her? Really, V? I thought you had better taste than that."

"Clearly not because I dated your psycho ass for six months. And, for fuck's sake, stop calling me V! I hate it. I've always hated it. And not that it's any of your fucking business, but no, I'm not dating her. Even still, she has more class in her little finger than you have in your whole body. Now, get your bony ass the fuck out of my trailer before I pick you up and throw you out myself, and then you'll really have a story to sell to the press."

My chest is heaving. I'm raging. And I need to find Charly.

"Fine, have it your way, *V*," she accentuates just to piss me off. "Have your fun with your little chippie. You'll be crawling back to me soon enough when you get bored."

I grab a T-shirt that was hanging over the back of the sofa. Not caring if it's dirty, I pull it on. "Honestly, I'd rather chop my nuts off, fry them in a hot pan, and eat them than ever get back with you."

"Fuck you!" she snaps.

"And there's the girl I never loved." I laugh, pushing my feet into my sneakers. "Now, get the fuck out of my trailer, and don't ever come back, you crazy bitch."

"You'll regret this, Vaughn West!" she yells like a bad movie villain before slamming her way out of my trailer.

I grab my cell and call Charly's number, but it just rings and then goes to voice mail.

I wait for a beat, making sure Piper is gone, before leaving to find Charly. I don't trust Piper, and I sure as hell don't want her following me to Charly. Knowing Piper, she'd take pictures of me with Charly and sell them to the highest bidder.

I head straight for the wardrobe trailer, hoping she'll be there.

And she is, but she's not alone. Ava's there.

"Hey, Vaughn, what can we do for you?" Ava smiles at me.

Charly hasn't looked at me. She's over on the other side of the trailer, looking through a drawer.

"I just need Charly for a minute."

"Oh, yeah, sure. Charly, Vaughn needs you," Ava calls to her before disappearing into the back.

I see Charly's body stiffen.

"Is it important, or can it wait?" she says without even looking up, her voice as rigid as her body. "I'm busy right now."

Pretending to look through a drawer. Right.

Wardrobe Malfunction

"It's important," I say in a voice that means I'm not fucking around.

I won't have her avoiding me and hurting over something that she thinks happened that definitely did not when I can fix this with a few words.

She pauses and then slowly rights herself before turning to face me. The hurt in her eyes that she's trying to hide slays me.

"Fine," she says tonelessly, her eyes narrowing, her hands going to her hips. "What's so important that it can't wait?"

If she wasn't hurting and this wasn't a fucked up situation, I'd be turned on right now.

Okay, maybe I'm a little turned on, but she's hot as fuck. And, when she's angry, she's off-the-charts hot.

"I ripped my shirt," I lie, knowing that Ava could be listening to what we're saying right now.

"Okay, give it here, and I'll fix it for you." She sticks her hand out, knowing full well I don't have a ripped shirt and that I definitely don't have one with me.

"It's in my trailer."

"Convenient."

I step closer to her, and she steps back.

I hate that so fucking much.

I grit my jaw. "We need to talk," I say in a whispered voice. "And we can't do that here with Ava listening."

"Maybe I don't want to talk to you," she hisses.

"I don't care if you do or not; you're going to. I won't have you thinking something that's not true when I can clear this up for you right the fuck now."

She laughs, and there's not a trace of humor. "I'm not an idiot. I know what I saw, Vaughn."

"And I know what happened." I step toward her again, and she doesn't back away this time—probably because there's nowhere for her to go. "I'm going nowhere, so you'd better come with me to my trailer if you don't want me to cause a scene and let everyone know what's going on between us."

Her eyes narrow to slits, and her lips pinch. "You won't do that because you have more to lose than I do."

I fold my arms across my chest. "Right now, I don't fucking care if the whole world knows about us. I care that you hear me out."

"Fine," she huffs as she shoulders past me. "Let's get this over and done with."

"Oh, we won't be done," I mutter behind her. "Not by a fucking long shot."

"I'm popping out for a few minutes, Ava," she calls out before stomping out of the trailer.

Arms folded, she marches her way to my trailer, ignoring me the whole way.

The minute we're inside and alone, I lock the door. "What you saw isn't what you thought it was."

She laughs bitterly, her face reddening with anger. "You couldn't have used a more cliché line if you'd tried. But whatever, Vaughn. You're free to do whatever you want. We're not together. We're just fucking."

Well, if that doesn't sting.

I know she doesn't really mean that. She's hurt and angry, and she's lashing out, but it still pisses me the fuck off.

"That's bullshit, and you know it," I bite.

"Do I?" Her voice pitches higher. "Because, from where I'm standing, that's all we seem to be doing."

"I told you last night that I'm serious about you!"

"And I thought you were just messing around!" she yells back at me.

I grab her arm, crashing her into my body, and I slam my mouth down on hers. She fights me for all of a second before wrapping her arms around my neck and kissing me back.

Wardrobe Malfunction

I break off, breathing heavily and pressing my forehead to hers. "Does this feel like I'm just messing around?"

"No," she whispers.

I take her face in my hands, tipping her head back, forcing her eyes to meet mine. Knowing I have her attention, I say what I've needed to since she walked in on Piper and me, "Pins...Piper just turned up here and let herself in. I was in the shower, hence the lack of a shirt. I told her to leave, but she wouldn't listen. She said she wanted me back. But I don't want her, Charly." My words are clear, so there's no misunderstanding. "You just walked in at the worst moment possible. I was just about to shove her off me, I swear. I don't want her. I don't even fucking like her. Honestly, I don't know what she thought she would achieve by turning up here."

"You loved her once, not so long ago, and she broke your heart. I saw the news stories, Vaughn, about how you were out nursing your broken heart with drinks and...women." She looks away.

"You're wrong. I never loved her, and she definitely didn't break my heart. What happened with her and Cain...it was his betrayal that hurt me." Her eyes flash back to mine, and I know she's still listening, so I continue, "With Piper, I felt humiliated because she'd been screwing around with my best friend behind my back, and I had no clue until it was outed on live TV. I never loved her. I know that for sure. But Cain...that fucking hurt. He was supposed to be my best friend. I trusted him. I'd known the guy for ten years. And, when it came down to it, I didn't know him at all. That was what the partying was about. *He* broke my heart. Not her."

Her expression softens, and she touches her hand to my face. I close my eyes at her touch.

"I'm sorry he did that to you," she whispers.

"And I'm sorry you walked in on that psycho trying to get grabby with me." I open my eyes. "But I swear to you, it was all her, not me."

"I believe you," she says.

I can't tell you the relief I feel at that.

"Thank you." I take hold of her hand and kiss the palm.

"I'm sorry I acted like a jealous person," she says.

"Don't be. If I'd walked in on the same scenario with you and an ex, I'd be in jail right now."

She giggles.

"My trust took a real battering when all that shit happened, but I trust you, Pins." And I do.

"I trust you, too. I'm sorry I reacted badly. Just seeing her and you…"

"Like I said, Pins…*jail*."

I grin, and she laughs again.

"If I'd known she was groping you without permission, I would have stabbed her in the ass with a pin."

"And I would have really liked to see that." I laugh.

Then, I kiss her—because I can and because I have to.

Honestly, I can't imagine a day when I won't be kissing her.

Vaughn

I'M RUNNING LINES WITH Alex in my trailer when there's loud hammering on the front door. Before either of us gets to say anything, the door flies open, and Charly comes stomping through it.

"What the hell is this?" she asks, waving her cell phone around in the air.

I'm getting the distinct vibe that she's pissed off about something. I'm just not sure what the something is.

"Um...your cell phone."

"I know it's my cell phone, smart-ass! I'm talking about what's on my phone."

"And what's on your phone?"

She glares at me. "You tell me!"

I glance at Alex, and he shrugs. Lot of fucking help he is.

"Pins, have you been drinking?"

It's a valid question but probably not the best one to ask because her nostrils flare, and she gets this crazy look in her eyes. I genuinely shit my pants.

"No, I haven't been drinking, you ass! A first-class plane ticket, West. What the hell were you thinking?"

Ah. Now, we're getting somewhere.

I upgraded her flight to Vegas from coach to first-class and put her on the same flight as me. We leave in two days to go to Vegas to film the rest of the movie.

I thought she'd be happy. Apparently not.

"And I'll take that as my cue to leave." Alex gets up, putting the script down. "I'll get some coffee."

"Deserter." I glare at him.

He laughs. "Go easy on him, Charly." He pats her shoulder as he passes. "His intentions were good. He's just a bit dim at times."

"Hey! What the fuck?"

"Can I bring you coffee back?" He pulls his jacket on.

"Where are you going?" Charly asks him in a nice-as-pie voice.

"Starbucks."

"Ooh, I'll have a caramel latte then, please. Thanks, Alex."

I buy her a first-class plane ticket and get yelled at. He offers to buy her a four-dollar cup of coffee—that I'll actually pay for—and she's all *please* and *thank you*.

Honestly, I don't understand women.

"Black coffee, Vaughn?" he asks me.

"Yeah." I sigh. "And one of those toffee cookies."

"A Toffeedoodle?"

"Ooh, I'll have one of those, too," Charly says.

"Got it. See you in ten."

We both watch him leave. Then, Charly turns back to me, her face like thunder.

Seems her happy moment left with Alex. *Great.*

Wardrobe Malfunction

"Pins...I thought you'd be happy about the ticket." I get to my feet, walking toward her.

"It was a nice thing to do—"

"I'm a nice guy."

"But it was also dumb."

"Hey!" I frown. "Go easy there, Pins. My ego is fragile. I wound easily, you know." I slap a hand to my chest.

Her lips crack into a smile. But she's soon back to scowling at me. "Did you even think when you booked the ticket?"

"I didn't book it. I had the studio do it."

"Yeah, and nothing says we're sleeping together like a first-class plane ticket on your flight."

Oh, yeah. She has a point there.

"Do you want people to know we're sleeping together?" she asks.

"Maybe I do."

What?

Her eyes widen with surprise. Honestly, I'm a little surprised myself.

I didn't know I was there yet.

But...maybe I am.

Is that why I had her ticket changed?

"Vaughn..." She swallows, moving closer to me.

I watch her closely. Her eyes...something in them isn't sitting right with me.

"Are you sure that's what you want? Because I thought you wanted the focus to be on the movie right now. Not your sex life."

"Personal life. I thought we had established that you and I are more than just sex."

Even though we haven't discussed exactly what we are. But I know I want her. I know I'm serious about being with her. I know I want more from her than just sex.

"I know we are, but..." She looks away.

"But what?" I ask, dipping down to look her in the eyes, my heart starting to beat just that little bit faster.

She lifts her head. "I just think the focus should be on the movie and not us."

"It's not just that though, is it?"

"Of course it is." Her response is too quick, and I know she's not being entirely truthful.

"Charly...if you're not ready for us to go public or to have your life changed, then it's fine. I do understand."

She stares at me for a long beat. Then, she bites her lip. "Are you angry?"

"No." I wrap my arms around her. "So long as you're not ashamed to be with me."

"As if." She laughs, fisting the back of my shirt in her hands. "I'm pretty sure the embarrassment should be on your part."

"What?" I pull back from her, looking at her like she's lost her mind because she clearly has. "Why in the fuck would I be embarrassed about you?"

"Because I'm just a wardrobe assistant." She lifts her shoulder.

"You're an artist. I read lines that other people write and pretend to be a different person for a living. It's not as big of a deal as people seem to think it is."

"I think it's a big deal." She slides her hands into my back pockets.

"I think you're a big deal. When we finally go public, I'll be wearing an *I'm Sleeping with Her* T-shirt, you know, just so everyone knows we're screwing."

"You're so romantic." She laughs, squeezing my ass.

"And you love it." I brush my lips over hers.

"Mmhmm," she murmurs.

"I'll have the ticket changed back," I tell her. "I'll have you stuck back in coach, if that's what will make you happy."

"You make me happy, West."

Wardrobe Malfunction

"Right back at ya, Pins." I slide my hands down to her ass. "So…Alex won't be back for another eight minutes. I can do a lot in eight minutes."

She tips her head back and smiles. "Oh, yeah? You have me intrigued with that statement."

"I'm an intriguing kind of guy."

She pulls her hands from my pockets and steps back. "Guess you'd better show me then, Mr. Eight Minutes." And she takes off for the bedroom.

I'm seconds behind her, shutting the door behind me. Grabbing her around the waist, I tackle her down to the bed, making her laugh.

Then, I'm lifting her skirt and pulling her panties off and pressing my mouth to her pussy, making her moan my name, and it has never sounded better than it does coming from her lips.

I lick her and fuck her with my tongue until she's coming around my mouth and begging for my cock.

Moments later, I'm suiting up and slipping into her from behind, and then we're fucking up against the wall and on the floor and, finally, the bed where we both come hard and together.

I'm still not done because I can't get enough of her.

So, I flip her onto all fours and start to fuck her with my fingers, making her come again and again. Then, I'm back inside her, and I never want it to end.

I never want my time with her to end.

So, those eight promised minutes turned into an hour. Seems I'm Mr. Sixty Minutes.

And our coffee is waiting for us when we finally emerge from the bedroom. It's cold, and it's the best fucking cold cup of coffee I've ever had.

Charly

WE'VE BEEN FILMING IN Vegas for a week now, and it's hot. Hotter than the summers I'm used to in New York.

Things with Vaughn and I seemed to have moved up a level after the Piper thing.

Neither of us has come out and said we're dating, and we can't exactly go out on dates in public, but it feels like we're dating. It's more than just sex.

The fact that he wanted to go public with us said a lot. A hell of a lot.

But it also reminded me of the difficulty of the situation that I find myself in right now.

I never thought, when I started this thing with Vaughn, that it would move beyond anything other than sex for him. I knew I was falling for him; it's impossible not to. But, when he said he wanted people to know about us, it made me realize that, when he'd said he was serious about me, he really meant it.

Honestly, in that moment, I panicked. I acted like a coward. I used a half-truth to keep things the way they were, keep our relationship hidden from the world.

I don't know how to tell him the truth about my situation. If I can tell him the truth. I trust him, but telling him…explaining it is a whole different story, and it would also mean putting him in a position that I don't want him to be in. But, if he finds out any other way, he won't understand. He'll be hurt, and I don't want that either.

So, for now, until I can figure this out, it's best to keep our relationship as it is—between us.

I need to talk to Nick. He'll know the best way to handle it. I just don't seem to have time to call him at the moment. Between nights spent with Vaughn and going out on the odd occasion with Ava and Logan to see the sights of Vegas, we've been filming nonstop.

Filming has stepped up, as Vaughn has a three-day break in his filming schedule coming up.

Apparently, it was written into his original contract. I found out about it from Ava when I got the shooting schedule for next week, but she doesn't know why he's off or where he's going in those three days.

And I don't know because he hasn't told me. He hasn't even mentioned that he'll be gone for three days, which has left me feeling a little weird. I mean, why hasn't he told me where he's going? But I'm not going to ask him. I'm going to wait and see if he tells me.

I'm on set now. We're out in the desert, and it's nighttime.

They're filming a scene where Vaughn's character, Drew, and Natasha's character, Lexi, are burying a body in the dead of night in the desert. Natasha's character killed someone, and she called Drew to come help her.

We already filmed those scenes back in the hotel yesterday. Now, we're filming the burying-the-dead-body scene. I spent most of the day getting Vaughn's clothes ready for it. He needs sets of the same suit but in different degrees of dirtiness.

As he won't actually be burying the body, he won't get as dirty as his character would, so I had to prepare five different suits, dirtying them up to varying standards with blood from the dead guy when he's lugging the body around and dirt from the digging.

They're getting ready to film. Vaughn and Natasha are in makeup, but I need to go get him from there, as it's time to put him in his first suit of the night. I also said I'd retrieve Natasha for Logan, as he's just putting some final touches on the dress she'll be wearing for the first part of filming. I have no clue where Ava is. She went to go get coffee, and she hasn't come back yet.

I step out of the wardrobe trailer, and the heat hits me immediately. It's nine p.m., and it's boiling. I'm just glad I'm dressed in jean shorts and a T-shirt. I can't imagine what it's going to be like for Vaughn wearing those suits. He'll be melting.

I head over to makeup, knock on the door, and step inside. But Vaughn and Natasha aren't there.

"Where are Vaughn and Natasha?" I ask Grace, one of the makeup artists. "They're needed for wardrobe."

"Oh, they're out on set with Brandon. He wanted to go over some things with them before they started shooting."

"Cool. Thanks."

I head back out of the trailer and around the back, heading for the set, which is lit up with floodlights, and the car Vaughn's character drives the dead body out here in is set in position.

People are milling around on set, but I don't see Vaughn, Natasha, or Brandon.

I head over to John, one of the camera crew guys, who's setting up his camera. "Hey, John." I smile.

"Hey, Charly."

"Have you seen Vaughn and Natasha? I need them for wardrobe."

"Coffee." He jerks his head in the direction of the catering van.

"Thanks."

I head toward the van, coming up to the side, where I hear Vaughn and Natasha talking before I see them.

"So, not long till Sasha's wedding then?" Natasha says.

I know Sasha is one of Vaughn's sisters, but I didn't know she was getting married.

"I bet she's getting excited. I remember what I was like in the run-up to my and Carter's wedding."

"Yeah, she's driving my mom nuts. Bridezilla at its worst."

"Are you taking Charly with you?" she asks in a lower voice.

The mention of my name makes my feet stop just before I'm about to round the corner.

Natasha knows about us? He never told me that.

"I don't know. I haven't mentioned it to her."

"You haven't told her that your sister's getting married?"

"No. Why?"

She laughs. "God, you men are clueless. Do you want to take her with you?"

I hold my breath, waiting for his response.

"I don't take women home."

"Yeah, I know that. But I didn't ask if you took women home. I asked if you wanted to take Charly home with you."

There's a long pause.

His lack of a response makes my chest ache. I rub a hand to the spot.

Then, Natasha speaks again, "Well, if you do decide you want to ask her to go with you, don't leave it much

Wardrobe Malfunction

longer because, otherwise, she'll feel like you just asked her as a last-minute choice."

I don't want to hear any more, so I trace my steps back and go around the back of the van.

I stop at the other side and paste a smile on my face, shrugging off the hurt I'm feeling.

Then, I step out. Vaughn's eyes instantly come to me. He smiles at me. That secret smile he always gives me, one that usually turns me to jelly...not this time though.

"I need you in wardrobe," I say to him, fake smile on. Then, my eyes move to Natasha. "Natasha, Logan asked me if I would bring you along, too."

"Sure thing," she says, tossing her coffee in the trash.

Vaughn follows suit, tossing his coffee.

And we all walk over to wardrobe, Natasha and Vaughn talking over their upcoming scene while I totally zone out.

His sister's getting married, and he didn't tell me. Okay, that's not such a massive thing because he's a man, and men don't think like women.

But Mr. I Don't Take Women Home doesn't want to take me with him? Well, okay, he didn't exactly say that. But he didn't say he wanted to take me either. He didn't say anything.

I mean, rationally thinking, he probably hasn't asked because I pushed to keep us a secret, and if I go to his sister's wedding, we definitely wouldn't be a secret...which brings me to the fact that Natasha knows!

How many other people has he told?

And why do I feel so weird and bent out of shape about this?

Why is it bothering me so much that he hasn't asked me to his sister's wedding?

I'm being stupid.

I must be due for my period. I'm hormonal. It's the only reasonable explanation for why I'm acting like a wack job.

Because, honestly, I'm not bothered that he hasn't asked me.

I'm not bothered at all.

Vaughn

CHARLY'S ACTING WEIRD. SHE'S been weird since last night. It's like she's here, but she's not actually here.

I've asked her countless times if she's okay, and I get the same answer every time.

"I'm fine."

Like now, we're in my trailer where she's stitching up a shirt that got ripped in a fight scene, and I've been talking to her, but she's not actually listening. She's doing the *um*s and the *ah*s in all the right places, but I know she's not taking in a fucking word I'm saying.

"So, yeah, I was thinking of asking Natasha about the three of us having a threesome. What do you think, babe?"

"Hmm."

"Or we could have a foursome with her husband. I'll do Natasha. You do Carter. How does that sound?"

"Mmhmm."

See what I mean?

I get up from the sofa and walk over to the dining table. Sitting down in front of her, I pull the shirt from her hands.

"Hey! I nearly stuck myself with the needle then!"

"What's going on?"

"Nothing." She pulls the shirt back from my hands.

"I just suggested having a threesome with Natasha or maybe a foursome with her hubby, and your responses were all *hmm* and *mmhmm*."

"You want to have a three-way with me and Natasha?" she all but yells at me.

"No, I don't want to have a three-way, you fucking tool. That's my way of proving you haven't been listening to a word I said, and you haven't since yesterday."

"Did you just call me a fucking tool?" She frowns.

"What is going on with you? Why are you acting all weird?"

"I'm not," she says with shifty eyes. Looking down at the shirt, she carries on with sewing it.

Jesus! Fucking women!

I growl with frustration, "That's it. I'm withholding sex until you tell me what's going on."

Her eyes lift, and she laughs. "Yeah, okay," she says in a mocking voice.

"I'm serious." I fold my arms.

She puts the shirt down. "You'll last a day, max."

"Oh, ye, of little faith. I went dry for three months before I met you."

"Okay," she hums, picking the shirt back up. "We'll see."

"We will."

"Okay."

"Okay then."

Well, fuck, that didn't go as I'd planned, and now, I've screwed myself out of sex for God knows how long.

Nicely played, West.

Wardrobe Malfunction

My cell starts to ring in my pocket. I pull it out, seeing it's my mom.

"Hey, Mom," I answer.

I see Charly glance up, but she quickly looks away again.

"Hey, baby," my mom says, sounding exhausted. "I need a favor."

"Sure, anything," I tell her.

"Do you know of any clothes people, like designers, who could fix your sister's wedding dress?"

"What's wrong with Sasha's dress?"

I know she was having a local wedding dress designer make one for her.

"Jester happened."

Jester is my mom and dad's six-month-old golden Labrador. He's awesome. Just a bundle of energy. He makes me want a dog, but as I'm not home much, it wouldn't be fair. But, hopefully, one day.

"Your sister picked up her dress and brought it over to ours, and I hung it up in her old room. I don't know how, if someone left the door open or what, but Jester got in there."

"Oh no!" I laugh.

"Don't laugh, Vaughn. It's not funny. Your sister is freaking out," my mom says, sounding exasperated.

"Sorry." I bite my lip. "How bad is it?"

"He got it outside. God knows how. That dog, I swear. The dirt, I can get off, but the bottom is all torn."

"Shit. Well, tell her that I'll just buy her a new one. I can probably get her a Vera Wang shipped in."

"She doesn't want anything but this dress, Vaughn. She designed it with the dress designer. She has her heart set on it. It's all just a mess right now. She said she's canceling the wedding. Your dad is going mad about the expenses if she cancels, and Greg's at a loss for what to do. It's just a nightmare." She sighs.

"So, can't she get the woman who designed her dress to fix it?"

"She's in Hawaii."

"Oh."

"Right." She sighs again.

"So, I was hoping you might know some dress designer who could fix it up."

I lift my eyes to Charly. "Actually," I tell my mom, "I have one sitting right in front of me as we speak. She's really talented."

Charly's eyes flash to mine.

"You do?" My mom's voice lifts with hope.

"Yep. She works on wardrobe here. Charly. She's an amazing seamstress. I bet she could fix it, no problem."

Charly's brows lift. I fight back a smile.

"We'll pay her."

"I'll sort that, Mom."

"You're my star, Vaughn."

She's been saying that to me since I was a kid. It never fails to warm my insides. Because she means it in a whole other way than the rest of the world does. She has always said that I'm her little star, that I brighten her world. And I might be a grown-ass man, but when your mom says something like that, you revert back to the five-year-old kid who thought she was the only woman in the world you would ever love. Well, that still is true because I haven't ever been in love.

My eyes drift back to Charly, a different kind of warmth spreading across my chest.

"Tell Sasha it's going to be fine. Take a picture of the dress, the damage, and send it to me. I'll have Charly take a look and see if it's fixable. And, if it is, FedEx it to me out here, Charly will fix it, and I'll bring it back with me."

"I'll take the picture now. Sasha will be over the moon!"

Wardrobe Malfunction

"Don't tell her until Charly says for sure if she can fix it."

"Okay. I'll send the pic now and then call me back once Charly's had a look. And tell her not to worry if she can't; we appreciate it all the same."

"Will do, Mom. Love you."

"You, too, baby."

We hang up, and I put my cell down on the table.

"So…from the gist of that, I got that you need me to fix your sister's wedding dress. I gather it's for a wedding because of the Vera Wang comment."

"My parents' puppy went to town on my sister's wedding dress."

"Crap," she says.

"Yeah, Sasha's apparently freaking out."

"Well, I'll take a look and see what I can do."

"I'll pay you."

She stares at me. "Don't be stupid, West. I don't want your money. I'm happy to help your sister."

I reach across the table and take ahold of her hand. "You're the best." I lean down and kiss her hand.

"I know." She grins, and I smile.

"And I'm totally lifting the sex ban for this, Pins."

"That lasted all of five minutes!" She laughs. "I knew you'd cave before I did!"

"I did not cave." I frown. "I'm being generous, you know, because you're being so generous with fixing my sister's dress."

"If I can," she says.

"You'll be able to."

"You have a lot of faith in me."

"Because I know how amazing you are."

Her eyes soften at my words.

"So…now that the sex ban is lifted, you wanna go and break the bed with me?"

She laughs, bright and loud, making me smile. "You're one of a kind, Vaughn West."

"So are you, Charly Michaels."

And she is. My one of a kind.

"Isn't your mom sending over the picture for me to look at to see if I can fix the dress?"

"Oh, yeah. We'll wait till she sends it over, and you've had a look. Then, we can go fuck."

"God, you're romantic, West."

"I know." I shrug, grinning. "You're a lucky, lucky woman, Pins."

Truth is, I'm the lucky one to have her in my life.

Charly

VAUGHN LEAVES FOR HIS sister Sasha's wedding in two days.

I fixed the dress. It was a bigger job than I had initially thought from the look of the pictures. There were some really fine tears within the lace of the bodice, and some crystals were missing, but I managed to get ahold of some that were almost identical from a store in Vegas. I finally finished fixing the dress late last night, and I did an amazing job, if I do say so myself.

I text a picture of the now-fixed dress to Sasha. I've been keeping her updated with my progress on it. She's been so grateful, constantly offering to pay me money for doing it, but I keep refusing. Honestly, I enjoyed working on it, and it kept my mind off my silly feelings of rejection over Vaughn not wanting to take me to the wedding with him.

Because I am being silly.

We might be more than just sleeping together now, but that doesn't mean he wants to take me home to meet his family. And, of course, it would expose our relationship, which I don't want.

So, the dress is safely inside its garment bag in Vaughn's hotel room, where I am right now, and it's ready to go with him to Oregon.

We finished filming at six p.m. Vaughn and I were starving, so he had Alex order room service for when we got back, and we had dinner together in his room.

We're now lying on the bed, watching an episode of Julian's show *Dead Cop*. I'll admit, I'm totally addicted. Logan and I are always talking about it at work, but because Logan's ahead of me, he's careful not to spoil it for me. But the one thing we do agree on is that we want Julian's character, Mason Banks, to get it on with his costar character Meredith Castle. And I also want them together in real life. But Logan reckons that Julian is gay. He said his gaydar was flashing loud and bright when he met Julian.

I don't think Julian is gay, and I think he and Sara Parks, who plays Meredith, would be perfect together.

I keep meaning to ask Vaughn if Julian is gay. I guess now would be as good a time as any.

"Vaughn?"

"Mmhmm?"

"Is Julian gay?"

His eyes flick to mine. "What made you ask that?"

"Because Logan thinks he is. He said Julian set his gaydar off when they met. But I think he's straight."

"Why does it matter?"

"It doesn't. I just really want him and Sara to get married and have babies."

He laughs, shaking his head. "Sadly, Julian won't be having babies with Sara."

"So, he's gay?"

Wardrobe Malfunction

"Yes. But that has to stay between you and me, as Julian's in the closet."

"Why?" I frown.

"Because he has a hell of a lot of female fans who watch the show because of him and his pretty-boy looks. Coming out could damage the ratings, as his female fan base could drop when they realize that he's not fishing in their gender pool, and the network doesn't want that."

"That's stupid."

"That's reality, babe. Women like to see the men they watch on-screen as available."

"Yeah, but it's not like they're ever really going to get with them."

"You landed me, didn't you?" He shrugs.

"Ass!" I poke him in his side.

"Hey! No need to go crazy and start attacking!" He holds his hands up in surrender.

"Drama king."

"No, babe, *your* King."

"God, you're so arrogant." I roll my eyes.

"Just the way you like me." He chuckles.

Shaking my head, laughing, I settle back down beside him and start watching the show again.

"Anyway, it's only like you and me," he says.

"What is?"

"Julian in the closet. We're in the closet, albeit together. People don't know about us."

"For a completely different reason." I can feel my insides starting to tense.

"Yeah. But whatever the reason, we're still hiding. Just like Julian."

I don't say anything because…what can I say?

I'm partly doing it for him—the movie and keeping his reputation clean, not attracting attention to his love life again—but I'm also nervous about us going public, which is the truth but not for the reason he thinks.

I feel like I'm deceiving him.

I am deceiving him, and I hate it.

I just don't know quite what to do about it yet. Well, I do know what to do, but at the end of the day, even when that's done, I'll still have to tell him the truth. I'm just not sure what version of the truth to tell him.

"So, I've been wanting to ask…" He pauses the show and shuffles down the bed.

He turns on his side to face me, so I do the same.

"Sounds ominous. It doesn't involve something kinky and dirty, does it?"

"No, but it can if you'd like?" His eyes flash at me.

"I'm not averse to kinky and dirty, but let's put a pin in that for later, so you can ask me what you wanted to ask me."

"Will you come to Sasha's wedding with me?"

He's asking me to the wedding?

My heart soars.

"I mean, I know the dress is fixed, but I thought she might need you there, just in case, you know."

And then it drops like a rock in water.

"You want me to come to help with the dress?" My voice is stilted. I know it is. I can hear it, but I can't seem to help it. "The dress is fine. Sasha won't need my help." I sit up and start to get off the bed.

"Hey, where are you going?" He tries to tug me back to lie down, but I resist.

"Back to my hotel."

He moves across the bed, so he's sitting beside me. "Why?"

"No reason."

"For fuck's sake, Charly." His voice is tense. "Don't play games. Just tell me what's wrong."

I turn my eyes to him. He looks irritated.

So, I tell him the truth, "I overheard you talking to Natasha on set last week."

Wardrobe
MALFUNCTION

His brows pull together. "About?"

"Sasha's wedding. You hadn't even told me, which was fine because you didn't have to."

"Clearly, it's not fine." His tone is resolute.

"Well…it just would've been nice if you'd mentioned it, considering all the time we spend together."

"It wasn't a conspiracy to keep it from you, Charly. I'm a guy. I don't think of shit like that."

"Natasha knew. And she knows about us. I thought we weren't telling anyone."

His eyes flash anger at me. "I didn't tell her about you and me. She guessed I liked you back in the beginning when I yelled at you on set. And I trust Natasha. She's not a gossip; she's good people. And, as for Sasha's wedding, Natasha already knew that, too. I've known her for a long time. She knew when my sister got engaged, hence her knowing about the wedding."

"Okay," I say.

"What else?"

"Who says there's more?" I frown at him.

"Your body language." He gestures at me, and I realize I'm pointing my body away from him.

"Fine. I heard Natasha ask if you wanted to invite me, and you didn't answer. You didn't say anything." I stare at the carpet beneath my feet. "And I know I'm not getting paid for doing Sasha's dress because I don't want to get paid," I quickly add. "But, even still, I don't want to go to your family's home, feeling like the hired help." *And I don't want you to take me when you really don't want to.*

"Jesus, Charly." He grabs my face and turns my eyes to him. The look in his is fierce and determined. "I want you there."

"No, you don't. I heard you, Mr. I Don't Take Women Home." I mimic his voice. "And that's fine, Vaughn, but just don't make out that this is something it's not. You don't want to take me home as the girl you're dating; it's fine. And, like you said, we're still in the closet, so it makes sense anyway."

"First off," he growls, "I'm glad you finally said we're dating because that's exactly what we are doing. And there are no worries about taking you home to my family as my girl."

His girl.

It's stupid how crazy my heart goes at that.

"My family knows better than anyone how my life is. They don't talk about my private life or me—ever. And not just my family, but also the people in the town I grew up in Oregon. Keno is a small town and a safe place for me. My family has lived there for generations. After I got famous and my status started to rise, the press began turning up in town, trying to get dirt on me. The townsfolk quickly made them aware that they weren't welcome there. And, yeah, the press knows I'm from Keno, but they don't know I still live there now. Not many people do."

But I do, and he trusts me with that information. I feel a confliction of happiness and shame because he doesn't know everything about me.

"My house is well hidden. Exactly how I want it. And second"—he ticks off his finger—"I want you there as my date for the wedding. I want my family to meet you—"

"But—"

"Let me finish, Charly." He presses his fingers to my lips, silencing me.

"Yes, I didn't say anything in answer to what Natasha said because I hadn't thought about it. I'm a guy. I'm slow, and I don't consider these things. It's not out of malice. And then my mom called about the wedding dress, and that took over. But I have thought about it…taking you home. I've thought a lot about it, and I do want to take you to meet my family. And I've wanted to ask you for a while now, but I'm a chickenshit. It seems like a big deal, asking

Wardrobe Malfunction

you to come to my sister's wedding with me and meet my whole family. I was worried that I might scare you away."

He wants me there. He didn't want to scare me away.

He wants me there.

My heart has fluttered out of my chest and straight into the palm of his hand. And I'm not sure if it's ever coming back. Or if I want it back.

"You could never scare me away," I whisper, toying with the hem of my top.

"What if I told you I wanted to spank you with a paddle?"

My eyes flick to his, and I see the playful look in them.

"Okay. So, maybe you can scare me away." I grin.

He chuckles and then tugs me back down to the bed. This time, I go with him, and we're back to lying face-to-face.

"So, will you be my date to the wedding?" He brushes my hair back off my cheek, tucking it behind my ear. "I really want you to be there."

Then, it stupidly dawns on me that, after all the fuss I just made, I can't go anyway.

"I want to go." I grimace. "But I'm scheduled to work those three days."

"But I won't be here." He frowns, like he expected I wouldn't have to work if he wasn't.

"I do dress other actors aside from you, superstar."

"Yeah, well, I'm changing that," he says, still wearing the frown. "I don't want you accidentally pinning anyone else's balls."

"Asshole." I slap his chest.

He catches my hand, kissing it. "Another of the many things you adore about me. And don't worry about getting the time off work. I'll sort it out."

"You will? Well, okay," I say, "if you really want me there—"

"I really want you there," he says softly, his eyes caressing my face, making my insides gooey.

"Then, yes, I would love to go."

"Good." He smiles.

Then, he kisses me with that smile, and I let myself absorb that happiness, making it mine, too.

"Vaughn—"

"I was kidding about the paddle spanking."

"Oh, good."

"But let's talk about the kinky and dirty that you're not averse to," he says, lifting my leg and hooking it over his hip.

"Cool. But, first, can we talk about what I'm going to wear to your sister's wedding? Because I have two days and nothing to wear."

"Oh God," he groans, falling to his back, covering his face with his hands.

"What?" I say, laughing. I climb over him and straddle his hips.

He pulls his hands from his face. "I want to get it on, and my woman wants to talk clothes."

"Hey, you knew what you were getting into when you got involved with me." I smile, loving that he just called me his woman.

He sits up, putting us face-to-face. His big hands grab my hips, and he yanks me onto his cock, which is hard.

"Oh," I say, my eyes widening.

"Yeah, *oh*. So, do you still want to talk about clothes? Or do you want me to make you come? Multiple times."

I scrunch my nose up, like I'm thinking about it. "I guess…we can talk about clothes later."

"That's what I thought," he growls. Then, he attacks my mouth with those gorgeous lips of his.

Vaughn

MY DAD IS WAITING for us in the parking lot at Klamath Falls Airport.

We flew by private jet, like I always do when I go home. Charly had never flown private before, so she was pretty excited. It was cute to see. She kept taking photos of the plane and the views.

We left Vegas at two thirty, and we landed at four thirty, so we made good time. And, now, I have three days off, which also means three days alone with Charly at my house. I can't deny that I'm looking forward to being free about our relationship here.

"Hey, Dad." I walk over to him.

He's standing by my car. He puts out his cigar. He thinks my mom doesn't know he smokes them.

I put my bag down and hug him. It's been a while since I last saw him. A few months at least.

"Good to see you, son." He hugs me, patting my back. "How was your flight?"

"Good." I smile, stepping back. "Dad, this is Charly."

She's lingering back a little and steps forward when I introduce her.

"Nice to meet you, sir." She waves.

God, she's cute.

My dad smiles at her. "Call me Anthony. And it's nice to meet you, too, Charly. You've stopped my daughter from canceling her wedding, which has cost me thousands of dollars, so you're my new favorite person."

"Oh." She blushes. "Thank you."

"No, thank you." He opens up the trunk of my car and picks my bag up, putting it in.

I take Charly's bag and the garment bag containing my sister's wedding dress from her. She didn't let me carry it at all on the way here. I kid you not; it had its own seat on the plane, next to her. I was relegated to sitting across from her the whole way here, which wasn't too bad, because the view was pretty as hell.

"It was real good of you to fix Sasha's dress on such short notice."

"Oh, it was no problem." She waves him off, her face reddening further.

I open the back passenger door for her, and she climbs inside.

"You driving or me?" Dad asks, closing the trunk as I shut Charly's door.

"I'll drive."

He tosses me the keys, and I go around to the driver's side. Climbing in, I buckle up.

"Nice car," Charly muses as my dad climbs in. "Yours?"

"Yep," I answer, smiling, as I start my car. She purrs like a kitten.

Wardrobe
MALFUNCTION

My Range Rover Sport is top of the line. She cost a pretty penny. I bought her a year ago when my Dodge pickup had seen her final days. I love this car, and I don't get to drive her too often.

"So, your mom's stocked up your fridge. Steaks, chicken breasts, pork chops, sausages, and God knows what else," he tells me. "She went a little crazy at the store."

"She does realize I'm home for only three days, right?" I chuckle, pulling out of the parking space and heading for the exit.

"You know your mother. She likes to make sure you're well fed when you're home."

"Well, considering I eat mostly at your house, Jester's gonna be in meat for weeks. How is Jester? Still in the doghouse?"

"Sasha still hasn't forgiven him, but hopefully, when she sees her dress—thanks to Charly here—it will put him back in her good graces."

I glance at Charly in my rearview mirror to see her blushing again.

She's being oddly quiet.

Maybe she's just nervous about meeting my dad. Feeling a little out of her element. Once she gets to my parents' house, she won't have time to feel shy. Not with the women in my family.

I drive the usual route on the OR 66, heading west, soaking up the greenery of home.

I can feel the dirt of Hollywood falling away from me and the clean of Oregon seeping into my pores.

Charly starts to chat a little more on the drive, asking questions about the place I call home.

She seems enthralled by the roaming fields and greenery that sit off the highway.

We cross the bridge over Klamath River into Keno, and I'm home.

I drive past my old elementary school.

"Is that where you went?" Charly asks.

"Yeah." I smile.

"Looks like a nice school," she observes.

I wonder what her school was like back in Philadelphia.

"So, where are you from, Charly?" my dad asks.

"Philadelphia originally. But New York is home now."

I know the question is coming, but I can't stop it.

"And your family? They still back in Philly?"

"No, sir." She clears her throat. "I was raised by my grandma, but she passed years ago."

"I'm sorry to hear that," my dad says.

"Thank you," she says politely.

I glance back at her in my rearview, but she's not looking my way, her eyes on the window. Something pulls in my chest for her. Protectiveness. I feel like I should've protected her from my dad's innocent questioning.

I've never felt this protective over a woman before.

Maybe it's because Charly was dealt such a bad hand in life, and I was raised with a great family.

Or maybe it's just because I'm crazy about her.

I turn on the long drive, taking me up to my parents' house.

When I pull up outside, Jester, the dress destroyer, comes bounding up to the car, attacking me the moment I step out of the car.

"Hey, buddy." I crouch down, picking him up, and he covers my face in sloppy licks.

Charly comes over, scratching Jester's ear. "So, this is the little man who caused all the problems."

The moment he sees her, I'm totally forgotten about. He all but leaps into her arms and starts smothering her in doggie kisses.

She laughs, scratching his ear, and he's putty in her hands.

I know how you feel, bud.

"I'll get the dress," Dad says.

Wardrobe Malfunction

"Oh, can I?" Charly says, putting Jester down. He's at her feet, following her to the trunk of the car. "No offense," she says to my dad, "but I wanted to give this to Sasha. When I do a job, I like to be the one to deliver it."

"No worries." My dad winks at her, handing the garment bag over.

He shuts the trunk, leaving our bags in there, as we'll be driving over to my house soon.

"Now, Jester, no chewing on this dress again, do you hear me? It took me a long time to fix it after your last playtime with it," she chats away to Jester as we walk up the steps of the porch, making me smile.

Jester is just trailing along behind her, gazing up at her, like a puppy in love.

"We're home," Dad calls out as we step through the door.

My mom comes bustling out of the kitchen. "Vaughn!" she calls, walking toward me, arms outstretched for a hug.

"Hi, Mom," I say, stepping into her hug.

"Missed you." She kisses my cheek and then cups it, leaning back to look me in the face.

"Missed you, too," I tell her.

"You look good, baby. Really good."

That's a change from what I get every time I come home. I usually get the spiel that moms generally give once you've left home. *You look tired. Are you eating properly? Sleeping enough?* It's probably thanks to all the sex I've been having with that little vixen back there, but I'm not going to say that to my mom.

Her eyes move past me to Charly.

"Charly!" my mom greets her like a long-lost friend. "I'm Everly, Vaughn's mom, but everyone calls me Evie. Is this it?"

Charly looks down at the garment bag hanging over her arm. "Oh, yeah," she says almost shyly.

"Oh, wonderful! You're our lifesaver, Charly! Come here." My mom bundles Charly into a hug.

I see Charly freeze the instant my mom's arms go around her, and then she slowly puts her one free arm around my mom, hugging her back.

I know Charly has issues with hugging. I don't know where it comes from. Maybe it's from a lack of affection growing up; she told me her grandmother wasn't that loving. I'm not going to question her about it. She'll tell me if she wants to. But that's why I make sure to hug her as often as possible—for all the years she wasn't hugged.

"Where are Gran, Meg, and Sasha?" I ask Mom.

"Meg's in town, running some errands. She'll be back soon. Sasha's out back, and your gran is in the kitchen."

"No, I'm not. I'm here."

I turn at the sound of my grandma's voice.

I love all of my family, but my gran is just that little bit more special. She's impossible not to adore. She's outspoken, a bit crazy, and fucking awesome. Kind of like Charly.

"Hey, Gran." I go over and kiss her cheek.

"I'll go let Sasha know you're here," my mom says before disappearing off.

"I'm going back to work," my dad tells us.

I watch him go out the front door, and I'm just about to introduce Charly to my grandma, but I don't get a chance.

"So, Charly, are you sleeping with my grandson?"

My head snaps back to Gran. "Jesus Christ, Gran!"

"Don't curse, Vaughn Anthony West." She directs a look my way. "And how many times have I told you to call me Phoebe? Calling me Gran makes me sound old."

"You are old. You're eighty. You've got three grandkids and four great-grandkids."

"And I would have five great-grandkids if you'd get your ass in gear and give me a grandson who'll carry on your granddaddy's name."

I groan, rolling my eyes. Like I haven't heard that before.

"*And*," she emphasizes, "you're as old as the man you're feeling, so according to that, I'm seventy."

"Jesus." I groan briefly, closing my eyes in disgust. "I just threw up in my mouth."

She rolls her eyes at me. My eighty-year-old grandmother rolls her eyes at me.

Charly laughs.

"So, are you sleeping with my grandson?" she asks Charly again.

Charly glances at me and then looks at my grandma. "Define sleeping," she says with a curve of her lips.

My eyes nearly bug out of my head. Just when I think I've got Charly pegged, she does something to surprise me.

My grandma hoots out a laugh. "I like this girl, Vaughn. I think we should keep her. Now, come get a drink with me, honey. Do you like Long Island iced teas? Because I just learned how to make them. I bought this cocktail-making kit, and I've been making all the cocktails from the book that came with it."

"How far through the book are you?" Charly asks her.

"Oh, I've already made them all. I'm on my second trip through it."

Charly giggles, and my gran laughs.

And I watch them walk away. Charly tosses me a smile over her shoulder before disappearing into the kitchen with Gran and Jester at her heel. I'm left wondering what the hell just happened and why exactly I am turned on right now.

You're a sick man, West. A sick, sick man.

I follow them into the kitchen. Gran already has a cocktail in Charly's hand, and she's finally put the garment bag down, hanging it over the back of one of the kitchen stools at the breakfast bar.

I watch her take a sip.

"Ooh, this is really good," she tells my gran. "Try this, Vaughn. It's delicious."

She hands me the glass, and I take a sip. She's right; it's good.

"You'll have to get a job as a bartender, Gran," I tell her.

She pours me out a glass and hands it over. Apparently, we're drinking early today in the West household.

"You're here! Can I see?" Sasha comes bursting into the kitchen from the back door, advancing on Charly like she's known her forever.

My family is a friendly bunch.

"Sasha?" Charly checks.

"And you're Charly! God, Mom was right. You're gorgeous! What are you doing with my little dweeb of a brother?"

"Dweeb? Um, what the fuck?" I frown.

"Language!" my mom and gran scold at the same time.

"Sorry," I mutter. "But, um, *Glamour*'s Hottest Guy of 2016 right here," I say to Sasha, pointing a finger at myself.

She ignores me and turns back to Charly. "A stunner like you could pull Brad Pitt."

"Brad Pitt's old!" I scoff. "He's well over fifty."

Amazing actor though.

Sasha throws me a dirty look. "Brad Pitt is *hot*. He's a hot older man. No way will you look that good when you're fifty."

"Love you, too, sis." I scratch my forehead with my middle finger.

"Right back at you, bro." She sticks her tongue out at me, and then she comes over and hugs me. "I missed your ugly face," she tells me, patting my cheek as she lets me go.

Wardrobe Malfunction

Then, she's back to Charly, who looks like she's just been hit by a whirlwind. Well, she has. Whirlwind Sasha. Wait until she meets Meg. Meg is like Santa on ecstasy.

"My dress is in here?"

"It is." Charly smiles. "Do you want to try it on now and make sure everything is okay for you? And, if any more alterations are needed, I can do them tonight."

"You're the best." Sasha picks up the garment bag. "Will you come upstairs with me? Help me get into it?"

"Sure," Charly says, following her out of the kitchen, giving me a smile before she goes.

"I love your hair," I hear Sasha saying to her. "I've been thinking about getting some color put in my hair, but I don't know if I'm too old."

"How old are you, if you don't mind me asking?" I hear Charly ask.

"Thirty-five," Sasha groans, her voice trailing off as they head upstairs.

A cell phone starts to ring.

"Ooh, that's me," Gran says, picking up her phone and disappearing out of the kitchen.

I suspiciously eye her. *I wonder if that's her boy toy on the phone.*

It's weird, Gran having a boyfriend. She's not had anyone since my granddad passed ten years ago.

"Charly seems really nice," my mom says.

"Yeah, she is." I sit up on a stool and start picking at the grapes in the fruit bowl. I pop one in my mouth and chew.

"And so damn pretty," my mom adds.

"Yeah." I smile.

She's more than pretty. She's beautiful. Stunning.

"So, you guys are dating?"

"Mmhmm."

"Well, she must be good for you. You look a lot better than the last time I saw you. You look happy."

My mom…well, my whole family was worried about how I was dealing with Cain's betrayal, which obviously wasn't well.

"I was hurting back than. I needed to get it out of my system."

"And it's out now?" she checks.

"Yep." I put another grape in my mouth.

"Good."

I watch my mother move around the kitchen, chopping up vegetables, which I'm assuming are for tonight's dinner.

"So, you brought Charly home; that's a first," she says.

I was wondering how long it was going to take her.

"She must be special."

"She is. But don't go getting carried away, Mom."

"What? I'm not," she protests innocently.

"Sure you're not." I laugh. "Charly and I are having fun together. I like her a lot. But I'm not looking to get married anytime soon."

"That's good. But you don't fool me, Vaughn." She points her chopping knife in my direction.

I put my hands up in surrender. "I have no clue what you mean."

"I was watching the way you looked at her."

"And how do I look at her?"

"The way your father looks at me. And the way your grandpa used to look at your gran. The way Greg looks at Sasha. And Vic looks at Meg. Like there's no one else in the room when they're there."

My mother is too damn observant for her own good.

"Did you know that Gran has a boy toy?"

"Nice subject change. And he's hardly a boy toy." She laughs.

"Gran is ten years older than him!"

"How old is Charly?"

"Nice switch back."

"Thanks." She grins.

"She's twenty-five," I tell her.

"You're nearly five years older than her, Vaughn. You'll be thirty soon. Does that make you her sugar daddy?"

"What the hell, Mom?" I groan. This conversation is seriously going in entirely the wrong direction. "I'm twenty-nine, for crying out loud, not fifty-nine. I'm not old enough to be anyone's sugar daddy."

My mom is doubled over, laughing, at this point. She thinks she's hilarious.

"It's not funny," I grumble.

"It kind of is." She wipes her eyes with the back of her hand. "And be happy for your gran. This is the first man she's shown any interest in since your granddad passed. It's been ten years, Vaughn."

"God, it has, hasn't it?"

I was away, working on my first movie, when he passed. He never even got to see my first film. I've always regretted not being there when he died. My granddad was the best kind of man. His family was everything to him.

He was the kind of man I aspire to be. Just like my dad is.

"Your granddad was and always will be the love of your gran's life. She's just having some fun in the time she has left. We can't begrudge her that."

"Yeah, I get it." I sigh. "Is Dad okay with it?"

Gran is my dad's mom. I can only imagine it'd be weird for him.

"Well, he doesn't exactly have a choice. You know your gran." She chuckles. "But he wants her to be happy. And Ed's a good guy."

Ed. So, that's his name.

"And where is Ed from?"

"Over in Klamath Falls."

"Mmhmm," I say. "Well, I want to meet him before I leave."

"You will, at the wedding. He's your gran's date."

Well, thank God I did bring Charly with me; otherwise, I would have been the only one flying solo at this wedding.

Charly

"YOUR FAMILY IS AWESOME," I tell Vaughn as we drive the few minutes over to his house, which is on the same land as his parents' place. They have a heck of a lot of land.

"Yeah, and they love you," he says.

"Yeah, well, I helped with Sasha's dress." I lift my shoulder.

"No, they love you because you're smart and funny and amazing."

He picks up my hand and kisses it, and my heart starts to beat double time.

"My gran especially loved the 'define sleeping' comment." He laughs. "What the hell was that?"

"I'm funny. What can I say?" I give a careless flick of my hair. But I don't feel careless.

I try not to think about what my life might have been like if my dad hadn't been a murdering sick bastard and my mom were still alive. But seeing Vaughn with his family, it was hard not to let my mind wander there.

I'd like to think I would've had a family like Vaughn's. Loving and happy with people who genuinely liked each other. Not because they felt like they had to because they were family, but because they actually liked each other.

His family has made me feel so welcome. I was nervous to come, and it was a little overwhelming at first, but I really enjoyed being in their company.

I can see where Vaughn gets his dry sense of humor—from his gran. She is awesome. And his mom is beautiful, and Vaughn looks just like his dad. Sasha is lovely. I can't wait to meet Meg at dinner later.

When I showed Sasha her dress, her eyes filled with tears. At first I thought she was sad, but then I realized they were tears of happiness. Then, she hugged me tight.

I've come to quickly realize that the West family is a hugging family. It's taking some getting used to, but I'm getting there.

Sasha was just overjoyed with her dress. She told me that I was a magician with a needle and thread. I'm not so sure that Vaughn's once-punctured ball sack would agree, but it was nice to hear.

Watching how happy I made her just from my ability to fix her dress had my heart full and my chest glowing with pride.

Glancing up, I see a huge gorgeous-looking ranch in our approach. "Is this it?" I ask.

"Yeah, this is home." He smiles.

If I thought Vaughn's mom and dad's farmhouse was big, this place is ginormous.

It's an L-shaped two-story ranch with a front porch. There's a two-door garage, a grassy front area with shrubbery, and a purpose-built driveway, off the track of his family's land, which we're currently driving up.

"It's amazing," I breathe, staring at it.

He parks the car in front of the house and turns off the engine, and we both climb out of the car.

I follow him around to the back of the car. He pops the trunk and then pauses.

"So, I have this rule about my house…" He scratches his forehead, staring at me.

"It's not a no-clothes rule, is it? Because your house has a hell of a lot of windows, West, and I wouldn't want to have the girls out on display when a member of your family comes a-knocking."

"No." He chuckles. "Although that is a really good idea, Pins." He rubs his chin with his hand. "The no-clothes rule…yeah, I think—"

"No way, West." I fold my arms over my chest. "So, what's the original rule?"

"I don't have any electronics in my house."

"You don't have any electronics in your house?" I slowly repeat back to him.

"Yeah. No cell phones. No laptops, tablets. Anything. My home is an electronic-free zone."

"Um…why?"

"Because I spend most of my life in Hollywood, surrounded by the fucking press and news stories about myself and where I went to take a piss the night before. When I come home, I don't want to see any of it. I don't want to see stories about myself. My home is my sanctuary. I come here for peace. Here, I get to be a normal person."

"Normal people have cell phones."

"Funny," he says. Then, he puts his hand out. "You wanna come into my home, you've got to hand over your cell phone."

"Really?" I grimace.

"Really."

Jesus, he's serious. How the hell am I going to live without my cell? It's an extension of me.

"What if Nick calls? If he can't get ahold of me, he'll be worried."

"He knows where you are, right?"

"Yeah."

"Then, I'm guessing he won't think I've killed you. But, if you need to call him or Ava or anyone, then, by all means, come out here and make your call. But not in my house. So, phone, please." He wiggles his fingers at me.

Sighing, I get my cell from my bag. I stare down at it. "I'll see you soon," I say to my cell.

"It's a phone, not a baby."

I stick my tongue out at him. "She's my baby. And my best friend."

"Pins, that's really fucking sad." He grins.

"Whatever." I slap my cell in his hand.

He laughs. Then, he puts my cell in the trunk of his car. Pulling his own cell from his pocket, he sets it next to mine. Then, he gets our bags out of the trunk, and I follow him over to the front door.

"Do you have a TV?" I ask hopefully.

God, please have a TV.

"Yeah."

Wahoo!

"But I don't have it connected for any stations. I just use it to watch movies."

"What? No TV?" I whine. "Seriously?"

"You'll survive." He laughs. Pulling a key from his pocket, he unlocks the front door, letting us in.

"What do you do if you get bored?" I follow behind him and step into a huge hallway, which opens into a massive living room, and in front of me is one of those big staircases that branches off to both sides.

Wowzers.

"I read a book. Watch a film. Go for a run. Play pool; I have a game room."

"I always thought you were weird, West. Now, I know you're certifiable. No electronics? I mean, what the hell?" I sigh dramatically.

He laughs and puts our bags down at the bottom of the stairs, and then he comes over to me, putting his arms around my waist, smiling down into my face.

God, he's pretty. I don't think I'll ever get used to how pretty he is.

"You'll be fine, Pins. The peace and quiet. The ability to sit and be with your own thoughts. You're gonna love it."

"I don't have any thoughts. That's why I use my phone—to create thoughts for me."

He laughs again, louder this time. "You might surprise yourself. Just give it a try. It's only for three days. And, if you really need a phone fix, it's just right out there, in the trunk of my car."

"Okay." I snuggle into him, pressing my face to his chest. "You're weird. But I still like you."

"I like you, too. And, if you get really bored, we can just have sex all the time. Also, I have a hot tub out back."

That perks me up. "Oh, hot tub! And sex. Okay, I can live with that."

"Good," he hums, brushing his lips over me. "So, that's the living room." He nods his head in the direction of it.

I turn in his arms and take the living room in. There's a big leather L-shaped couch filled with cushions. And the TV he mentioned is mounted up on the wall. And framed pictures of old movie posters, like *The Godfather*, are up on the walls. None of his movies are up there though.

And scattered around are tons of pictures of his family.

"Kitchen's through there." He turns me around to face an open door, and I can see the kitchen through it. "Game room is there." He points to a closed door. "Downstairs bathroom." He points to another door. "The door next to it is where the gym is. The bedrooms are upstairs—master and two guest suites. Of course, you're in the master with me."

I tip my head back to look up at him. "Of course."

His lips brush my forehead. "Right. I'll get these bags upstairs. Make yourself at home."

I watch him pick up our bags and walk up the stairs, admiring his tight ass as he goes. He veers off to the left, and I turn around on the spot.

I walk over to the kitchen and poke my head through the door.

Wow. Nice.

It's a very manly kitchen. Dark gray cupboards, a huge black fridge. I spy a built-in coffee machine.

I wander back out. Can't say I really have an interest in the gym, so I go to the door I think is the game room. I open the door and walk inside.

Double wow!

It's awesome in here. He has not only a pool table, but also an air hockey game, a basketball-throwing game, arcade machines, one of those motorbike racing games, a super Mario Kart game, and a dartboard up on the wall. It's like a kid's heaven. Or a big kid's heaven.

"You like?" His voice comes from behind me.

"I love! It's so cool." I beam, turning around to him. "I definitely won't get bored in here."

"No, there's plenty that can be done in here." The words sound innocent, but I know that look in his eyes. It's predatory.

A shiver runs through me.

"Oh, yeah? And what would you like to do in here?" Biting my lower lip, I step back, and my ass bumps into the air hockey table. I curl my fingers around the edge.

He steps close to me and picks me up, sitting me on the hockey table. "You," he says. "I'd like to do *you* in here."

"I can live with that."

His eyes on mine, he skims his hands up my bare legs and under my short pleated skirt.

Thank God I wore a skirt today.

He slides my panties down my legs.

Pushing my thighs apart, he drops to his knees. Vaughn is never selfish when it comes to sex. He always makes sure to take care of me first.

His hand taps the heeled ankle boots on my feet. "The boots stay on the whole time."

"What is it with you and boots?" I tease.

"It's *you* in the boots. Turns me on like crazy."

He presses a kiss to the inside of my thigh and starts to kiss a slow path upward until I'm trembling with need.

When he reaches the top, my needy hands slide into his hair.

He stares up at me. "What do you want?" he asks, his voice husky with sex.

"You, making me come."

He puts his mouth on me, and I sigh with relief.

He works me over, licking my clit, pushing a finger inside me and then two.

"I'm so close, Vaughn…so close. Keep doing that…yes…"

Then, without warning, his mouth and fingers are gone.

"What? I was so close to coming."

"I want us to come together." His nimble fingers are unfastening his jeans, and then he's kicking off his shoes, pulling his T-shirt off, and getting a condom out of his wallet. His jeans and boxers drop to the floor, and he's naked.

"I could have come then and then come again." I pout.

He rips the condom packet open with his teeth and rolls it on his cock. Then, he tugs on my bottom lip with his finger and thumb before replacing it with his lips. "I'll make the wait worth your while," he murmurs. Then, he steps back. "Strip for me," he commands.

"You want the sexy dance or the clothes just gone?"

"You do a sexy dance?" His brow goes up.

"Oh, yeah, totally." I grin.

"That, I definitely want to see...but later. Right now, I just need to be inside you. So, clothes off, Pins."

"Yes, sir." I salute.

I pull my top off over my head before quickly removing my bra. I unfasten my skirt at the back and lift my ass. Sliding it down over my hips and down my legs, I flick it aside with my foot.

Vaughn's eyes rake over me. I'm naked, except for my cute little boots. He looks like he wants to devour me whole, and I want to be devoured. I want him to swallow me up. I want every single part of him.

He doesn't seem to be moving. Just frozen to the spot. His cock is hard and ready, his breathing labored.

So, I slide my hand over my chest, letting my fingers play over my breast, my nipple. Then, I slide my hand lower, down over my stomach, coming to rest on my pussy. I already know how wet I am. I'm always wet with Vaughn. All he has to do is look at me.

I dip my finger inside and moan, my eyes briefly closing.

When they open back up, I find Vaughn's eyes on fire.

"Taste yourself," he says roughly.

I lift my finger to my mouth and put it inside, sucking myself from it.

"Mmm," I murmur.

His hand goes to his cock, gripping it. He starts to move it up and down, jacking himself off. "You like the taste of yourself, dirty girl?"

"Yes. But I like the taste of you better."

He covers the distance between us in two strides. He's between my legs, thrusting his cock inside me. His hand fists my hair, tipping my head back, as he takes my mouth in a hard kiss.

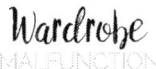

It's rough. It's passionate. It's everything.

He's everything.

"Yes," I moan as he pulls my hair, his hips slamming against mine.

"I can't get enough of you," he growls into my ear. "I've never needed anyone like I need you."

"God, yes!" I cry out.

He sticks his tongue in my ear, sending dizzying sensations spiraling through me.

No one has ever made me feel like he does.

Needing more, needing to be closer to him, I grip ahold of his ass. Digging my nails in his skin, I push my hips harder against his. His tongue trails a path down my neck. His hand comes up to grab my breast, and his mouth finds it, sucking on my nipple hard.

I come like a rocket. "Vaughn!" I scream.

My orgasm seems to trigger his, and he's moaning my name amid curses, his hips pumping in short, fast strokes against mine.

Then, he finally comes to a stop. His hands slide up my back, pulling me to him, and he hugs me. I lift my hands from his ass and wrap them around him.

We're both silent, trying to catch our breaths.

"That was intense," I whisper.

"Yeah," he says into my neck, "it was."

I don't know what triggered the intense sex, but I'm not complaining even if I do feel a little knocked by it.

It feels like every time we have sex, I fall a little more for him. It's scary as hell.

"We need to clean up." I pat his back.

"Yeah," he says, sounding reluctant to move. Then, he sighs and releases me, pulling out of me. He kisses me one last time. "I'll get you a cloth," he says, heading toward the door.

"No, it's fine. I want to freshen up a bit anyway," I tell him.

He stops and looks at me. "Okay, well, you use the master bathroom. Your things are up there in the bedroom. I'll clean up down here."

I gather up my clothes and make a naked dash for the stairs. I head left, the way I saw Vaughn go, and I soon find the master bedroom. It's freaking huge with a massive bed facing the floor-to-ceiling windows. My case is sitting on the bed. The view is amazing. And I'm naked in front of it. I grab my toiletry bag from my overnight case and go into the bathroom.

A quick freshen-up and brush of my teeth, I head back into the bedroom. I put on fresh underwear and pull on my jeans and gray cashmere V-neck sweater.

I head back downstairs to find Vaughn and see him through the window, sitting out on the porch. I let myself outside and pad over to him.

He's sitting on one of the comfy-looking wicker sofas out here, a bottle of beer in his hand.

"Hey, handsome."

He turns his head, smiling at me. "I got you one." He picks up a beer bottle off the table next to him and holds it out for me.

I take it from him and sit next to him. I bring my feet up to rest on the sofa and rest my head on his shoulder. He lifts his arm and puts it around me, so I rest my head on his chest.

"It's so pretty here. I can understand why you like being here."

Honestly, looking out at the view, just acres of greenery and trees beyond, the peace and tranquility of it, I could stay here forever.

Okay, well, not forever because I'd miss New York and Nick and the clothes and everything New York. But I could definitely stay here for an extended period of time.

"Yeah, it is beautiful." He presses a gentle kiss to my hair.

I tip my head back, looking into his face. "How did you get into the movie business?" I ask.

It's something I've wanted to ask him for a while now. And seeing him here, where he's from, has piqued my curiosity. I know Vaughn modeled prior to acting, but that's all I know about his step into the world of movies.

"Meg was studying at UCLA, doing her nursing degree."

"She's a nurse?" I ask.

"Yeah, she works over at Sky Lakes Medical Center in Klamath Falls. Anyway, I was eighteen years old, on school break, and I went out to visit her. She took me to this club in LA. I was underage, but she got me a fake ID. Mom and Dad would have had a seizure if they had known." He grins. "So, we were in this club with her university friends, having fun, and this woman came up to me. She was a model agency scout. Said that I had a great look. That I should consider modeling. She gave me her card. Told me to call her the next day.

"I knew I was a good-looking guy—I'd never had a problem with getting girls in school—but modeling wasn't something I'd ever considered. Honestly, in my mind, I was going to go to graduate college, do a horticultural and business degree, and then work for my dad on the farm until I took it over one day.

"So, I took her card, put it in my pocket, and didn't think about it until I pulled the card back out when I was getting my wallet the next day. I was looking at the card, thinking, *What if?* You know?"

He looks at me, and I nod.

"So, I called her. Thought it couldn't hurt anything. Her assistant answered and asked me if I could come into the agency the next day. Turns out, she was a scout for LA Models. I went in, and they took some test shots. Then, I left. They called me the next day, asking me to come back in for a chat. A few days later, I was signed to their books.

"There was nothing at first. No calls. And I came back home. Then, the phone rang, and I had my first booking. And that was it after that. The jobs started rolling in, and staying in Keno wasn't doable, so I ended up moving to LA and staying with Meg. I was getting busier and busier by the day, traveling all over the world.

"After being in the business for a year, I was at a party, and that was when I was introduced to Jack Hanson, my manager," he tells me.

"Jack asked if I'd ever considered acting. I told him I hadn't, but I was willing to give it a try. I signed with him and enrolled in some acting lessons. He started getting me auditions for small roles, like ads and that kind of thing. Then, he called me up one day and said he had a role in a movie he thought I'd be perfect for. He sent me the details. Of course I liked the looks of it. I mean, it was a movie. If I got the part, I knew it'd be a huge step in my career. I just didn't realize how huge. So, a week later, off I went to audition for the part of Talion in *All the Pretty Ones*."

"But you played Zander in the movie."

Zander was the lead role. Talion was Zander's rival in the movie. *All the Pretty Ones* was a dystopian film based on the novel of the same name. That movie was when the whole world fell in love with Vaughn West.

"Yeah, but when I went in to audition for the part of Talion, Jeff saw me—Jeff Burke, the director," he explains. "Took one look at me and said I was exactly what he was looking for, for Zander. He asked me to read for the part. I did, and he offered me the role on the spot. And, as they say, the rest is history."

"Wow," I say.

"Yeah," he says, but he doesn't sound as enthused as he should.

"You don't sound happy about it."

"I am." He takes a swig of his beer. "But, sometimes, I just wish…"

Wardrobe
MALFUNCTION

"What?"

He looks at me again.

"I wish I had my anonymity back. I wish I could just walk around, unknown."

"You can here, in Keno."

"I know. But I wish I could just go anywhere without being recognized. Without someone stopping me to ask if I was Vaughn West, if they could take a photo with me, if they could have my autograph. I wish I could go to the fucking grocery store without the press following me there. Without my whereabouts being tweeted and shared among people, and then a crowd turns up, and I have to have a security escort out of there. To meet a pretty girl, take her out on a date, have a relationship without every detail ending up on the nightly fucking news. I just…I don't know." He sighs. "I love my job. I love acting. I'm fucking good at it. But, sometimes, I wonder what my life would have been like if I hadn't made that call."

"Sometimes, I wonder what my life would have been like if my dad hadn't murdered my mom."

Jesus, I can't believe I just said that.

"Fuck, Charly. Jesus." He scrubs a hand over his face. "Here I am, whining like a little bitch about my privileged life…and you lost your mom. I'm sorry."

"Don't be sorry. I guess…I think everyone's problems are individual to them. No one else's problems are bigger or more important than the next person's, you know. I think we all deal with things differently. We all have different levels of coping abilities."

"And you have the dealing ability of a lioness. And, still, I'm a whiny dick who's not worthy of you. I'm sorry, Pins."

"Like I said, don't be. That's not why I said it."

Why did I?

"Then, why did you?" His words echo my own thoughts.

I look down at my hands. "I don't know. I guess, it kind of just popped out because I feel safe with you. I know I can talk to you. Tell you anything. I trust you, Vaughn."

I finally look back up at him, and the warmth in his eyes coats my skin like a blanket.

"I trust you, too, Pins."

He kisses my forehead, and then I lay my head back down on his chest and take a sip of my beer.

And I realize something in this moment.

I get to see the real Vaughn West. One not many other people get to see.

I can't tell you how incredibly privileged that makes me feel because he's so very special. He's so much more than what people see on-screen.

He's smart and witty and beautiful, inside and out, and he's incredibly talented. I've never known a man who loved his family more.

He has such a big heart. A heart that I want to keep all for myself.

I don't ever want to let him go.

I'm just not sure how I can keep him forever.

Vaughn

IT'S A WARM EVENING, so Charly and I decide to walk over to my parents' house, as it's only a ten-minute walk.

She's wearing this sexy strappy, knee-length pink dress that I can't wait to take off her later. Surprisingly, she doesn't have heels on her feet; instead, she has on a pair of flip-flops.

She looks beautiful.

I catch hold of her hand as we walk.

She smiles up at me and wraps her other hand over my arm, bringing herself closer to me.

It's good to be able to walk outside and hold her hand. Okay, so it's on my parents' land, not in the middle of town, but still, it feels good.

"This is nice," she murmurs.

"Yeah, it is."

And it really is. Not just the hand-holding. Being here with her. I'm usually here on my own. I don't bring anyone here. I thought it would be weird, her being here, but it isn't. Having her in my home feels as natural as breathing.

We reach my parents' house and head on inside. As usual, the noise is at an epic level.

"Uncle Vaughn!"

A swarm of kids run at me, hugging my legs and stomach.

"Hey," I say to my nieces and nephews. "Kids, this is Charly."

They all let me go, and four sets of eyes all stare at Charly.

"Charly, this is George." I pat his head. "He belongs to Meg and Vic. These three are Parker, Thomas, and Nora. They're Sasha and Greg's."

"My mama and daddy are getting married," Nora tells her.

Nora's three and beyond cute. I adore her.

I know you're not supposed to have favorites, but she's my favorite.

"I know," Charly says, crouching down to Nora's level. "It's so exciting. I bet you're a bridesmaid, right?"

"Uh-huh," Nora replies. "My brothers are page boys. I'm three, you know."

"She doesn't care how old you are," Thomas says to her. "Are you Uncle Vaughn's girlfriend?" he asks Charly.

Charly looks up at me and then back at Thomas. "Yeah, I guess I am."

"Mama said you were his girlfriend," Nora says. "She was telling Aunt Meg how pretty you are and that she thinks that Uncle Vaughn is going to marry you."

"And that's enough of this conversation." I scoop Nora up in my arms, carrying her through to the living room, blowing a raspberry on her stomach.

"Stop, Uncle Vaughn!" she squeals, grabbing my hair.

Then, I feel arms grab me from behind, and it's Parker. I drop to my knees, placing Nora on the floor, and take

Wardrobe Malfunction

hold of Parker, bringing him over my shoulder. I go down to the floor with him. The next thing I know, I'm under attack from four kids, who are all on me. Three are tickling me while Nora is blowing raspberries on my stomach.

"Uncle Vaughn, why is your tummy so hard? Daddy's tummy isn't this hard when I blow raspberries on it. It's all squishy."

"Thanks, baby." I hear Greg's voice, followed by his laughter.

"Sounds like you need to get to the gym, man." I look up at him, grinning.

He picks Nora up from off me, gives her a kiss, and puts her to her feet while I continue to wrestle with the boys.

"Grandma wants you all in the kitchen to wash up for dinner."

They all groan in unison, and then, one by one, they clamber off me and head into the kitchen.

Greg offers me a hand, and I get to my feet.

"Good to see you." I give him a one-armed hug. "Greg, this is my girl, Charly."

Charly's lingering in the living room doorway with this odd look on her face.

I raise a brow in question, but she just returns it with a smile.

"Hey," Greg says to her, giving her a polite nod. "Good to meet you."

She walks over and stands beside me. I sling my arm over her shoulder.

"Congratulations on your upcoming wedding," she says to Greg.

"How are you feeling about signing away your life to my sister?" I joke with him.

"I signed it away years ago." He chuckles, making us all laugh.

"Where is everyone?" I ask him.

"Your dad's out back with Vic, showing him the tent. Sasha, your mom, Gran, and Meg are all in the kitchen."

"I guess we should go let Mom know we're here," I tell Charly.

We leave Greg in the living room and head toward the kitchen.

"You okay?" I quietly ask her.

"Yeah"—she smiles—"I'm good. Your nephews and niece are adorable."

"They get it from me."

"Of course they do." She rolls her eyes, making me laugh.

I push open the door, seeing the familiar sight of the women in my family in the kitchen. As usual, Meg's sitting at the breakfast bar, reading a magazine and sipping a glass of wine; she's not a cooker. Gran, Mom, and Sasha are working in perfect sync.

"We're here," I announce.

"Vaughn!" Meg hops off her stool and runs at me, throwing her arms around me like she hasn't seen me for a year. "Missed you, movie star."

"Missed you, too, Nutmeg."

"And you must be Charly!" She lets go of me and advances on Charly, sweeping her up in a hug.

I think Charly must be getting used to the hugs, as she doesn't seem to freeze up this time.

"I love your hair! Sasha said it was gorgeous, and it really is. Come sit with me." She grabs Charly's hand, leading her over to the breakfast bar.

"Hey, Mom." I lean over and kiss her cheek.

"Hey." She smiles.

"Sasha, Gran." I smile at them. "You doing okay?"

"I would be if your sister didn't keep trying to give me the easy jobs." Gran frowns at Sasha.

"I'm not!" Sasha holds her hands up in innocence.

"Do you want a glass of wine?" Meg asks Charly.

"Sure. Thanks."

"Movie star, grab us a glass for Charly. So, you're the girl who finally tamed my baby brother."

"Hey! Who says I'm tamed?" I put the wine glass down and pick up the bottle, pouring some into the glass for Charly.

"Thanks," she says to me, picking it up and taking a sip.

I rest my arm around her shoulder.

Meg is staring at us with a big smile on her face.

"What?" I say to her.

"Nothing."

"You're acting weirder than usual, Nutmeg."

"You just look so adorable together." She presses her hands to her chest.

"And, on that note, we're going to say hi to Dad and Vic. Come on, Pins." I reach for her hand, helping her off the stool.

"Oh my God, you have a nickname for her! That's so sweet! Did you hear that, Mom? Vaughn has a nickname for Charly. It's so cute."

"Run," I whisper into Charly's ear. "Before she starts getting out Sasha's bridal magazines for us to take a look at."

Charly looks at me. There's a beat of hesitation in her eyes, which she quickly covers with a smile. And, as we make a hasty exit from the kitchen and away from my overly romantic sister, I wonder where the hesitation came from, but before I can think too much about it, the second we step outside, we're under attack from Jester. Well, Charly is. He practically leaps into her arms. She giggles, cuddling him, while he licks her face.

I think Jester's in love. He's not the only one.

Wait.

What?

Charly

"MEGS, DO YOU REMEMBER when Vaughn was obsessed with *Bugsy Malone*?" Sasha says with a smile on her face.

We've just finished dinner—or I should say, a feast of epic proportions—and I'm stuffed to the rafters. I won't need to eat for another week. Vaughn's family has been telling me funny stories all night.

The meal and company have been amazing. I've had such fun. Although I do keep catching Vaughn staring at me with this odd look in his eyes. One I've never seen before.

"Oh my God, yeah!" Meg laughs.

"Oh God, no," Vaughn groans from beside me.

I glance at him, but he's too busy giving his sisters the evil eye across the table.

"He used to make us watch it with him all the time," Sasha tells me.

"It is a great film," I say. "Maybe being an actor was in your blood all along, not just a happenstance." I nudge his elbow with mine, and he smiles warmly at me.

"Yeah, but not only did he used to watch it daily, he also used to get us to watch it with him. We'd have to dress up like the characters and perform the musical routines," Meg adds.

"Aw, I bet you made a cute Bugsy," I say.

"Not Bugsy!" Sasha laughs.

"I'll feed your wedding dress to Jester," he says to Sasha. "And I'll make sure it's not fixable this time."

"Ha!" Sasha laughs. "You wouldn't dare."

"Try me." He narrows his gaze at her.

"Children," his mom chastises.

"Well, I have nothing to lose," Meg says quickly. "Vaughn didn't dress up as Bugsy. No, he insisted on being Tallulah every time! He used to get Mom's dresses and shoes and put them on! He even wore lipstick!"

"Oh my God!" I laugh.

Vaughn picks up a roasted potato off his plate and throws it at Meg. She ducks, and it misses her.

"You're such a *see you next Tuesday*." He frowns at her, but I can see that he's also fighting a smile.

"Mama, why is Uncle Vaughn saying he's going to see Aunt Meg next Tuesday? He's seeing her right now," Nora asks innocently.

"Yeah, Tallulah, why are you going to see me next Tuesday?" Meg teases him.

Vaughn scratches his forehead with his middle finger. Meg sticks her tongue out at him.

I swear, he and his sister act like kids around one another. It's funny to watch. And it makes me wish that I'd had a sibling growing up. But I have Nick, and that's all that matters.

"Uncle Vaughn's just being silly," Sasha explains to her daughter, giving Vaughn a dirty look.

Wardrobe Malfunction

He just smirks at her.

"We have some photos of Vaughn dressed up as Tallulah," his mom says.

"No, we don't. I burned them," Vaughn says.

"Don't tell lies, Vaughn. You never burned them. I know exactly where they are." His mom gets up from the table. "I'll go get them now before we have dessert, so Charly can have a look. I'll get your baby photos, too."

Dessert? Good God, I might die from overfeeding.

"Jesus Christ," he complains. "Can't you stop her, Dad?"

"I wish I could, son. But this is the first time you've brought a girl home. Your mom and sisters have been waiting years for this."

He looks at me with a help-me expression on his face. He looks so adorable, I can't help but smile.

"Sorry, West. But I really want to see your baby pictures. And, of course, the ones of you dressed as Tallulah."

"Traitor," he grumbles.

I can see a smile teasing the corner of his lips.

I tug on his bottom lip, and that smile finally makes an appearance. His eyes soften on me, and he takes hold of my hand and kisses it.

When I turn back to the table, his sisters are looking at us like we're magic.

Honestly, I feel like magic when I'm with him. This whole thing with Vaughn feels like magic. Not real. I keep expecting to wake up at any moment.

Being here is so wonderful. I did worry that being in a family environment like this would be weird for me. It's not something I'm used to, so I wasn't sure if I would know how to act around his family, but they make it easy. They're so warm and friendly. I feel lucky to be a part of this even if for a short time.

"Got them!" Vaughn's mom comes bustling back into the dining room with a stack of photo albums in her arms. She hands them to Meg, who gives a wicked grin to Vaughn.

"Oh God," Vaughn grumbles.

"Girls, why don't you take Charly into the living room to look through these? The men and kids can help me clear the table. And we'll have dessert in there."

"Can I go with Mommy, Charly, and Aunt Meg to look at the pictures?" Nora asks.

"Sure you can, baby."

"That's not fair!" Parker complains.

"Life ain't fair sometimes, kiddo." She ruffles his hair.

I get up from the table, pressing a kiss to the side of Vaughn's head.

He catches my hand. "Whatever you see in that living room stays in that room, Pins. I never want to hear of it again."

I grin. "Sure thing, Tallulah."

I head off toward the living room with his sisters and Nora, who catches hold of my hand, surprising me.

Jester jumps up from his spot in the hallway. Vaughn's mom put him out here, as he wouldn't leave me alone at dinner. He kept trying to climb onto my lap.

I felt so bad for him. He's so cute.

He comes trotting over to me, tail wagging.

"Hey, Jester." I lean down, patting his head.

"Jester likes you a lot," Nora says.

"Yeah. I like him, too."

"And I think Uncle Vaughn likes you a lot," she whispers to me. "I've never seen him with a girl before."

I smile down at her. "I'm glad 'cause I like him a lot, too."

I take a seat on the floor where Sasha and Meg have set up camp with the photo albums. Nora sits down beside me. Jester climbs into my lap. I give his ear a scratch.

Wardrobe Malfunction

"Okay"—Meg gleefully rubs her hands—"let's get this show of embarrassing my brother on the road."

She opens a photo album, and the first picture is of a glammed up Tallulah-looking Vaughn. Oversized dress, too-big high heels, and bright red lips.

"How old was he here?" I ask.

"Eight. Wasn't he such a pretty boy?" Sasha says.

And we all burst out laughing.

Vaughn

"You made such a pretty Tallulah," Charly murmurs, sounding sleepy, her arm linked through mine, head resting against my shoulder, as we walk the short distance back to my house.

We've got Jester with us. He's trotting on up ahead, sniffing every blade of grass possible. He was at the door, following us out when we were leaving, so I said to my mom that he could stay at mine. He wouldn't leave Charly alone all night. He's obsessed with her. As it turns out, I am, too.

And wasn't that revelation earlier just a little shocker?

Since realizing how I felt about her, I kept sneaking looks at her all night to see if she looked different to me. But she just looks the same, and it makes me wonder if I've been in love with her all along.

"I thought we talked about this, Pins," I say in a mock-annoyed voice. "What you saw in my parents' living room stays in my parents' living room."

She giggles softly. "Sorry, West."

"You're forgiven. Just don't do it again." I kiss the top of her head, breathing in her raspberry and vanilla scent.

I don't really care about the embarrassing story and photographs because I saw how much fun she had while hearing them and seeing the pictures. I loved making her laugh. I want to make her happy.

And, honestly, this is what I love about being home. Here, I'm just me. My sisters' kid brother who they take the piss out of.

That's why I made the decision to build my house here and keep Oregon as my permanent home. When you live in a place like LA, a place where people call you special, tell you that you're a star, that you're important, it's easy to believe it. It's easy to forget that you're the same kid who dressed up as Tallulah and acted out *Bugsy Malone* with your older sisters. It's easy to believe your own hype. It's easy to forget who you really are in Hollywood.

And it's not that I'm ungrateful for the opportunities that my profession affords me.

But the person I want to be is the person this place keeps me being.

I have a great family who treats me the same as they always have. They are the reason my feet stay firmly on the ground, where they belong.

And, despite the shit I endured a few months ago, I've always thought of myself as a happy guy. But I didn't know happiness until I met Charly.

And I've never been more myself than I am with her.

We reach my house, and I let us in. Jester shouldn't need to pee. He took about twenty pisses on our way over here.

Wardrobe Malfunction

Charly kicks her flip-flops off. "Mind if I go straight up?" she asks. "I'm super tired after all that food."

"Yeah, sure, babe. I'll just get Jester settled for the night, and I'll be up."

She starts up the stairs, and Jester follows her.

"Jester," I call after him.

He stops on the stairs.

"Back down here, buddy. You know the rules."

"Sorry, Jester," Charly says to him. "Not my house, not my rules. But, if it were my house, I'd totally let you upstairs."

"You're not helping," I tell her.

She smiles at me and then crouches down on the stairs. "Night, Jester. See you in the morning, cutie." She kisses the top of his head and then gets to her feet, turns, and goes upstairs.

Jester sighs and then comes back down. I swear to God, he gives me a dirty look.

Jester trots into the living room, hopping up onto the sofa.

"Don't make yourself comfy there either. You're in the kitchen," I tell him as I head into the kitchen, through to the utility room to get out his bed and water bowl that I keep here for him.

I set them up for him and go back into the living room to get him. "Jester," I call.

No sign of him.

I instantly know where he is.

"Little shit," I mutter to myself. I jog upstairs and walk into my bedroom, stopping in the doorway.

Charly is passed out on my bed, fast asleep. She didn't even get undressed. And Jester, the sneaky little bastard, is snuggled up beside her, his head on her shoulder.

Honestly, in this moment, I wish I had my cell phone, so I could take a picture.

"You," I whisper, pointing at Jester, "downstairs."

Fucking dog just ignores me.

I go over to pick him up, and Charly rouses.

"Can he stay?" she mumbles sleepily, hugging Jester to her.

I stare down at Jester, giving him the evil eye. He just smugly stares back.

"Sure thing, Pins. But let's get you undressed."

I lift her dress up her body, and she moves, helping me get it over her head. Jester grumbles because he has to move. I actually chuckle at the cheek of the dog.

My cock hardens at the sight of her in just her pale pink lacy underwear, but it looks like he's not getting any action tonight.

"Where are your pajamas?" I ask her.

"Bag," she mumbles.

I dig out a pair of shorts and a tank that she's worn to bed before. I slip the shorts up her legs, and she lifts her butt, helping me get them on her. Then, I lift her head, slipping the tank over her.

"Bra," she says. Then, she lazily undoes it and pulls it off, giving me a great view of her fantastic tits, making my dick painfully harder.

I'm considering tugging one out when I go in the bathroom.

I help her slip her arms through the armholes, and she's done.

I pull the duvet down from underneath her and cover her. Jester is just about to get in with her.

"You. Floor." I point in the direction of the floor.

Jester stares at me and then slowly gets off the bed, lying down on the floor at Charly's side of the bed. He lets out a loud sigh.

"Fucking dog." I chuckle to myself, hitting the light, plunging us into darkness.

Wardrobe Malfunction

I make a quick trip to the bathroom, take a piss, brush my teeth, and then come back into the bedroom. I strip my clothes off, leaving just my boxers on, and I climb into bed.

I reach over for Charly to pull her into my arms, and instead, I get a furry dog.

"For fuck's sake, Jester," I grumble.

"Sorry," Charly mumbles sleepily. "He got in when you were in the bathroom. Shall I move him?"

"No, it's fine, babe." I throw daggers at Jester in the dark, realizing I'm not winning this battle tonight.

I've been edged out by a fucking dog.

I lean over and press a soft kiss to her lips. "Night, babe."

"Mmhmm. Love you," she mumbles.

I freeze.

She loves me.

My heart starts to pound in my chest.

Does she realize what she just said?

Even still, I can't resist saying it back, testing it out loud. I guess I'll know if she means it when I tell her that I love her, too. That I'm crazy about her. She's all I think about. She's all I want.

From the minute I saw her dancing around, twerking her cute ass like she was Nicki Minaj, I knew she was going to be different. I just didn't know *how* different.

Now, she's everything.

I brush my fingers over her forehead, sweeping her hair back, my heart beating so fast, as I whisper, "I love you, too, Pins."

I wait a second, but she doesn't respond, and when she starts to snore softly, I know she's asleep.

The disappointment I feel is surprising. But I guess this just wasn't meant to be the moment to say how we feel.

I'll tell Charly how I feel about her when the right moment arises. And I pray to God I won't scare her away.

Hopefully, she really does feel the same way I do, and she's not just speaking meaningless words in her sleep.

Charly

I HAD THIS DREAM last night where I told Vaughn I loved him.

Thank God it was just a dream; otherwise, that would have been embarrassing.

But I do love him. I'm crazy in love with him.

It's just not the time to be telling him. Especially when he doesn't know everything about me.

He's taking me to a place called Crater Lake today. He said it was this really huge lake that came from a volcano that had collapsed thousands of years ago. He said it was a really beautiful place. I'm looking forward to seeing it. We've packed up a picnic with some of the food that Vaughn's mom had stocked his fridge and cupboards up with.

We're dropping Jester back at his mom and dad's. I think Vaughn's had enough of Jester monopolizing my time. I think he's feeling a little jealous and left out, which is seriously cute. Also, it's an hour's drive there, so Jester might get bored in the car for that length of time.

Vaughn also wants to check if his mom needs us to do anything for the wedding before we head out. I can't believe the wedding is only hours away. I bet Sasha is getting so excited.

I can't wait to see the look on Greg's face when he sees Sasha in her dress. She looks stunning in it.

Vaughn puts the picnic basket along with a picnic blanket in the backseat. I sit in the front with Jester on my lap.

I'm dressed sensibly today. Well, as sensible as I can. I didn't bring any sneakers with me, not that I have any, so I'm wearing my flip-flops, knowing that we'll be walking a bit. And I'm wearing jean shorts and a tank, as it's really warm today. I've put on sunscreen as well, as I don't want to burn. Vaughn is wearing khaki shorts, a tank, and sneakers. He looks hot, like usual. He's also wearing his ball cap, and he has sunglasses on.

I tug his cap off and put it on my head. "You worried about people recognizing you when we're out?" I ask him, referring to the cap. I know he wears it as a disguise of sorts.

"We shouldn't run into anyone. It's a big place, and I'm taking you to one of the quieter areas, but you never know." He shrugs, putting the car in drive.

I can't imagine how it is for him, always having to worry about being recognized.

We stop at Vaughn's parents' house. I get out, carrying Jester in my arms.

"He can walk, you know," Vaughn teases as we head over to the house.

"I know, but he's so cute, like a little baby." I snuggle Jester and get a lick on my face in return.

I wish I could have a dog. But it's not feasible, as I travel a lot for work, and even though Nick is always home,

it'd be stuck inside while he was at work all day. That, and we live in a small apartment, which isn't really practical for a dog.

"It's us," Vaughn calls as he walks through the front door.

Is it silly that I get all glowy when I hear him say that? *Us*. I've never been part of an *us* before. Except with Nick, but that's different.

"Hey." His mom comes out of the kitchen, drying her hands on a dish towel. "Has he been okay?" She gestures to Jester.

"No trouble at all." I smile at her.

"Except for hogging the fucking bed all night."

"Ignore Vaughn." I shake my head. "He's been a little gem."

"Maybe for you," he grumbles. "Jester thinks the sun shines out of your ass."

"You saying it doesn't?" I tease, checking my behind.

Vaughn's mom chuckles and takes Jester from my arms.

"We're just heading up to Crater Lake."

"Have you ever been, Charly?" she asks me.

"No." I shake my head.

"You'll love it. Such a pretty place. Do you need any food to take with you?" she asks.

"No, we're good. We packed a picnic. Before we go, I just wanted to check if there's anything you need us to do or to pick up before the wedding?"

"Nope. All taken care of," she tells us. "Go have fun."

"Okay. We'll see you later." He kisses the side of her head.

"Bye," I say. "Bye, Jester."

I wave at him, and he whines and wriggles in Vaughn's mom's arms. I feel mean, leaving him behind.

I follow Vaughn out the door.

"That dog fucking loves you," he says as we walk over to his car.

"I'm very lovable." I give a comedic flick of my hair, sashaying my hips as I walk.

"That, you are," he says. There's something different in his voice. He doesn't sound as light as he did a second ago.

I glance at him, but whatever expression he was wearing is gone, and his face is schooled. "And, of course, you have a hot ass," he adds with a grin.

"That the sun shines out of," I remind him.

"Yeah, we should check that out later."

"The sun shining out of my ass?"

"Mmhmm. For scientific purposes, of course." His hand finds his way to my butt, giving it a squeeze.

"Scientific purposes? Sure, West." I laugh. "Well, check away, buddy, but there'll be no sticking of anything in my sun-shining ass."

"Spoilsport." He sighs dramatically, making me laugh again.

We both climb in the car and buckle up.

"You want some music on?" he asks me when he fires up the engine.

"What have you got?"

"There are some CDs in the glove box," he tells me as he puts the car in drive.

I open it up and pull out a CD case. I start flicking through it. "I didn't know you liked Nirvana," I say, coming across *Nevermind* in his CDs.

"The question should be, who doesn't like Nirvana?"

"Right?" I smile. "Nick doesn't like their music."

"And you're friends with him why?" He takes his eyes off the road for a second to look at me, giving a teasing smile.

My stomach fills with warmth. I love that we both love Nirvana.

"It was a bone of contention in the beginning of our friendship, but because he understood my love of clothes, I decided to overlook it." I twist in my seat, bringing my knees up, so I can look at him. "Which is your favorite song?"

"'Lithium,'" he states. "Yours?"

"I'm always torn between 'Come As You Are' and 'Heart-Shaped Box.'"

"Both are great," he says.

"What do you think of the Foo Fighters?"

"That they're life."

I smile, agreeing. "Dave Grohl's kinda hot, too," I admit.

"Nah, he's not my type." He glances at me, smiling. "I like 'em cute and blonde. Oh, yeah, and female."

"With pink and lilac highlights."

"Of course." He reaches over and tugs on a lock of my hair. "There should be a couple of Foo Fighters albums in there as well," he tells me.

"We'll listen to them on the way back. I kinda want to listen to Nirvana now." I pull the CD from the case and insert it into the CD player. I put the case back in the glove box just as "Smells Like Teen Spirit" starts to play.

I relax back in my seat and reach over to rest my hand on Vaughn's thigh, squeezing it. He takes ahold of my hand, linking our fingers together, and he doesn't let go for the rest of the journey.

Charly

VAUGHN PULLS INTO A parking lot. There are hardly any cars here. He parks the farthest away from the other cars and turns the engine off.

He takes his hat from my head and pulls it on. "Come on, gorgeous," he says to me.

We climb out of the car. He gets the picnic basket and blanket from the backseat.

I meet him around the back of the car. I take the blanket from him, leaving him with the picnic basket.

Taking my hand, Vaughn leads me off, and we start to walk up the road together.

"We'll take one of the trails up to the picnic area," he tells me.

"Cool."

We venture off the main road and onto one of the trails, which gives me a view of the lake.

"Holy shit." I come to a stop, tugging on his arm.

"Amazing, right?"

"It's stunning." And it is. It's a beautiful huge hole in the earth filled with the bluest water I've ever seen. The forestry surrounding it is spectacular.

"Come on." He tugs on my arm. "You'll be able to get a better view when we get to the picnic spot. It's just a little further up."

We walk for a little while longer and then come to a clearing. He wasn't kidding; the view is spectacular.

"I have to take a picture." I go to my pocket to get my phone, and then I realize it's still in the trunk of Vaughn's car.

Weird that I haven't felt the urge to use it until now.

"Crap, it's still in your car," I tell him.

"Do you want me to go get it?"

"No, it's fine. Don't worry."

I set the blanket out on the grass, and Vaughn puts the basket on it.

I step a little closer to the edge. "What's that in the middle? An island?" I ask him.

He comes up behind me and slides his hands around my waist. "That's Wizard Island. And that tiny one over there…" He points a finger, and my eyes follow the direction.

"Where?" I squint.

"Right over there." He gestures with his finger again.

My eyes pick up on something, but it's not very clear. "I can just about see it," I tell him.

"That's Phantom Ship."

"Sounds spooky," I say.

Then, I make a ghost noise, and he chuckles. I feel it rumble against my back.

"Why's it called that?" I ask.

"Because people say it resembles a ghost ship."

I slide my hands over his, linking our fingers, and lean my head back onto his shoulder. I turn my face to him and press a kiss to his neck.

"Are you happy?" he asks me, staring down into my eyes.

"Very. Are you?"

"I've got the hottest girl in the world in my arms, and her ass is currently pressed up against my cock. I'd say I'm extremely happy."

"You're such a charmer." I giggle.

"And don't you just know it?" He laughs, kissing my forehead. "Come on, let's eat. I'm starving."

I kick my flip-flops off and sit down. Vaughn sits beside me, opens the basket, and gets the sandwiches out that we made earlier—turkey and mayo.

Yum.

Then, he pulls out a bottle of wine and a plastic glass from the side of the basket.

"When did you sneak that in?" I ask.

"I put it in when you were in the bathroom. I just forgot to tell you. Thought you might like a drink."

"Aren't you having one?"

"I'm driving." He gives me a duh look.

"I know you're driving, smart-ass, but you can have a glass, can't you?"

"I only brought the one glass."

"Then, I'll share mine with you."

He pours the wine out, and I take a sip and then hand it to him.

"Thanks for bringing me here," I say before taking a bite of my sandwich. "It really is beautiful. And kind of romantic if you think about it."

"I'm a romantic kind of guy." He grins.

"Can you ever be serious for just a minute?" I nudge his thigh with my foot.

He stares right into my eyes. "Like I told you, I'm serious about you."

Butterflies swoop into my stomach, going nuts. "I'm kind of serious about you, too, West."

We eat and drink—well, I do most of the drinking—and we talk about everything and laugh. I laugh so much when I'm with him.

I think humor is such an attractive quality in a man, and Vaughn has it in spades. That, and a gorgeous face and smoking-hot body.

I'm a lucky, lucky girl.

I'm just nibbling on a strawberry when I remember something that I've always wanted to ask him. "West, can I ask you something?"

"Is it dirty or kinky?"

"No." I giggle.

"Sounds boring to me, but go on then. I'm listening."

I shake my head at him, my lips curved into a smile. "Why didn't you have me fired when I stabbed you?"

He furrows his brow. "Why would I have?"

"Because you had Millie fired for incompetency. I stabbed you in one of your balls. Seems kind of worse than being incompetent. Even though she is incompetent."

"Who's Millie?"

"The girl who did the job before me." I put the rest of the strawberry in my mouth and chew.

"Oh, her. I had her fired because she kept hitting on me."

"Oh." I swallow it down. "Well, it makes sense. She always did seem to like the men I did." Even if she did see Vaughn first, it doesn't count because I don't like her.

"Do I smell a history there between you two?"

"I just don't like her. She's crap at her job. And she slept with my ex after I dumped him."

Wardrobe
MALFUNCTION

"Ah. Well, Pins, I wouldn't have fired you for an accident even if it hurt like a motherfucker. And you intrigued me. I liked your fire. And you made me a cock warmer, so…"

"Oh my God! It wasn't a cock warmer! It was—"

He cuts my words off with a soft kiss.

His lips part from mine, his thumb brushing gently over my mouth. My eyes flutter open to his warm stare on mine.

"It wasn't a cock warmer," I utter softly.

"Sure it wasn't, Pins." He winks.

"Kind of ironic that you fired her for hitting on you, and then you ended up sleeping with me."

"It's different."

"How?"

"Because, first off, she was seriously inappropriate. You never behaved that way with me."

"True."

"And, secondly, I wanted to fuck you the moment I laid eyes on you."

I hold back a smile. "You were quite standoffish when I first met you."

"Because I wanted to fuck you, and I knew I couldn't, hence the hard-on when you stabbed me."

"I knew you had an erection!" I exclaim. "And you were all, 'I didn't have a boner. You're not my type,'" I say, mimicking his voice.

"What was I supposed to say? *Oh, yeah, I got a boner while you were on your knees in front of me because I couldn't stop imagining you sucking my cock.* I'm sure that would have gone down really well."

I laugh. "You said I wasn't your type."

"I lied. You're more than my type."

"You seemed very convincing."

"I'm an actor, Pins. I'm paid to be convincing."

"So, how will I actually know when you're telling me the truth or lying?" I'm teasing, but his face instantly turns serious, surprising me.

"Because I would never lie to you. You're far too important to me for me to ever do anything to fuck this up."

My own secret thumps me hard in the chest. I swallow, my mouth suddenly dry. "I know," I whisper. "I was just teasing."

"Sorry." He grabs ahold of my hand and tugs on it. "I just…after what happened with Cain…I just…I would never do that to you."

"I know you wouldn't. And I would never cheat on you. You know that, right?"

He looks at me for a long moment. "I know, babe. I trust you."

I take a sip of wine.

Vaughn gets a strawberry and puts it in his mouth, biting into it. Some of the juice runs down his lip. He catches it with his tongue. "So, tell me about this ex-boyfriend."

"Huh?"

"The ex who Millie slept with."

"Oh, Michael."

"Sounds like a prick."

I laugh. "He is. A prick who was a drug dealer, which I found out about after six months of dating him. The second I found out, I dumped his sorry ass."

"How did you find out that he was dealing?"

"I was working on a show, and an actor told me to thank Michael for the coke and that it was good shit, that'd he be telling all his buddies about him."

"Sounds like a charmer."

"Oh, yeah, a real charmer."

"You've really gone up in the world with me, Pins."

I glance at him, and he's grinning.

Wardrobe Malfunction

"I know, right? But then there wasn't exactly anywhere for me to go but up after Michael."

His brow furrows. "I don't know if that was actually a compliment or not."

"It was. Well…a backhanded compliment—argh!"

I squeal as he dives on me. Taking me to my back, he pins my hands over my head.

"Your smart mouth is going to get you in trouble one of these days, Charlotte Michaels. Hey, do you realize you've got the same surname as your douche ex's first name?"

"Of course I realized." I laugh.

"If you'd married him, you could've made him change his surname to yours, so he'd have been called Michael Michaels."

"You're a fucking comedian, West. And why exactly are you talking about me marrying another man? My ex, to be precise."

"I have no clue." He frowns. "The thought actually makes me want to punch a hole in that tree over there."

"You'd have to be pretty strong to punch a hole in a tree. Like Hulk strong."

"You're killing the romantic in my words."

"Sorry." I bite the smile on my lips, but I can't stop the laugh that comes out.

"You suck." He frowns, climbing off me, sitting down.

I sit up next to him. "I do suck. Very well, according to you."

He slides a grin at me. "You do have a mouth like a vacuum."

"Was that another one of your romantic statements?"

"Yep."

"Uh, well, thanks."

He laughs. "You're welcome."

We're quiet for a moment as we stare out over the view. Vaughn brings his knees up and links his arms around them.

"Can I ask you something?" I say.

He turns his head, resting his chin on his shoulder. "Shoot."

"Does it, um, bother you that I dated someone who was a drug dealer?" I'm asking to test the water now that he knows. I want to know what he's willing to tolerate. "I mean, if we went public and the press were to find out, would it bother you?"

"Not at all."

"What about my past? My father murdering my mom. My father being in prison. If the press found out, they would have a field day."

"The only thing I would be worried about is you." He drops his arms and turns around to face me, putting his legs on either side of me. He cups my cheek, turning my face to him. "Is that why you want to still keep us a secret?"

I glance away, looking down.

Maybe. Partly. Not really.

Tell him the truth, Charly.

He slides his fingers under my chin, lifting, forcing my eyes up. "Pins, what happened…you had no control over. You were a kid. I don't care what the press has to say about it. *Nothing* about *you* could ever embarrass me. You're amazing. I'm crazy about you."

I stare back at him, my heart beating with love and fear and everything else that I feel for him.

I lean forward and press my lips to his. He moans a sound that hits me straight between my legs. His hand moves from my face to cup the nape of my neck. He shifts in closer, deepening the kiss, taking control.

And, as it always does with Vaughn and me, things get heated fast, and I'm straddling his lap, pressing myself up against him.

And I tell myself that I don't need to tell him now, that there's no rush. And Sasha's wedding is tomorrow. I don't want to do anything to spoil it for him. He might be okay with what I have to tell him, but just to be sure, I'll wait.

I'll tell him when we get back to Vegas.

Vaughn

"You having fun?" I ask Charly.

"So much fun. Thank you for bringing me with you."

"Yeah, well, it was between you and Doris, who cleans my trailer, but Doris was busy today, so you lucked out."

"You jerk." She chuckles, and I grin.

"I'm glad I asked you, too, Pins," I say in a lower voice.

I kiss the tip of her nose as we dance to an acoustic version of Lady Gaga's "The Edge of Glory" being played by the band my sister hired for her wedding.

The day has been awesome. My mom and sister did an amazing job with putting the whole thing together. The ceremony went off without a hitch. They got married under the willow tree by my parents' house. The tree had lights hanging from it. An altar was just beneath it, covered in white flowers. It looked really cool.

Sasha looks beautiful. Greg even cried when he saw her walking up the aisle, which he is going to get so much shit for but not today. Today, I'll let it slide. I'll just mock him tomorrow. And for the rest of his life.

We've done the sit-down, had our meal in the tent, and laughed at my dad's bad jokes during his speech. And, now, we're partying until the night is over.

But, for me, the best part of today has been Charly. She looks totally fuckable in her dress—a long, floaty dark gray number that is fitted over her breasts, making them look magnificent. Her hair is down and curled, and I desperately want to get my hands all tangled up in it. And her lips are tease-me red. It's been killing me all day because all I've wanted to do is kiss that lipstick right off her mouth and then carry her back to my house and fuck her all night long.

She's been glowing all day. Like she's lit up from the inside out. And, the moment when my sister thanked her in her speech for saving the day by fixing her dress…I honestly thought she was going to cry.

Being here with her has been amazing. Being free to be with her, I never want it to end. I don't want to go back to Vegas tomorrow and go back to pretending that we're not together in front of people.

I just don't know how to ask her again. I don't want to push. But I want it. I want her.

I feel a tug on my pants and look down to see Nora.

"Hey." I smile at her.

"Uncle Vaughn, will you dance with me? My brothers won't dance with me."

"Course I will, beauty. You don't mind, do you, Charly?"

"No, of course not. I need to use the little girls' room anyway."

I pick up Nora in my arms and start to dance with her as Charly makes her way through the dance floor that is filled with my family and friends whom I've known all my life.

Wardrobe
MALFUNCTION

That's another thing. She fits in so effortlessly with my family. They all love her. She couldn't be more perfect for me.

The more I think about this, the more determined I become about wanting to go public. I just need to figure out how to get her on board.

"You look so serious, Uncle Vaughn." Nora's chubby little hands press to my face. And they're sticky. I'm pretty sure with cake.

"I was just thinking."

"About Charly?"

Kid is smart for a three-year-old.

"I like her, Uncle Vaughn. She's really pretty and funny."

"Yeah, she is."

"I think you should marry her. But don't wait as long as Mommy and Daddy did."

I laugh. "Because you want to be a bridesmaid again?"

"Course." She smiles. "I love being a bridesmaid. Look how pretty my dress is."

"You look beautiful, Nora."

"There you are. I've been looking for you."

I turn to my sister, and her eyes are on Nora.

"You feeling tired yet? 'Cause Nanny Porter said she'd put you to bed in Gran and Granddad's house, and she'd sit with you."

"No, I don't wanna go to bed." Nora pouts, arms wrapping around my neck, clinging to me.

"Okay, baby." Sasha laughs. "You don't have to go to bed yet. Wanna come and dance with me and Daddy?"

Nora looks at me and then her mom. "Okay," she says, letting me go.

I hand her over to Sasha.

"Where's Charly?" Sasha asks.

"Bathroom."

"Have you met Ed yet?"

"No." My eyes narrow. "When did he get here?"

Apparently, he couldn't make it to the ceremony because it was his granddaughter's sixteenth birthday, and they were having a party for her. Sounds suspicious if you ask me.

"A few hours ago," Sasha tells me.

"Where is he?" I scan the dance floor.

"In the tent with Gran. They were chatting with Dad."

"Right." I kiss Sasha's cheek and then Nora's. "See you in a few. Oh, and if you see Charly, will you tell her I'm in the tent?"

"Will do," Sasha answers.

I head off the dance floor and in the direction of the tent.

I spot Gran and Ed. They're not with Dad anymore. They're sitting at a table not too far from the bar.

I make my way over, staring at Ed. He's got a lot of hair for a seventy-year-old guy. Probably a wig.

"Hey, Gran," I say as I approach the table. I lean over and kiss her cheek, giving Ed the evil eye as I do.

"Vaughn, this is Ed. Ed, this is my grandson, Vaughn."

"Nice to meet you." He gets to his feet and shakes my hand.

Weak handshake.

I sit on the chair by my grandma.

"So, your grandmother told me that you're an actor."

I glance at my gran, and she's just smiling at Ed.

I look back to Ed. "Yeah, I'm an actor."

"What kind of actor? Theater? I used to do a little amateur theater when I was younger."

Is he taking the piss?

"Ed doesn't watch movies," Gran tells me.

"Not unless they've got Frank Sinatra in 'em." Ed chuckles.

Wardrobe
MALFUNCTION

Ah, okay. He doesn't know who I am, and my gran clearly hasn't enlightened him. I love her a little bit more in this moment. I relax a little toward him.

"So, you do movies then?"

"Mmhmm."

"Interesting." He nods and then looks off across the room.

And that's the end of that conversation for Ed.

"So, how did you two meet?" I ask him.

"On Tinder," my Gran says.

"Tinder."

"Yeah, you know, the dating app that you swipe left or right on. Well, let's just say Ed didn't get swiped left." She winks at him.

And I want to vomit.

Aside from the fact that my gran just winked, she's on Tinder. I have no clue what swiping left or right has to do with anything, and I'm not sure I want to know.

But my gran is on a dating site.

What the fucking fuck?

"Gran, I know what Tinder is. But what I mean is…" I scratch my head. "Why were you on there?"

"Gosh, Vaughn, you do ask some silly questions sometimes. I was trying to find a man, of course." She gives me a knowing look. "So, I downloaded the app onto my phone. Your mom helped me set it up. And that's how I met Ed."

Mom helped her set up a dating app on her phone. What planet am I on right now?

"Hey."

The sound of Charly's voice from behind me is a welcome reprieve. I get to my feet.

"Ed, this is Charly, my grandson's girlfriend."

"Nice to meet you, Ed." Charly gives him a smile.

"You, too," he says.

"Drink," I say. "We're going to the bar. You want anything?" I ask them both.

They shake their heads.

I steer Charly over to the bar.

"Ed seems nice," Charly comments.

"He's on Tinder," I say.

"What?"

I turn to face her. "My gran met him on Tinder. And my mom helped her set up her profile."

She smiles wide. "Go, Grandma! Tinder, eh?"

"You know how it works?"

"Not really. Why?"

"Because my gran said something about swiping left, and then she winked, and—actually, forget it. I don't want to know. Bartender, whiskey. Now."

Vaughn

"I STILL CAN'T BELIEVE Gran is on Tinder," I grumble as I pull my tie off, tossing it to my bedroom floor.

Charly comes over to me, pressing her hands to my chest. "I think it's nice that she's got someone. And she's not on Tinder any more now that she has Ed."

"Semantics," I sigh.

"Your protectiveness over your gran is looking really attractive to me right now."

"You always look attractive to me." I take her face in my hands. "You're beautiful," I tell her.

Then, I do what I've wanted to do all night. I kiss her red lips.

One hand pushes into her hair, and the other slides down her back to her ass, pulling her toward me.

"Let me get out of this dress," she whispers against my mouth.

"That was kind of the plan. Not that you don't look gorgeous in that dress, but I've been looking forward to seeing it on my bedroom floor all day."

She laughs softly and eases back from me. "Five minutes," she says.

"Four, and it's a deal."

"Four." She smiles, kisses me one more time, and disappears off into the bathroom.

I undress, stripping all my clothes off. I switch off the light and climb into bed to wait for her. I sit with my back against the headboard and rest my eyes.

It was a long day but a good day. I realize that I'm the only one left of my siblings who is not married and doesn't have kids.

I think about that for a moment. *What would it be like to be married and have kids? What would it be like with Charly?*

I reckon it would be awesome.

And, apparently, I've turned into a chick, thinking about kids and marriage with the woman I've barely known two months.

I hear the bathroom door click open, and I open my eyes to see Charly standing in the doorway. The light from the bathroom spills out into the bedroom, shining around her.

She looks like an angel.

A purely hot-as-fuck angel that I'm going to dirty right up.

She's wearing a white sheer lace tunic-style slip that falls off her shoulders. It barely skims the tops of her thighs, showing off those gorgeous long legs of hers. Beneath it, she's wearing white lace panties that I plan on tearing off with my teeth. And I know for a fact that she's not wearing a bra because I can see her nipples through the fabric.

I'm instantly as hard as a rock.

I sit up on my knees. "Come here," I tell her.

Wardrobe
MALFUNCTION

She pads across the room, her breasts bouncing gently. I can't wait to get my hands and mouth on them.

Reaching the bed, she climbs onto her knees and meets me in the middle of the bed.

"Hi," she whispers.

"Hi yourself." I reach out and stroke my fingers over her bare shoulder before moving them down to her chest. I run my fingertips over the tops of her breasts through the soft fabric.

"You like?" she asks quietly.

"I like."

I circle her nipple with my finger. It hardens against my touch. Her breathing starts to change. I move my hand lower, smoothing my palm over her stomach. I cup her over her panties.

She's soaking wet.

"You're ready for me," I groan.

"I'm always ready for you."

I push her panties aside and slip a finger inside her.

"Ah," she moans, throwing her head back.

My mouth finds her neck, and I lick a path upward. She lowers her head, bringing her mouth to mine, and she kisses me, deep and wet. Her hands clutch my hair as I fuck her with my finger, palming her with my hand, but I can't get proper access to her clit, as these fucking panties are in the way.

"Are the panties new?" I ask.

"Yes."

"I'll buy you a new pair." Then, I tear them from her body.

"Oh God." She shivers.

I don't miss a beat. I keep fucking her with my finger, my palm now pressing against her clit.

She grinds down onto my hand. "Yes, Vaughn, yes," she moans.

Her hand reaches out, taking my cock in it.

I hiss at the feel of her touching me. It always feels incredible when Charly touches me, each time seeming to get better.

She starts jacking me off. I push another finger inside her. She parts her legs wider, giving me more access. She's absolutely soaking wet.

"I want you on my mouth," I tell her. "Climb on my face, baby."

I lie on my back, expecting her to crawl up, but instead, she turns around and straddles my body.

"Sixty-nine?" I say.

She grins back at me in answer.

"God, you're so fucking hot." I grab her ass and pull her toward my mouth. Lifting my head a little, I lick a path from her hole to her clit and then back again.

I plunge my tongue inside her at the exact same moment that she puts my cock in her mouth.

It's like fucking heaven. Her sweet pussy in my mouth and her mouth on my cock. She sucks me hard, just like I like, jacking me with her hand as well, but then she moves her hand away and takes more of me in…nearly all of me in, deep-throating me.

"Jesus, fuck," I groan, my eyes rolling back in my head.

I lick and tease her clit while she sucks me like a porn star.

Fuck, life is good.

I feel her legs start to tense around me, and I know she's close.

"Come for me, baby," I tell her.

She moans around my cock and starts to move against my tongue, grinding on my face. I grip ahold of her ass, licking her hard.

My cock falls from her mouth. "God, Vaughn…I'm gonna…I'm coming!" she cries, her trembling legs locking around my head as she comes against my mouth.

I keep licking her because I can't stop. I can't get enough of her.

She sags against me. "I don't think I can again."

"You can." I lift her off me, putting her beside me on the bed. "I want this off." I tug on her slip. "And then you on your back."

I'm a bossy fuck.

But she obeys immediately.

She's naked and waiting for me, and I am one lucky bastard.

I spread her lips open with my fingers and put my mouth back on her pussy. She moans loudly, her hips coming up off the bed. I hold her down with my hands on her thighs, and then I start fucking her with my tongue again.

I reach up, grabbing her tit in my hand. I tease her nipple between my thumb and forefinger. My other hand pushes two fingers inside her.

She's moaning and writhing and panting beneath me, and I'm so hard, I could cut glass. My hips are pressed against the bed, trying to find some relief. I need to come so badly, but it's more important that I get her off again. Getting Charly off is what turns me on the most.

"God, Vaughn!" she screams, coming without warning.

I ride through the orgasm with her, licking up everything she gives to me.

She sinks into the bed, her body looking relaxed, but I'm not giving her a reprieve. I need inside her tight body more than I need my next breath.

"On your knees. Now," I command.

Her eyes open, looking at me. They're heavy with desire.

She pushes up to a sitting position. Then, she takes hold of my face with both her hands and kisses me hard, pushing her tongue into my mouth. Then, she lets go and turns away, getting on her hands and knees, giving me her ass.

She looks fucking perfect.

I reach for my nightstand to get a condom. I never had them in my house until Charly. I never needed them here until her.

"Wait," she says just as I've gotten one from the box, staring back at me.

Wait? Is that even a word?

I look at her, confused. She moves across the bed to me.

Her hand curls around mine that has got the condom in it.

"I want to feel you inside me," she says.

"That was the plan all along." I grin.

"Bare," she whispers.

Oh.

"You don't have to if you don't want to, but I wanted you to know that I want to, in case you wanted to, too."

"That was quite a run-on sentence." I smile.

She laughs softly.

"I've never before," I tell her. And it's the truth; I haven't.

"I'm on the pill, and I'm clean. I've never slept with a guy without a condom before either. But I want to with you. There's no pressure. I just wanted you to know the option's there if you want it. I trust you, Vaughn."

I love you.

The words are right there on the tip of my tongue.

She's so fucking amazing.

And I want her so badly. I want to feel her.

"I trust you, too." I toss the condom aside and kiss her.

I lower her back, lying between her legs. She brings them up around my hips. My cock is pressed up against her pussy, hot and bare.

And I can't wait a moment longer.

I break away from her lips. "You're sure?" I check.

"I'm sure. Are you?"

I answer that by pushing inside her.

"Jesus, Charly," I groan, closing my eyes to the feel of her around my cock, hot and snug and so fucking wet.

"I know," she says, her hands sliding into my hair.

"You feel incredible." Lights are dancing behind my eyes. I've never felt anything like her before.

She tugs me down to her mouth and kisses me. I push my tongue into her mouth, taking control of the kiss.

Then, I very slowly pull my cock out of her, drawing out the sensation. When I reach the tip, I ease back in up to the hilt.

"This feels…I've never…not with anyone…God, Charly, you feel like fucking heaven."

Her hand comes up to my face, her fingers dusting over my lips. I catch hold of her middle finger and suck it into my mouth.

I watch as her pupils dilate.

She pulls her finger from my mouth and traces a wet path between her breasts. My cock swells.

I pull back out again and reach my hand between us, taking hold of my dick, and I move him up and down her slit, wet and slippery. I tease her clit with the head of my cock.

"Vaughn." Her back arches off the bed, her fingers gripping ahold of the bed cover. She fixes me with a stare. "I need you to fuck me."

Moving my hand away, I slam back inside her.

"Yes!" she cries.

I take her mouth with mine and start to fuck her slow.

Only it doesn't feel like fucking anymore. It feels like I'm making love to her.

I want to take my time with her because I want this to last. I want to stay here, inside her, for the rest of my life.

Her legs wrap around my back, the heels of her feet digging into me. "Harder, Vaughn. Faster," she moans.

"Impatient." I smile against her mouth.

But, in the end, I give her what she wants. I can't seem to say no to her.

I pull all the way out and thrust back in hard.

"Yes! Again," she cries.

So, I do it again.

I give her more. I give her all of me.

I make love to her in a mixture of hard and fast, slow and gentle until we finally come together, falling apart in each other's arms.

I lie there, breathing heavily against her neck. I lift my head and brush my mouth over hers. "I don't want to move."

"So, don't." She brushes her fingers through my hair. "We can clean up later."

But we don't clean up. We fall asleep there together, wrapped up in each other.

Charly

"You got everything?" Vaughn asks me as he puts our bags in the trunk of his car.

"Yep."

It's time to head back to Vegas. We're driving over to Vaughn's parents', and then his dad is going to drive us to the airport and bring Vaughn's car back.

I'm really sad to be leaving. I've had the best time here with him. I don't want it to be over.

"Here's your cell," he says, handing it to me.

God, my cell.

I can't believe I haven't used it all weekend. I didn't even come out to the car to check my messages. I was too busy having fun with Vaughn and his family. Three days without it, and I survived. And I didn't even miss it. Go figure. I didn't even miss watching TV. They have a TV at his mom and dad's house, and it was on during the times we went over there, but I didn't even bother watching it.

I enjoyed the quiet at Vaughn's. The disconnection to the outside world. Maybe I should do it more often.

Part of me doesn't even want to go back to the real world yet. But I guess I have to sometime.

I press the button to wake my cell up, but the screen stays black. I push it again, and I get the red battery sign.

"My phone's dead," I tell him.

"Yeah, mine is, too." Vaughn chuckles, looking down at his. "That always happens when I come here. Leave it turned on in my car, and the battery just drains. You can charge it in the car if you want. I have a charger in there for occasions such as this."

I smile at him and then drop my phone in my bag. "No, I'm good. I'll wait till I get back to Vegas. Charge it up there."

"You sure?" he checks. "I know how much you love it."

"Not as much as I've loved being here."

He stares at me for a moment and then comes over, resting his arms over my shoulders. I tip my head back, looking up at him.

"I've loved having you here," he tells me.

I smile, my heart doubling in size.

"And I'm not going to charge my phone either."

"No?"

"No. I'm not ready for this weekend to be over." His eyes smile at me.

My insides light up. "Me neither." I lift up on my toes and softly kiss his lips. "Let's drag it out for as long as we can."

"Forever?" he says.

I touch my hand to his face. "If only."

He presses a kiss to the palm of my hand. "We'd best get moving. We've got that flight to catch."

We get in the car, and Vaughn drives us over to his parents'. His dad is already outside, waiting on us.

Wardrobe Malfunction

"They're here," he calls out.

Every member of Vaughn's family piles out of the house to see us off.

"You're coming back once the movie's wrapped?" Vaughn's mom asks him.

"Yeah. I'll be back soon."

She hugs him and then comes over to me. "It was so lovely to meet you, Charly."

"You, too. Thank you for making me feel so welcome."

She hugs me. "I hope to see you again."

"You will," Vaughn says, smiling over at us.

"Guess I'll see you soon then."

His mom smiles and winks at me, and I laugh.

"I'm taking bets on how long it is before he asks her to move in with him," Meg announces.

"I'll put twenty on a month," Gran says.

"I'll take two months, babe," Vic says to his wife.

"For fuck's sake!" Vaughn grumbles.

"Vaughn! Delicate ears!" Sasha's hands go over Nora's ears.

"Too late, Mama. I already heard Uncle Vaughn say the naughty word."

"Fuck's sake!" George mimics.

"George!" Meg covers her hand with her mouth. Then, she narrows her eyes at Vaughn as she reaches over and punches him in the arm.

"Hey! No need for violence."

"If he goes to school saying that, I'm telling his teacher where he learned it."

"Sorry." He laughs, rubbing his arm.

We continue saying our good-byes to everyone.

I feel like I'm in an episode of *The Brady Bunch*, receiving hugs left, right, and center. But in no way am I complaining.

I actually enjoy each and every hug I receive. Weird. Must be Vaughn rubbing off on me. He's a huggy guy.

281

Then, we're done, and it's time to go.

I climb in the backseat, and Vaughn hops in beside me.

Vaughn's dad gets in the driver's seat and turns the engine on. "Ready to go, kids?"

Vaughn takes hold of my hand, linking our fingers. I look at him, and he smiles at me.

"Yeah, we're ready," he tells his dad.

His dad puts the car in drive, and I wave to Vaughn's family as we go, as they're all waving us off.

The farther away we get, the more I start to feel this weird tugging in my chest.

It takes me a moment, but then I realize that tugging in my chest is because I don't want to leave here. Or them.

It's not only Vaughn that I've loved being here with, but his family, too.

Not only have I fallen in love with him, but I've fallen in love with them, too.

And I want this with Vaughn. I don't mean a family...well, maybe in time, but I want this, what we have right now, and more.

I want to share his life and share mine with him. I want us to live in each other's worlds and make our own world together.

I don't want to hide anymore.

I want everyone to know that we're together.

Not because he's Vaughn West, movie star. But because I'm crazy in love with *him*.

I'm in love with the Vaughn West who takes care of me and calls me Pins and makes me laugh and drives me crazy and fucks me like no man has ever done before.

I want to tell him that I'm in love with him.

But none of that can happen until he knows the truth.

He has a right to know. I should have told him weeks ago when I realized things were getting serious between us instead of hiding like a coward.

When we get back to Vegas, I'm going to put my big-girl panties on and sit him down, so I can tell him everything. And then I'm going to pray to God that he understands why I have kept it from him for so long.

Vaughn

"JACK'S BEEN TRYING TO get ahold of you," Aiden says, taking the bags from me and putting them in the trunk of the blacked-out Mercedes he's picked us up at the airport in.

"Hey, Aiden." Charly smiles at him as she climbs in the back of the car.

"Hi," he says flatly.

"My cell's dead," I tell him. "What does he need me for?"

"Not sure." He shrugs, shutting the trunk.

He's acting a little weird. He won't even make eye contact. Seemed a bit off with Charly just then.

"Everything okay?" I ask him.

"Uh-huh. Let's get you back to the hotel." He holds open the back passenger door, waiting for me to get in.

I climb inside, sitting beside Charly and taking her hand. Aiden shuts the door with a soft clunk. A minute later, we're pulling out of the airport.

I rest back in my seat. The peace I always feel after I've been home starts to ebb away, like it always does when I come back to work. Back to the reality of my life.

But having Charly here beside me makes it feel easier somehow. She makes everything feel easy. Better.

We drive through Vegas and reach the hotel in good time. As we drive up, I notice the press is loitering outside.

"For fuck's sake," I sigh.

"What's wrong?" Charly asks, leaning forward to look at what I'm looking at.

"Press is out front of the hotel." I wonder if they've found out I'm staying here. Or it could be for a number of reasons. This is Vegas after all.

"We'll go in through the underground garage," Aiden says.

He drives around and pulls in the parking lot, taking a spot close to the elevators.

I climb out. Charly gets out behind me.

"I'll bring your bags up," Aiden says.

"Okay. See you up there."

We walk toward the elevator, and I catch hold of Charly's hand.

"Weekend's not over yet," I tell her. "Not until we get upstairs."

She smiles warmly at me. I press the call button and wait.

The elevator's empty. We get in, and I press the button for the penthouse. Then, I get my private access card and swipe it. The doors close, and the elevator starts to ascend.

I turn, taking her in my arms, and I press a soft kiss to her lips. "So, I've been thinking."

"Sounds dangerous."

Wardrobe Malfunction

"Funny. Look, I know we've talked about this before, and I know all your reasons for wanting to keep our relationship private, but I don't want to anymore. I want the world to know that you're mine. I've just had the best weekend of my life with you. I've had the best few months of my life with you. I want to take you out on dates. I want to kiss you in public. Yes, I initially asked for us to be a secret, but things have changed now. I didn't know we would become more…this. I know I'm asking a lot. I'm asking you to give up your privacy to be with me. But…" I take a deep breath. "I love you, Charly. I'm in love with you."

She's staring at me with a mixture of emotions on her face. I can definitely pick out happiness in there, but there's fear, too, and that worries the shit out of me.

"God, Vaughn. I…" She squeezes her eyes shut.

"Okay, I'm gonna be honest here, Pins. Not the response I was hoping for."

She opens her eyes. "I'm sorry." And she really looks it. "There's just something you need to know. Something I need to tell you before we go any further. It's important."

"Okay." My head starts to ring with warning bells. I step back from her just as the elevator reaches our floor. "We can talk inside."

I turn to step out of the elevator, and Jack is standing there, waiting for me.

"Jesus, Jack! You scared the shit out of me. What are you doing here?"

His eyes flicker past me to Charly. "I've been trying to get ahold of you for hours."

"My cell is dead."

"I called your mom, but she said you'd already left."

"Well, I'm here now. What's the problem?"

His eyes go to Charly again, who's still standing behind me. I don't like the way he keeps looking at her.

Did the press find out about her and me? Do they know that her dad murdered her mom?

Would make sense with the way that Jack has a face like thunder.

"Let's go inside and talk." Jack jerks his head in the direction of my suite.

"How did you get in?" I ask, following him.

Charly is lagging behind me. I reach back and take hold of her hand, pulling her to my side. I give her a reassuring smile. She gives me a tight one in return.

"Alex let me in. He's here, too."

He looks at me holding Charly's hand, and his expression tightens.

Guess the cat's out of the bag. Oh well.

We step inside, and I shut the door behind us. Alex is sitting on the sofa. He stands when he sees us. I jerk my chin in greeting at him.

His smile is tight.

"Okay, so what's the problem? I'm guessing you know Charly and I are together—"

"Vaughn."

"I'm not just fucking her. I'm in love with her."

"Jesus." Jack rubs his face. "He doesn't know, does he?" He's looking at Charly.

I feel her tense beside me, and I hate that Jack is making her feel uncomfortable.

"Jack, let me stop you there." I hold a hand up. "If you're talking about Charly's dad, then I already know everything."

"Do you want to tell him, or should I?" He's talking to Charly again.

"Tell me what?" I look down at Charly, and she's paled. The expression on her face makes my stomach sink.

Then, her words in the elevator ring clear in my head.

"There's just something you need to know. Something I need to tell you before we go any further. It's important."

Wardrobe
MALFUNCTION

Releasing her hand, I step back to face her. "Charly? What's going on?" My voice betrays me and wobbles, giving away the fear and dread I'm feeling inside because I know for certain that, whatever this is, it's not going to be good.

"I, um..." She runs a hand through her hair.

I see that it's shaking. She glances over at Alex and Jack.

"Charly?" I say her name.

But she doesn't look at me.

So, I say it again louder this time, "Charly."

Her eyes snap to mine.

"Just tell me what the fuck is going on."

"I'm married."

The words drop in the silence of the room, and they hit me like a wrecking ball. I feel pain in every part of my body.

"What?" I breathe.

"She's married," Jack pipes up.

"I fucking got that!" I yell at him. My eyes swing back to her. "You're married?" The words fall out of me.

"I'm sorry. I should have told you."

She steps toward me, and I step back.

"Preferably before you let me fuck you!" I roar.

She visibly flinches.

"It's all over the news, Vaughn. The press got pictures of you two together in Oregon. Intimate pictures. They somehow found out Charly's name, and they looked her up. Digby exposed it on his show a few hours ago," Alex says quietly.

"Oh no." Charly covers her face with her trembling hands.

"I don't fucking believe this!" My hands are in my hair, and I'm pacing.

Jack says, "We need to get on top of this, Vaughn. Put out a press release straightaway—"

"Stop! Just stop right fucking there." I point at Jack, silencing him.

I turn back to Charly. "You're actually fucking married?" I can't believe I'm saying this when, moments ago, I was telling her that I was in love with her.

"I am, but it's complicated."

"Are you separated or getting divorced?"

She briefly closes her eyes, biting her upper lip hard. "It's complicated," she repeats.

My head explodes.

"There's nothing complicated about the question! It's a simple yes or no answer!"

I see her eyes flicker to Jack and Alex.

"Don't fucking look at them! Look at me!" I yell, grabbing ahold of her by her upper arms, forcing her to look at me. "Are you separated or getting divorced?" I repeat.

There's this awful, painful silence where her eyes fill with tears, and her bottom lip quivers.

She shakes her head.

And my heart breaks. I actually feel it break in two.

I drop my hands from her like she's burned me.

Because she has.

"Then, we have nothing else to talk about." And I turn around and walk out of there to the sound of her crying out my name.

Charly

FOUR YEARS AGO, I made the best decision of my life.

I married my best friend, Nick.

Not because we were in love—though I do love him. I love him like a sister loves her brother. But I married Nick because he needed a visa to be able to stay in the country.

Nick is from Canada. He was here in the US on a student visa. When he finished studying, he couldn't find a company to take him on permanently. He was temping, going from job to job. He applied for a temporary work visa, but because he couldn't get a job with a fixed time period, it was denied.

So, he was either facing deportation or staying as an illegal.

He didn't want to do either.

You see, like me, Nick is alone in this world. Nick's parents were deeply religious. When he took the risk and told them he was gay, they rejected him. They threw him out of the only home he'd ever known. Nick couch-surfed for a while, staying with friends. Then, he made the decision to come to the US. So, he applied to some colleges and was accepted into The Art Institute of New York City. After being accepted, he was granted a study visa.

So, he bought a plane ticket to New York and left for the US.

I met him a month later.

I guess that's why we gravitated toward one another when we met. Two lost and lonely souls looking for something…looking for a home.

We found that home in each other.

From the moment I met Nick, he became my family, and I, his.

When it was looking like I could possibly lose him, I panicked. I couldn't lose Nick. He was all I had. I loved him. And, selfishly, I didn't want to go back to being alone.

So, I came up with the idea of Nick and I getting married. That way, he'd be able to stay in the country. When I told him about my idea, he shot me down. He said he wouldn't let me do that for him.

But I argued that it was no big deal. I was twenty-one, so it wasn't like I was going to be getting married anytime soon. And we just needed to stay married for two years until he got his permanent residency visa.

Okay, we were breaking the law. But keeping Nick in New York was more important. For me, the reward far outweighed the possible consequence. And, like I said to Nick, we were practically married. We lived together. Spent all of our time together. Knew each other inside and out. We were best friends.

We just didn't have the physical aspect that came with a relationship.

It would be easy for us to convince an immigration officer that we were in love. I adored Nick, and he adored me. We knew everything about each other. Convincing

someone we were marrying out of love wouldn't be hard because we were. It just wasn't the kind of love that people usually entered into marriages for.

So, after a lot of talking and me convincing Nick, we decided to do it.

We also agreed to stay married for four to five years to make it seem more real to the authorities. And we decided to keep our marriage to ourselves.

We were both temping at different jobs, so it wasn't like we had work colleagues that the immigration office could interview to find out about us. And we didn't have any other close friends, so it was easy to pass off.

A week later, we bought some cheap plane tickets to Vegas, left, and got married.

Nick got to stay in the US. He applied for permanent residency two years later and was approved.

We could have divorced then, but like we had agreed, to make it appear real to the authorities, we decided to stay married for another two to three years.

There wasn't any rush for us to divorce. Neither of us had met anyone special. We dated other people, of course. It was probably risky. But we figured, if we did get found out, then we would pass it off that we were swingers or had an open marriage. There's no law against that.

So, the time passed, and everything was great. We were actually approaching the time when we had agreed to get divorced, but it wasn't something that was at the forefront of my mind.

And then I met Vaughn.

And everything changed.

I didn't expect to fall in love with him. Or for the press to find out about us and expose my past before I had the chance to tell Vaughn the truth.

It was naive of me. I know that now.

I just didn't know marrying Nick all those years ago would cost me the love of my life today.

I don't regret marrying Nick. I wouldn't change what I did. I would marry him again in a heartbeat.

What I would change is telling Vaughn. I would have told him sooner. The moment I realized things were serious between us.

Because keeping it from Vaughn is ultimately what caused me to lose him.

I guess my only excuse is, apart from my cowardice, that being with Vaughn felt like a fairy tale. Too good to be true. Especially for someone like me.

But it was real, and I've lost it. I've lost him.

And, even now, he still doesn't know the whole truth. He left before I could tell him.

I felt trapped in that moment with Jack and Alex there. I couldn't tell him the real reason I was married in front of them and risk putting myself in jail and having Nick deported.

So, I had to let him believe the worst. I had to watch him walk out the door and leave, thinking that I'd betrayed him in the worst way possible. Just like Cain had.

And, now, Vaughn is gone. Took the car from Aiden, and I don't know where he is or how to reach him because his phone is still off.

But I do know one thing. I have to speak to him again. I have to tell him the whole story. Even if he doesn't forgive me, he needs to know that I didn't betray him in the way he thinks I did.

And that I'm sorry.

And that I love him.

Vaughn

I TAKE THE ELEVATOR straight down to the parking garage. If Aiden's not there, then I'll go out on the street and get a cab if I have to. I just need to get the fuck out of here.

When I exit the elevator, I see Aiden standing by the car, his cell phone pressed to his ear.

He looks up at my approach. "Jack wants to talk to you." He holds the phone out to me.

I take the phone from him and disconnect the call. Then, I hand the phone back to him.

"Key," I tell him.

He doesn't seem surprised that I want to leave.

He knew. Everyone knew. Everyone, except for me. Yet again.

Vaughn West, the dumbest fuck on the planet.

God, the press must be laughing their asses off at me right now.

My hurt and anger burn even hotter. "Give me the fucking car key, Aiden."

"Jack won't like this."

"I don't give a fuck whether Jack likes it or not. And Jack doesn't pay your wages. I do."

Aiden hands me the key. I get in the car, slam the door shut, turn the engine on, and squeal out of there.

I hit the street. Not knowing where I'm going or what the hell to do with myself.

I can't fucking believe this. She's married. Married! All this time, and she never said a word. How could she do this to me?

I'm so fucking stupid. First, Cain and Piper. Now, Charly.

I must have *Dumb Fuck* written on my forehead.

I took her to my home. Introduced her to my family. I let her in my bed. I fell in love with her.

And, all that time, she was married.

"Fuck!" I slam my hand against the steering wheel. "Fuck! Fuck! Fuck!"

Breathing heavily, I grip the wheel tight with both hands, trying to get a handle on my emotions.

How could she look me in the face and lie to me like that? Was she fucking me and then climbing out of my bed and calling him up? Telling him she loved him?

Because she sure as fuck doesn't love me.

Jesus.

I don't even know who her husband is. But I'm guessing he knows about me by now.

The whole world probably fucking knows.

Embarrassment covers me like a dirty black cloak.

I can't stay in Vegas. I need to get away. I need to go back home.

I turn the car in the direction of US-95, heading north to Oregon.

Once I'm on the highway, I turn on the radio.

"And, in entertainment news today, pictures are circulating of Hollywood sensation Vaughn West, who has been caught in an intimate moment with a married woman. The woman has been identified as Charlotte Michaels, a

wardrobe assistant on the set of West's current film, *The Lament*."

I reach out to turn it off when the sound of her husband's name stops me.

"Ms. Michael's husband, Nick Sharp, an interior designer, resides in New York with her. They've been married for four years. When approached, Mr. Sharp wouldn't comment on if he had any knowledge of the relationship between his wife and Vaughn West. We reached out to West's publicist, but we have yet to hear back.

"And, in other news, Patrick Dean is back in rehab—"

I turn the station off.

Nick Sharp.

She told me that Nick was her gay roommate, whom she'd known since college. God, she's a better fucking liar than me, and I get paid to do it for a living.

My head feels like it's going to explode. I can't think about it anymore.

I need music to fill my head, but Aiden doesn't have any CDs in here. I turn the radio back on, search through until I find a heavy metal station, and turn it up loud.

Twelve hours and two gas stop breaks later, I'm finally driving into Keno.

It's late. I'm tired. And my fucking head aches.

If I'm being honest, everything aches. My heart especially.

At the last rest stop, I decided to charge my phone, using the charger that Aiden had left in here.

I know Jack and Alex have been trying to call me. There are missed calls and countless messages from both of them.

There are missed calls and messages from Charly, too. But I won't listen to them.

I don't want to talk to anyone, and I especially don't want to talk to her.

What does she need to talk to me about? I think everything that needed to be said was said back at the hotel.

But I should call Jack. I know he'll be worried about me.

I press Call on his number and wait for it to connect.

He answers on the first ring, "Where the hell are you?"

"I'm fine. I just need some time alone."

I don't tell him I'm home. Even though Jack's never been here, I know he'd come charging down here and get me to go back to Vegas. And, right now, that's the last place I want to be.

"You need to get your ass back here. I've got the press on the phone nonstop. Brandon's freaking out. You're supposed to be back on set tomorrow."

I sigh. "Tell Brandon I'm sorry. And that I'll call him soon."

"You're sorry? What the hell is that supposed to mean?"

"It means I won't be there tomorrow, Jack."

"You can't just run out on a film, Vaughn. You're committed to this. You signed a contract."

"I know. I just need a few days."

"The delay will cost millions, Vaughn. Brandon could sue."

"So, let him sue me. Or ask him to just give me two days, and then I'll be back."

"He won't like it."

"I know. But he doesn't have a choice."

There's a pause.

Then, Jacks says, "Stupid question, but how are you doing?"

I laugh humorlessly. "I've had better days."

"She's gone," he tells me in a lowered voice. "Left not long after you did."

I want to ask if he knows where she was going. But part of me already knows. She's going back to him. Her husband.

"You should've told me—about you and her. I could've done a background—"

"Not now, Jack, okay?"

"Okay." He sighs. "So, I'll see you in a few days?"

"You will." I disconnect the call and turn my phone off.

I take the turn onto my parents' farm. Driving up the track, I see the lights are still on at their house. Then, I look at my house off in the distance.

The last time I was there, I was with her.

I turn off to my parents' house and park out front there. I can't stay in my house tonight.

My mom comes out the front door just as I climb out of the car.

"Hey, baby," she says, a sad smile on her face.

"Hi, Mom."

I walk over to her, and she wraps her arms around me, hugging me.

"It's going to be okay," she tells me.

"I know," I say, but I don't believe it.

Because nothing about this feels like it's ever going to be okay.

I thought what I felt after Cain betrayed me was bad. But this, with Charly...it's a million times more painful.

Charly

"I'M SO, SO SORRY," I tell Nick on the phone.

"Charly, it's not your fault."

It is. It's all my fault. But I don't bother arguing with him. I know Nick will never see the bad in me. Just like I never would in him.

After Vaughn walked out on me, I was left there in his hotel suite with Jack and Alex. *Uncomfortable* didn't even cut it. So, I walked out without a word to either of them and came to my hotel.

The room was too silent, so I made the stupid mistake of putting the TV on. The first thing that came on was *E! News*, and the presenters were discussing Vaughn and me. The moment I heard the word *cheater*, I switched it off and rang Nick.

"Are they still out there?" I ask.

"The press? Yeah, there's a bunch of them hanging around the front of our building."

I cover my face with my hand. "I can't believe this is happening."

"It's gonna be fine, gorgeous."

"No, it's not!" I cry. "The whole world thinks I'm a cheating whore. The press is camped outside our building, hounding you. And Vaughn hates me."

"He doesn't hate you."

"You didn't see the way he looked at me right before he left."

"You're impossible to hate."

"Stop trying to make me feel better."

"You want me to make you feel worse? Homewrecker. Is that better?"

"A little." I sigh. "What are we going to do, Nick?"

"Right now, we are going to do nothing."

"But what about immigration? They'll know what's happened with Vaughn. Everyone knows."

"I'm a US resident now, Charly. As far as immigration is concerned, you had an affair. Even if we get divorced, it won't change anything to do with my residency. We only stayed married to make it seem real. You having an affair seems real enough." He chuckles.

"Not funny."

"Sorry."

I let out a sad sigh, picking at the hem of my top. "He's never going to forgive me."

"Vaughn? He will when you tell him the truth."

"I was going to. I just didn't get the chance."

"You should have talked to me, Charly. Told me how serious it was getting between the two of you. I would have encouraged you to tell him about you and me. We could have started the divorce proceedings."

"I know. I fucked up. Big time. I'm sorry." I feel like that's all I've been saying. "I should have discussed it with you first before considering telling Vaughn. But the decision was taken out of my hands."

Wardrobe
MALFUNCTION

"Do you trust Vaughn?"

"Yes," I say without hesitation.

"Then, I trust him, too. Go see him, and tell him everything. He's gotta be hurting a hell of a lot right now. The very least he deserves is to know that what the press is saying isn't exactly the truth."

"But I don't know where he is, Nick. He left hours ago, and he hasn't been back since. Alex says he doesn't know where he is, that he can't get ahold of him. Not that he would tell me even if he did know where he was."

"I'm guessing he wants to be alone right now. Do you know of any places where he would go to do that?"

I don't even need to think about it. "He'd go home."

God, his family. What must they think of me? They're going to hate me for what I've done to him.

The thought makes my heart break just that little bit more.

"So, go there. Talk to him."

"What if he won't listen to me?"

"Then, make him listen. You can be pretty persuasive when you want to be."

"And you'll be okay there with the press?"

"I'll be fine."

"Nick?"

"Yeah?"

"I love you."

"Love you, too, gorgeous. Now, go get your man."

I hang up with Nick and look up flights to Oregon. There's one leaving in three hours. There are no direct flights. I'll have to fly from Vegas to Portland. Then, from Portland to Klamath Falls. It'll take five hours to get there. There's no private jet to get me there in two hours now. And the ticket is nearly four hundred dollars. But it's worth it. Even if I just get to see him one last time.

Using my credit card, I book the ticket.

I quickly pack my things into my case, and then I call down to the front desk and ask them to call me a cab, for it to pick me up outside the parking garage. I don't want to risk running into any press outside the hotel.

Before I leave my hotel room, I fire off a quick text to Ava, telling her that I'm leaving and that I'm sorry and I'll call her soon. I'm too chickenshit to call her right now.

I drop my phone in my bag and let myself out of the room.

I manage to make it to the lobby. I drop my key into the quick checkout box. The studio is paying for my room, so the hotel will just invoice them.

I take the elevator down to the parking garage. I walk up to the car entry and slip out under the barrier. Then, I wait by the wall for my cab.

It appears a few minutes later. The cabbie gets out and puts my case in the trunk.

"The airport," I tell him as I climb into the backseat.

I hear my phone beep a text.

My heart races. I wonder if it could be Vaughn, but I know it won't be.

It's Ava.

> *Ava: Don't worry. I understand. Just call me as soon as you can. Let me know you're okay. Love ya. xx*

In that moment, my heart swells. She didn't even try to question me about Vaughn. She just cares that I'm okay.

Maybe I do have more good friends than I realized.

Eight hours later, five of them spent on two different planes, and I'm back in Klamath Falls Airport where I flew out of a day ago with Vaughn.

I can't believe how much has changed in twenty-four hours.

I head outside to the taxi area and toward a waiting cab.

Then, I realize that I don't actually know Vaughn's address. *Shit.*

"Where to, love?" he asks me through the open window.

"Keno. About a mile past the elementary school. I'll know it when I get there."

"Okay," he says. "You want your case in the trunk?"

"Please."

He gets out of the car and takes my case from me. I climb into the backseat and put my seat belt on.

He gets back in the car, and then we're moving.

I sit on my hands and try to pretend that they aren't shaking and that my heart isn't racing.

Twenty minutes later, the cabbie is driving past the elementary school. I recognize the upcoming turn.

"Left here," I tell the cabbie.

He takes the turn and starts to drive down the driveway toward the farm.

"Keep going past the first house," I tell him.

He drives past Vaughn's parents' house and then up to Vaughn's house.

"Nice place," he comments.

I pay him the fare and climb out. "I'll get my case; don't worry," I tell him.

I lug my case from the trunk, and the cab pulls away.

I stare up at Vaughn's house.

You can do this, Charly.

I take a deep breath. Legs trembling, I pull my case up onto the porch and knock on his door.

It's silent. There's no movement.

I knock again louder and wait. After a few minutes, I finally accept that he's not here.

Shit.

What do I do?

I came all this way, thinking he'd be here, that I hadn't even considered that he wouldn't be.

I can go to his parents', but honestly, I'm afraid to face them. What they must think of me.

I can wait here, but if he doesn't come, then I'm stuck.

Fuck. I didn't think this through at all.

A lump thickens in my throat. And I feel like I might cry. Only I can't fucking cry. Not even yesterday when I had to tell Vaughn that I was married. My eyes welled with tears, but they never fell.

I'm broken.

I'm a screwed up, broken, fucking idiotic twathole of a person.

And I'm staring at his front door like it's somehow going to magically open.

I turn around, unsure of what to do, and then all thoughts fall from my mind. Because he's standing there at the front of his driveway, staring at me.

He looks beautiful. Tired but beautiful. My heart actually starts to ache from his nearness. My hands itch to touch him.

"What are you doing here?" he says in a low, hard voice.

I take a strengthening breath in. "I need to talk to you."

"I already told you back in Vegas that I heard all I needed to. Shouldn't you be in New York right now? I think you owe your husband a bigger explanation than you do with me. You did promise to honor him and not screw around behind his back."

"I've already spoken to Nick. And I wasn't screwing around behind his back."

"You're married! And you were screwing me! Most people would call that cheating, Charly. Decent people at least."

Okay, so that hurt. But it's nothing I don't deserve.

"You don't know everything." I take a step forward.

He takes one back. "And I don't want to. We're done here."

He turns to walk away from me.

"We're nowhere near done!" I yell. "I came all the way here, and you will listen to what I have to tell you!"

"The hell I will!" He turns back to me. "I don't have to listen to anything you have to say! You lied to me! Jesus! You even told me about Nick, that he was your gay roommate, and all along, he was your fucking husband! How fucking warped is your mind?"

"Nick *is* gay! And he is my roommate! He's my best friend and my family! And he's Canadian! He came here on a student visa, and when he graduated, he couldn't get residency because he didn't have a permanent job. He was looking at deportation, so I came up with the idea that we get married, so he could stay in the country because he was all I had in the world, and I didn't want to lose him!" I break off, panting.

Vaughn is just standing there, staring at me, saying nothing.

"I wanted to tell you," I say in a softer voice. "I was going to tell you when we got back to Vegas because I realized that I wanted...you. All of you. And I knew I couldn't have you without you knowing the truth. But the press beat me to it, and I'm so sorry for that, Vaughn. You don't know how sorry I am." I press my hand to my chest, making my way off the porch and onto the drive, so there are only a few feet left between us.

"I didn't mean for any of this to happen. I couldn't tell you in the beginning because we were just sleeping together, and what I did, marrying Nick...I broke the law.

If the authorities found out, then I would face jail, and Nick would be deported."

"So, why are you telling me now? I could go to the police. Tell them. Have Nick deported."

I swallow down. "Because you have a right to know the truth. The actual truth. You *deserve* to know. And I trust you. But, if you need to tell the authorities, then I'll face that, whatever happens. But Nick...he has no one back in Canada. His family threw him out when he came out to them. His whole life, his career, is in New York." My throat is starting to burn, my eyes stinging with tears. "Punish me for hurting you. But not him. He hasn't done anything wrong."

He sighs and scrubs his hands over his face. "Okay," he says, dropping his hands.

"Okay?"

"Okay. You've told me. I won't say anything to anyone."

"Thank you," I breathe.

"But you and I are done."

And my heart shatters into a million pieces.

"I admire what you did for your friend. Even though it's illegal, it was a selfless thing to do. But you lied to me, Charly. You lied for months. You looked me in the eye day after day and didn't tell me. I don't trust you anymore." He rubs his hands over his head. "And you humiliated me, and I have been humiliated enough this year to last me a fucking lifetime."

He doesn't want me anymore.

"You...you said you loved me...that you're in love with me." The words physically hurt me.

He looks away. "I don't trust you anymore. And, without that, we have nothing."

And there it is.

I'm never going to see him again. Except that I will see his face everywhere, in magazines and on-screen.

Wardrobe
MALFUNCTION

It's going to be so hard to be reminded that I had him and I lost him, and I only have myself to blame.

I'll never get to be close to him again. Never kiss him or hold him or make love to him.

A ball of pain forms in my chest and ruptures. I've never felt anything like it.

I press a hand to my chest, expecting to see blood there.

But there's nothing.

Then, something wet and hot runs down my cheek, hitting my lip.

I touch a finger to it. Pulling it away, I see a tear sitting on the tip of it.

I'm crying.

I swallow past the aching, burning pain I feel. "Vaughn."

He looks up at me.

"I love you. I'm not saying that to try and win you back. I know that I had my chance, and I ruined it. But I couldn't leave without telling you." I brush the falling tears away with the back of my hand.

Forcing myself to move, I go back up the porch and get my case.

It's time to go.

I walk toward him, not taking my eyes from him. He's not looking at me. His eyes are on the ground.

I will him to look at me, but he doesn't.

Reaching him, I stop a foot away. But the gap between us feels an awful lot bigger.

Silence stretches.

He finally looks at me.

I force myself to smile. I know it's a sad smile, but it's the best I can manage while my heart is breaking. "What we had…it was and always will be the most important time in my life. I'll remember it and you forever."

I go to touch him one last time. I step closer, just to touch my hand to his arm, but he moves away.

He doesn't even want me to touch him.

The rejection stings my cheeks and brings on a fresh set of tears. I force myself to smile through them even though my lips are trembling and my heart is dying.

"Have the best life, Vaughn West. Be happy. You, more than anyone, deserve it."

One last look at him, and then I walk away, pulling my case behind me. I don't look back.

Tears are streaming down my face. I bite my lip to stop the sob that wants to burst out of me.

All I want is to lie down on the grass and curl up into a ball, but I force myself to keep going while my hand rubs away tears that won't stop falling.

I guess, when you open the dam, a fuck-load of water comes rushing out.

I keep walking, not sure of what I'm doing or where to go. I can see Vaughn's parents' house coming up, and I don't want them to see me.

They must hate me. I kind of hate myself right now.

So, I keep my focus ahead and walk quickly.

I need to get a cab and get out of here. Only I don't know the numbers of any cab companies. I've just got to pray Uber works around here.

I just need to get off the farm and onto the main road, and then I can take a breath and figure out how to get to the airport.

I can just stay there until there's a flight out of here. God, I don't even know if there's a direct flight to New York.

"Charly."

The sound of Vaughn's grandma's voice brings me to a stop. I covertly dry my face on my hand and take a breath before turning to her.

"Hi," I say.

She smiles. "You're leaving?"

I glance back at Vaughn's house. "Yes. Look, I'm really sorry about Vaughn…what happened—"

"Can I tell you a secret?"

Her words surprise me.

But I answer her in the only way I can right now, "That's the one thing I am good at—keeping secrets." I make a self-derogatory laugh at myself.

"I was married once," she tells me. "Before I met Vaughn's granddaddy, I was married to a man I didn't love. Something tells me that you did the same. Probably for very different reasons, but we both married men we weren't in love with. Mine was for money to help save my family from bankruptcy. Your reason…I'm not sure of, but you definitely didn't marry for love. That, I know for sure."

"What makes you so sure?" My voice is small, timid.

"Call it intuition. Or because of the way you look at my grandson. You only look at one man in your lifetime the way you look at Vaughn. I know because it's the exact same way I used to look at Vaughn's granddaddy. Like the day began and ended with him. Well, that, and the fact that you came straight here to see Vaughn instead of going home to your husband."

She's got me there.

I stare at my feet, unsure of what to say.

"You want a cocktail?" she asks. "I just made up a jug of piña colada."

I lift my eyes to her. "It's pretty early in the day to be drinking."

"Nonsense." She waves my words away with her hands. "It's never too early for a cocktail." She turns and starts to walk toward the house.

I stay rooted to the spot, unsure if I should go inside. If I can go inside.

Surely, they all must hate me. I must be the last person on earth that his family wants to see.

I honestly don't know why his grandma is being so kind to me.

She stops and turns back to me. "Nobody's home, if that's what you're worried about. They're out for the day at the farmers market. So, do you want that piña colada or not?"

I glance at Vaughn's house, and my eyes start to sting with tears again. I realize that I'm not ready to leave just yet.

"Okay," I say, looking back at her. "A piña colada would be nice."

It's not like I have anywhere else to be right now. And a cocktail might be just what I need to take away this aching Vaughn-shaped hole inside my chest.

Vaughn

I'VE BEEN LYING HERE, on my sofa, for two hours now, staring at my ceiling.

After Charly left, I came in my house and lay down on the sofa, and I haven't moved since. Well, if I'm being precise, it's been more than two hours since she left. It's been two hours and seventeen minutes.

Only she didn't leave. I sent her away.

Shawn Mendes's "Stitches" ends, and Snow Patrol's "You Could Be Happy" starts to play on my phone.

I might have broken my own rule and brought my cell into my house.

I didn't want to sit in silence, so I only brought it in to listen to music. While I stare at the ceiling. Not thinking about Charly.

I didn't bring it inside in case she called.

Not that she would because I told her that we were over. She has no reason to call, except that she has no car.

And she left here on foot.

I'm guessing she got here by cab.

And I let her go and walk out of here, alone.

I should have driven her where she needed to go. I might be angry with her and not want to be with her anymore, but I shouldn't have just let her leave here to walk on foot.

I wasn't thinking straight at that moment.

I don't know if I should call her just to make sure she's okay. But I don't want her to get the wrong idea. I don't want her to think I've changed my mind about us.

Because I haven't.

I don't want to be with her. I don't trust her. She lied and humiliated me.

She'll be fine. Of course she will. I'm sure she called a cab.

But…what if she couldn't get a cab, and she got stuck? I know Pins; she's stubborn, so she won't ask for help.

And she definitely wouldn't ask me for help because, you know, I told her that we were done.

Because we are.

I am. Done, that is.

But I should call her to make sure she's okay. Not because I want to hear her voice one last time, but because I'm a good guy.

Sitting up, I turn the music off and go to her number in my Contacts. I'm staring at her number when my gran's voice calls into the living room as she comes in through the front door.

"Vaughn?"

"Living room," I tell her.

I put my phone down beside me.

She sits in the chair across from me and puts a flask on the table. "I brought you some piña colada. I had some leftover."

Wardrobe Malfunction

I swear, she's been turning into an alcoholic since she got that cocktail-maker.

"Thanks." I pick it up, open the lid on the flask, and take a sip. Wow, it's not lacking alcohol. Piña coladas are not really my thing, but it's got liquor in it, and I could do with some right now.

"Good?" she asks.

I put the flask back down on the table. "Strong."

"So, good then." She folds her hands in her lap. "So, should I take it that you're sitting here and feeling sorry for yourself?"

"I'm not feeling sorry for myself."

"Uh-huh. Of course you're not."

Silence.

"I saw Charly."

My eyes snap up to hers. "You didn't give her a hard time, did you? Because you don't know the full story."

A smile creeps onto her lips, but her eyes frown at me. "Of course I didn't give her a hard time. What do you take me for?"

"Protective. Like a guard dog, only Chihuahua-sized."

She laughs. "No, I talked to her. Invited her in the house. Gave her some piña colada."

"She's still here?" I tense.

"No. She left a little while ago. Called a cab."

Well, at least I know she got off safely. I don't need to call her now.

I glance down at my phone.

"Was she okay?" I ask.

"Do you care?"

"No." *Yes.*

"Then, why ask?"

"Because you drummed good manners into me while I was growing up."

"Good to know you listened. And you can listen to me now again."

315

"Please, Gran." I sigh. "I'm not in the mood right now." I flop back against the sofa, covering my face with my hands. "And you don't know the full story, so you can't pass comment on it."

"Charly told me."

I drop my hands from my face and sit up. "She told you what?" I ask carefully.

"Everything. About her marrying that gay Canadian friend of hers to get him a green card."

She told my gran.

"Gran, you can't tell anyone. It would get her in serious trouble if the authorities found out. She'd go to jail."

"Good Lord, boy, I'm not dumb. Of course I know she'd go to jail. You, on the other hand, are looking pretty dumb to me right now."

"Jesus, Gran. Kick a guy while he's down, why don't you?"

Even though she's not wrong. I do look like a dumb fuck. First, Piper and Cain. Now, Charly.

"Do you know what your problem is, Vaughn?"

"No, but I'm sure you're going to tell me."

"You care too much about what people think of you. You never used to, but when you got out there in Hollywood, it changed you."

"Of course I care what people think about me. My career depends on it. And, right now, I look like a fucking idiot—yet again. It'll probably be inscribed on my headstone—*Vaughn West, Dumb Fuck Who Didn't Know His Best Friend Was Screwing His Girlfriend Behind His Back for Months. And the Next Girl He Met and Fell for Turned Out to Be Fucking Married.*"

"That kind of wordage would be expensive on a headstone, Vaughn. And I don't think they allow curse words either."

I give her a droll look. "Then, I'll ask them to use an asterisk in *fuck*."

"God, you're dramatic." She laughs. "So, the world thinks Charly cheated on you? Big deal."

"I look stupid."

"You don't look stupid. People, if anything, feel sorry for you."

"I do look stupid," I argue. "And this could affect my career in a negative way. The stuff with Piper and Cain was bad enough, but at least I was the victim in it. In this, I look like the wife-stealer."

"Good Lord, Vaughn. Who cares what people think? Did you know that Eddie Fisher left Debbie Reynolds, his wife and the mother of his child, for Elizabeth Taylor, his wife's close friend? He married her the same year he divorced Debbie. Do you think that did any harm to their careers? No. People love scandal. That didn't do Eddie's or Liz's careers any harm."

"Things are different nowadays, Gran."

"No, they're not. There might be all this social media now, but it's just a different century with the same kind of people with the same opinions. And opinions are like assholes, Vaughn. Everyone has one, and everyone knows one. Stop caring what everyone else thinks, and think about what *you* want."

"I don't know if I can trust her," I tell her honestly.

"Relationships don't work without trust."

"I know," I sigh. "That's why I let her go."

"I guess you've got to think about if you'll look back at this and think you made the right decision by letting her go. Or if you'll look back and regret it."

"Do you have any regrets?" I ask her.

"None. Because every decision I ever made brought me to where I am now, and I've had a damn good life."

"You've still got a good life," I remind her.

"I don't have regrets, but I did have a choice to make a long time ago. And the one thing I do wish is that I hadn't taken so long to make it."

"But you made the right choice."

She looks at me and smiles with a softness in her expression that I rarely see on my Gran's face. "I made the best choice. Remember, you only get one shot at this life, Vaughn, so you gotta grab it by the balls and make the most of it."

Hearing my gran say *balls* makes me chuckle. And also reminds me of Charly and the first time we met.

Pins.

My Pins.

I rub my hands over my face.

Is my problem that I don't think I can trust her? Or is it about caring what everyone will think of me if I stay with her?

And I know it's the latter.

I've been letting my head…my ego…rule my heart.

I look at Gran. "You're right. I do care too much about what people think."

"The wrong people," she says.

And she's right.

When the only person I should be caring about is Charly. What she thinks of me.

My gran is right. Screw what everyone else thinks. I want Charly.

And I'm going to get her.

I stand up. "Do you know where Charly is right now?"

A slow smile spreads across my gran's face. "As a matter of fact, I do."

Charly

AFTER I WENT OVER to Vaughn's parents' house with his gran, we sat down in the living room. She gave me a piña colada. I downed the whole thing in one go, and then I started spilling my guts like a pig that had just been cut open for slaughter. I told her everything—the truth about my marriage to Nick.

But something tells me that I can trust Phoebe.

Or maybe it was just the two strong piña coladas telling me that.

Either way, it doesn't matter.

I lost Vaughn, so nothing matters to me right now.

I know I should ring Nick and tell him what happened, but I just can't bring myself to talk to anyone.

Every time I open my mouth to speak, I feel like I'm going to cry. So, I'm keeping it shut.

After I talked to Phoebe and cried my way through a box of tissues, I was embarrassed that I'd unloaded on her like that.

So, I thanked her for everything, and I looked up flights. Turned out, there wasn't a flight to New York until tomorrow night.

It's like the world is trying to punish me by keeping me here.

I asked Phoebe if she could recommend a hotel in Klamath Falls. She gave me the name of one, and then I called a cab.

The cab arrived fifteen minutes later. I hugged Phoebe and thanked her for everything. Then, I climbed into the cab, and it took me to the hotel.

I checked in for a single room. Took my case up to the room, sat down on the bed, and stared at the wall.

I knew I was going to cry again. After years of never crying, my eyes were sore, and I felt drained. I knew I wouldn't cry in front of people, so I got up to go outside, and I started walking.

I wandered around for a bit and then headed back in the direction of the hotel, but the thought of being in that room alone made my footsteps start to slow.

So, I went into the diner a few doors down from the hotel.

It was empty, bar the waitress. But it would do.

I sat down in a booth by the window and ordered coffee and a piece of pie. That was about an hour ago.

I've just finished my second cup of coffee, and the pie sits, untouched.

Charlie Puth's "Dangerously" is playing on the radio. I'm listening to the lyrics and staring out the window.

"Another refill, hon?"

I move my eyes to the waitress. She has a coffee pot in her hand.

"Sure." I push my cup toward her, using my fingers.

Wardrobe Malfunction

She refills it.

"Thanks," I say.

I get some creamer from the pot and pour it in before adding some sweetener.

I notice she's still hovering, and dread passes through me that she recognizes me. My face has been plastered all over the Internet since the news of my "affair" with Vaughn broke.

"Hey, are you—"

"No." I shake my head, cutting her off. I know I'm probably coming off as rude, but I just don't care at the moment.

"Oh. Get asked that a lot, do you? 'Cause you sure do look like her. But then I did think, *What would someone like her be doing in Klamath Falls?*" She chuckles to herself.

"Who?" I ask, curiosity getting the better of me.

The bell on the door behind me rings.

The waitress looks up at whoever just entered. She smiles. "Take a seat, hon. I'll be right with you." Then, she looks back at me. "Gigi Hadid. You know, the model who's dating Zayn. You're the spitting image of her."

Gigi Hadid, huh? I wish.

I smile at her. "Thanks for the refill and the compliment."

"Gigi Hadid," a familiar voice says, making my whole body freeze. "Nah, you're way prettier than her."

Vaughn.

I'm almost afraid to turn in case it isn't him. I think the disappointment would finish me off.

But I do turn. And it is him.

He's here.

My heart starts to beat triple time.

He smiles, and my heart breaks.

"Hey, Pins."

I can't speak, so I just sit there, mute, while he takes the seat across from me.

"What can I get you?" the waitress asks him.

"Coffee."

"Sure thing, hon. Anything to go with that coffee?"

He shakes his head but doesn't take his stare from me. He hasn't once looked away from me since I first locked eyes with him.

Well, he might be able to look at me for an extended period of time, but I can't look at him. Staring at Vaughn right now is like staring at the sun. My eyes are starting to burn and sting and fill with tears.

I suck in a breath and stare out the window.

"I'll be right back with your coffee," the waitress tells him.

Silence drags on between us.

He's right here.

I never thought I'd see him again like this. Never be close to him again.

Don't lose this chance, Charly, to have more time with him. You'll regret it if you do.

I just wish I knew why he was here. I'm too afraid to let my heart hope.

I move my eyes back to him. All thoughts fall from my mind.

"You're not saying anything, Pins. It's starting to freak me out." He gives me a tentative smile.

I lick my dry lips. "You're here." It's the best I've got at the moment.

"Yeah," he says softly, "I am."

"Why?" I want to kick myself for asking, but it's killing me, having him here and not knowing why.

I'm silently begging him to forgive me for lying to him. Begging for him to want me again.

The waitress brings his coffee over, interrupting us.

"Thanks," he says, briefly glancing at her. His eyes come back to me.

Wardrobe Malfunction

Silence hangs between us again. The tension is agonizing.

"I spoke to Jack," he says.

"Oh." That's why he's here.

Jack probably wants him to make an official statement to the press about our "affair."

"Tell the press what you need to, Vaughn. Tell them the truth. That you didn't know I was married. You don't need to be hurt in this any more than you have been."

"Oh," he says. "Well, I was kinda thinking that we'd tell them that you and Nick have been separated for a while now but still living together, as you couldn't afford to move out. I'm guessing you're in a two-bedroom apartment, that you haven't gotten around to filing for divorce yet, as it's another expense you couldn't afford. You and Nick are on great terms. And he knew all about you and me. About our relationship."

"You and me?" I breathe.

"Yeah, Pins. You and me." He reaches across the table, taking my hand in his. "I shouldn't have let you go earlier. I didn't mean any of what I said. I was still angry and hurting."

"You're not angry anymore?"

"No."

He smiles, and my heart soars.

"I'm just…"

"What?" I ask eagerly.

"In love with you. And nothing else matters but that. Everything else can go to hell, for all I care."

Tears fill my eyes, and my lips tremble. "I love you, too. So much."

He moves around the table and sits beside me. He takes my face in his hands. "What you said earlier, that you want me to have the best life, that you want me to be happy…the only way I can do that is with you."

A tear slides down my face. He wipes it away with his thumb. Then, he presses his lips to mine.

Happiness sets my skin on fire. I wrap my arms around him, kissing him back.

He breaks off, pressing his forehead to mine. "Let's get out of here." He kisses me one more time and then slides out of the booth.

I follow out behind him. He pulls some bills from his pocket and drops them on the table, way more than necessary.

He stares down at me and holds his hand out for me to take. Heart full, I slide my palm against his. He links our fingers, and we head for the door.

We've just almost made it outside when the waitress calls us back.

"Hey," she says.

We turn to her. She's standing on the customer side of the counter. She takes a step closer, looking…well, staring at Vaughn. She's made him.

"Can I ask…are you…Vaughn West?"

He chuckles softly and then looks back at me. "No," he says. "I'm just a normal guy who's in love with an extraordinary girl."

He thinks I'm extraordinary.

That's the most amazing thing anyone has said to me.

The smile on my face is so big, my lips are stretching. But, of course, me being me, I have to say, "Did you bang your head on the way here?"

He laughs loudly, eyes sparkling. "There's my girl." His fingers stroke softly down my cheek. "And, no, I didn't bang my head. But I plan on banging yours. Hard. Against my headboard. It's time you and I got reacquainted, Pins."

I step close and brush my smiling lips against his. "I can live with that, West."

I can live with that forever.

Four Years Later

Vaughn

THIS IS IT.

This is the moment I've been waiting my whole career for. The moment that will tell me if all my hard work has paid off.

Working on my last film, *Five Knots to Nowhere*, was amazing but hard as hell. I bled this film. I lived in the fucking desert and the worst places on earth you could think of for this film. I left Charly for three months while we were on location. I put up with Brandon again for this film. The guy was still needy as fuck, and he was at epic neediness level while doing *Five Knots to Nowhere*.

Surprised he wanted to work with me again? I'm not. *The Lament* did fucking brilliantly. We smashed it at the box office.

I look up at the stage where Natasha and Gabriel are standing, waiting to present the award to the winner, which they're going to announce at any moment now.

I mean, they're two of my closest friends. It has to be me. It's fate.

Right?

Please, God, let it be me. I'll stop cursing so much if I win this. Not altogether, of course, because that would be near on fucking impossible.

My heart is beating so hard in my chest, it feels like I'm going to crack a rib.

I haven't been this nervous since I stood up at the altar, waiting for Charly to appear and walk toward me.

Thank fuck she did.

I rub my thumb over her engagement and wedding ring.

She squeezes my hand. I glance at her.

Her look is encouraging. *You got this baby*, her eyes are saying.

I pray to God that I do. Because I'll suck at being a gracious loser. I'm not *that* good of an actor.

"And the Oscar goes to…" Natasha opens the envelope.

She smiles and shows it to Gabriel.

He grins. And looks at me.

Did he look at me? Or did I just imagine that?

For fuck's sake, just say who the winner is, or I'm going to—

"Vaughn West!" he yells into the microphone.

Holy…fuck!

I won!

I motherfucking won! Sorry, God.

But I'm an Oscar-winning actor.

An. Oscar-winning. Actor.

I close my eyes in sweet relief, happiness coursing through my body. The audience is clapping loudly all around me. I feel someone pat my shoulder from behind.

Wardrobe Malfunction

Charly is cheering and nearly squeezing my hand off.

I look at her and grin. She grabs my face in her hands and smashes her lips to mine, kissing me hard.

I get to my feet, hugging Brandon and my costar Jensen Fletcher.

"Well done, man," Jensen says in my ear. "You fucking deserve this."

I head to the stage, jogging up the steps.

Gabe hugs me first. "You did it, West, you fucker." He chuckles in my ear.

Natasha throws her arms around me. "I'm so happy for you!"

They step back, and I walk to the podium. I'm smiling like the Joker right now. My peers are still on their feet, clapping.

"Jesus, I'm feeling like I might cry here," I joke—well, only half-joke. "And you can ask my wife, I don't cry often. Only after sex."

I get the laugh I was after. I look at Charly fighting a smile, shaking her head at me.

I stare down at the gold statue in my hand, shaking my head in disbelief. Then, I stand the gold statue on the podium in front of me.

"But, seriously, I'm man enough to admit that I've cried in my lifetime. Twice, in fact. The first time was when that beautiful woman sitting there agreed to be my wife. And the second was the day she told me she was pregnant with our child."

Smiling up at me, her eyes shining, Charly rubs her hand over her huge bump where my son is sleeping soundly.

"And my third time crying will, without a doubt, be when I've drunk too much liquor, and it finally hits me that I've won an Oscar. I have to thank Brandon for trusting me enough to work on a second film with me. And my incredibly talented costar Jensen Fletcher. Thank you to my manager, Jack, who has been through thick and thin with me. My family—Mom and Dad, my sisters, and Gran—I love you all very much. Alex, my long-suffering assistant, whom I couldn't get through a day without, and if I did, I'd probably do it without any pants on."

The audience laughs again. I can see Alex sitting behind Charly, shaking his head at me.

"And, of course, my wife. My gorgeous, stunning wife, Charly."

I look right at her. I can see her eyes glistening with tears. In this moment, no one else exists, except for her.

"Pins, we got off to a crazy start. After the stabbing incident, you made me a stellar piece of underwear, and then you yelled at me and called me a few choice words. I kissed you to shut you up, and I've been lucky enough to keep kissing you ever since. I love you. I literally couldn't do any of this without you. You're my strength, my heart, and my soul. No one—and I mean, no one—can make me laugh like you do. My life was good before you. Now, it's beyond amazing. This"—I pick the Oscar up, lifting it high—"is for you and our unborn son."

I look out to the audience. "Thank you, everyone, and good night."

I step off the stage, and a glass of champagne is put in my hand.

"Congratulations," the guy says.

"Thanks."

I take a sip. Taking it all in, I look at the gold statue again.

I did it.

A minute later, I'm ushered out of the Dolby Theatre and into the adjoining Loews Hollywood Hotel where I do photographs and press.

The Oscars are over by the time I'm finished with the press. So, I meet back up with Charly in the limo. We're heading to an after-party.

Wardrobe Malfunction

"Hey," she says as I slip into the seat next to her. "Can I look?"

I hand the statue to her.

"Wow," she murmurs.

"Right?"

We look at each other and then both let out yelps of excitement.

Charly throws her arms around me. "You freaking did it, Vaughn! I knew you would!"

"You never doubted."

"Not a moment." She smiles, handing me the statue back.

I put it on the seat next to me. I consider actually strapping it in with a seat belt, but that would be weird, right?

"So, that was quite an acceptance speech you gave."

"You liked it?"

"I loved it. But I could've lived without you telling everyone that I stabbed you."

"At least I didn't tell them *where* you stabbed me." I gesture to my cock.

"True. There is that to be thankful for." She nods.

"And I didn't tell them that the underwear you made was a cock warmer."

"It wasn't a cock—"

I cut her off with a kiss, like I always do when we have this debate, which has happened *many* times over the years.

"Warmer," she murmurs.

"I love you," I tell her.

"I love you, too."

"How's my son doing in there?" I press a hand to her bump.

"*Our* son is doing good. Sleeping now, I think. He was on the move when you were giving your speech. I think he was excited for you."

"Not as excited as I am to meet him." I lean down to talk to my son. "Three more weeks, and we get to meet, buddy. Your mom and I are so excited. And your gran and granddad, great-grandma, aunts, and cousins are all excited. There are a lot of people waiting to meet you, Elijah."

We're naming him after my grandpa. When we told my gran what we were calling him, her eyes filled with tears. She muttered something about needing a drink, and then she went into the kitchen to make up some cocktails.

I sit back in my seat and take hold of Charly's hand.

"Happy?" she asks.

"I already was, Pins."

Her eyes soften, and she smiles. Then, she leans her head against my shoulder.

The split in her gown has parted, showing me inches of one of her gorgeous legs. I put my hand on her thigh and squeeze. I take a glance down at her cleavage, too. Charly has always had fantastic tits, but since she's been pregnant, they've gotten huge. And, I gotta tell you, I've had a lot of fun with them.

The gown is one of her own designs. She left the wardrobe and movie business and started her own clothing line. But not right away. The day after we got back together, Jack put out a press release, basically saying that Charly and Nick were already separated when our relationship started. Nick was fully aware that we were seeing one another, and blah, blah, blah.

After that, the media interest in Charly and me started to die down, as there was no great scandal for them anymore. And a few days after our press release went out, some squeaky-clean pop singer got high, stole a school bus—thankfully, it was empty—and totaled it into the side of a building. So, that kept the press busy for a while.

Charly came back to Vegas with me the day after the press release was issued and resumed her role in wardrobe while I finished filming.

She and Nick also started divorce proceedings. It didn't take long for it to be finalized. And, shortly after, Charly was legally a single woman again. Well, she wasn't single because she was mine.

And I made her officially mine a year later when we married in a small ceremony at the back of my ranch.

A few months after we were married, Charly opened up her own online clothes store, selling her designs. It got big fast. So, we had to expand and ended up opening up some stores—one in Portland and the other in New York.

We live permanently in Keno at my ranch. We also have another fixed member of the household—Jester. As soon as Charly moved in, so did he. There was no getting him away from her, but I understand that feeling. So, he lives with us and goes back to my parents' when we're away.

We also have an apartment in New York, as Charly needs to be there for her business quite often and, of course, to see Nick.

Nick lives in our apartment in New York, so we get to spend plenty of time with him when we're there. It's important that we do because he's Charly's family, and there is nothing more important than family. It helps that Nick and I get along great. He's a cool guy.

He spends every Fourth of July, Christmas, and Thanksgiving with us at my parents' house. My family loves him. Gran wants to adopt him. She's always trying to talk him into moving to Keno. I think he would if it wasn't for his business. He has his own interior design company now in New York, and it's going really well for him. He recently also just started seeing this guy whose apartment he redesigned.

And, talking of Gran, she's still with Ed. Four years and going strong. He's a weird guy, but he makes her happy, and I know that's what granddad would want for her.

So, life is good.

No, it's fucking great.

And, in three weeks, I'll be a daddy, and I can't wait.

The limo slows, and I hear the noise of the crowds of journalists and paparazzi outside.

My cell goes off in my pocket. It's been buzzing all night.

I pull it out and see a text from Gran.

> *Gran: Congratulations, Vaughn. You were always going to win. Those other films sucked.*

I chuckle.

"Who is it?" Charly asks.

"Just Gran congratulating me in her own unique way."

I can see she's writing me another text from the three dots at the bottom, so I wait for it to appear.

> *Gran: Oh, and Ed has just asked me to marry him. I said yes. And, like I told your mama and daddy, I'm not getting married in the back garden like you and your sister did, FYI.*

"Gran is getting married," I say, shocked.

"Vaughn?"

"Married! My eighty-four-year-old grandmother is fucking getting married!"

"Vaughn—"

"I can't believe this. I mean, who gets married at eighty-four—"

"Vaughn!"

"What?" I snap my eyes up to her, and I see hers are as wide as saucers.

"Well, I either just peed myself or my water broke."

I look down to see water trickling down to the floor near my feet.

My eyes dart back to her face. "Your water broke? Holy shit! Your water broke!"

Wardrobe Malfunction

Jesus Christ.

I'm about to become a dad.

I just won an Oscar. Found out my eighty-four-year-old grandmother is getting married. And my wife's water's just broke.

At least I can say that my life isn't boring.

She moans a sound of pain, her hand going to her stomach.

"Don't worry, Pins. I'll get you to a hospital." I press the intercom to the driver. "Driver, nearest hospital. *Now.* My wife has just gone into labor."

"Jesus," he says.

Yeah. No fucking kidding.

"I'll get you there as quickly as I can. Just hang on."

I take hold of her hand and look her in the eyes. "You got this, Pins. And I'm going to be with you every step of the way."

"It hurts," she groans.

"How bad?"

"Bad."

"Like a-pin-in-the-ball-sack bad?"

She pinches my nipple through my shirt, twisting it.

"Ow!" I yelp. "That fucking hurt." I rub at the pain.

"As bad as an eight-pound baby deciding it wants out of your body through a hole the size of a lemon?" She glares at me.

My lips twitch, and I fight the smile because I know she'll probably maim me if I do, and I really, really like my cock.

"Don't you dare fucking laugh, West."

"As if I would." I take her face in my hands and stare into her eyes. "I love you," I tell her. "And, no, it didn't hurt that much. You definitely win that one, Pins."

Then, I kiss her, the love of my life and soon-to-be mother of my son, as we speed through the streets of LA, hospital-bound, so my son can make his entrance into the world.

And I can't fucking wait.

Acknowledgments

WRITING A BOOK isn't a solo endeavor. Many people help me get my stories down onto paper and out into the world, and their help comes in many forms. Craig, Riley, Isabella, Trishy, Sali, Jodi, Jovana, Naj, Sue, Nicky, and Lauren—thank you. I couldn't do it without each and every single one of you. And another special mention to Craig—thank you for the *Bugsy Malone* story.

My Wether Girls—I'm so glad I created our group. It's my safe haven. And the best place to have fun!

Huge thank you to all the bloggers who work tirelessly to help promote books. I appreciate and adore you all.

And my readers—the best readers in the world!—Your continuing support makes it possible for me to do what I love. My biggest thanks goes to you.

About the Author

SAMANTHA TOWLE is a *New York Times*, *USA Today*, and *Wall Street Journal* bestselling author. She began her first novel in 2008 while on maternity leave. She completed the manuscript five months later and hasn't stopped writing since.

She is the author of contemporary romances, The Storm Series and The Revved Series, and stand-alones, *Trouble*, *When I Was Yours*, *The Ending I Want*, *Unsuitable*, and *Sacking the Quarterback*, which was written with James Patterson. She has also written paranormal romances, *The Bringer* and The Alexandra Jones Series. All of her books are penned to the tunes of The Killers, Kings of Leon, Adele, The Doors, Oasis, Fleetwood Mac, Lana Del Rey, and more of her favorite musicians.

A native of Hull and a graduate of Salford University, she lives with her husband, Craig, in East Yorkshire with their son and daughter.

Printed in Poland
by Amazon Fulfillment
Poland Sp. z o.o., Wrocław